REDEEMING HOPE

SHELL TAYLOR

Published by

DREAMSPINNER PRESS

5032 Capital Circle SW, Suite 2, PMB# 279, Tallahassee, FL 32305-7886 USA
www.dreamspinnerpress.com/

Redeeming Hope
© 2015 Shell Taylor.

Cover Art
© 2015 L.C. Chase.
http://www.lcchase.com
Cover content is for illustrative purposes only and any person depicted on the cover is a model.

ISBN: 978-1-63476-376-9
Digital ISBN: 978-1-63476-377-6
Library of Congress Control Number: 2015950125
First Edition October 2015

Printed in the United States of America
∞
This paper meets the requirements of
ANSI/NISO Z39.48-1992 (Permanence of Paper).

To my husband for his infinite love and support. Thank you for always encouraging me to be me.

Acknowledgments

Writing a book is truly a team effort and my words are so much better because of the advice, brutal honesty, and most importantly friendship of the following people: Adele, Amy, Beth, Meredith, Shelli, and Sue. Special thanks to Viv for all of your wisdom and huge heart regarding all things CPS, and to Jayme for talking me off the ledge and forcing me to hit Send. I love each of you.

Prologue

ELI CLUTCHED the glossy eight-by-ten as tears welled in his eyes. He could hardly believe the emaciated, washed-out figure in the picture was the same person he'd centered his entire world around just a few weeks earlier. Eli would recognize that face anywhere. God knows, he'd spent enough time staring at it—running his fingers over those soft lips, sucking on the kidney-shaped birthmark just below the ear. He never imagined he'd see those eyes so lifeless.

"It's him," Eli whispered, dropping the picture on the officer's desk.

His mother rested a hand on his shoulder. "E.J.—"

"Don't pretend to care, now that he's dead." Eli shrugged out of her grasp and clenched his jaw to hold in the gut-wrenching sobs brewing in his chest. "Will I need to identify the body in person too?"

The officer avoided Eli's eyes, but his voice was kind. "If you're certain, this is good enough for us. He'll be released in the next thirty-six hours. Will you be claiming him, or will the city keep him?"

Eli's eyes widened, and panic ripped through his heart. He'd never expected the search to end with a dead body, and there was no way he'd be able to give his boyfriend the funeral he deserved—the one Eli owed him for his own part in Brian's death. Prepared to beg, he turned and met his father's eyes for the first time since Brian disappeared from their house almost three weeks earlier.

"We'll take care of his arrangements." Eli's mother spoke quietly but firmly, and his father dipped his chin in silent agreement.

Relief carried Eli back to his parents' car, but grief consumed him as soon as he slid into the back seat. Burying his head in his knees, he shut out the rest of the world. Eli didn't leave the quiet safety of the car until long after he arrived home, his cheeks crusted with salty tears from mourning the loss of the future he'd been so sure of.

CHAPTER 1

SOMETIMES LIFE just sucked.

There was no rhyme or reason for why good things happened to bad people—or why bad things happened to good people, for that matter. Karma was nothing more than a myth, made up to trick everyone into doing good deeds. Life consisted of a random series of events that would inevitably occur whether you were generous enough to hold doors open for complete strangers or selfish enough to jam the Close elevator button when your boss came running around the corner.

But on days like this, Elijah couldn't help but wonder what the fuck he'd done to deserve the shitfest that had been dumped on him.

It started on his morning commute when the moron in front of him slammed on the brakes to avoid hitting a squirrel—a fucking *squirrel*—forcing Elijah to swerve off the road and spill hot coffee all over his Dior slacks. Fortunately Elijah kept a spare suit in his office, but as soon as he sat down at his desk, he was assaulted with a list of ten "friendly" reminders from the "former but not quite ready to give it up" CEO of Langley Lumber and Construction—also known as his father. Then the head of his accounting department—the man he'd been training to officially take over the role of CFO so Elijah could cease wearing both hats—put in his two weeks' notice.

When a conference call ran over, Elijah missed lunch. By the time some environmentalist freak who didn't think Langley Lumber was doing enough to save the planet showed up in his reception area, he wasn't even surprised that she'd demanded an audience with "whoever's in charge."

Elijah was tired. His nerves were shot, and for the first time in… well, ever… he wanted to cut out of work early, go home, and do absolutely nothing. But it was Wednesday, which meant dinner with his parents, and they always ended the same way—a lecture from his father about everything Elijah needed to do for the business and apologetic looks from his mother while she sipped her wine.

Shoving the cuff of his shirt back to check the time, Elijah saw he still had twenty minutes before his next appointment, and he needed a break to survive his last meeting as much as he needed a quick bite to eat. Shrugging on his suit jacket, he walked down the short hall to reception.

Elijah rapped one finger on his secretary's desk. "Sherri, I'm heading to Etman's to get a sandwich. I should be back in time for the four-thirty meeting. If I'm not, tell them to start without me."

Oblivious to his sour mood, Sherri offered her tight, patented almost-smile and nodded.

Elijah dipped his chin once, a habit he'd only grudgingly acquired from his father, and started toward the door. He stopped in his tracks when the front doors opened and laughter ushered two strangers inside. A young woman, maybe midtwenties, with a pretty, oval face and choppy, shoulder-length blondish-brown hair nudged the kid beside her as if reprimanding him for whatever he'd just said. When she turned her smile toward Elijah, her entire face lit up, making her even prettier than Elijah had first thought. But once he got a good look at the kid beside her, she could've been J. Lo and Elijah wouldn't have noticed. The kid's hair was different—darker, shorter, and artfully swept to the side—but Elijah would have sworn he was staring at a younger version of the guy he once thought he'd spend his life with.

"Hi," the woman chirped to Sherri. "I'm Kirsten and this is Kollin. We're making rounds in the neighborhood, dropping off some information about The Center for HOPE. It's the LGBT center over on Leftwich. HOPE stands for Healing, Opportunity, Protection, and Equality, and we're committed to providing a safe place for queer youth to feel accepted and help prepare them for their futures. We're having a fundraiser in a few weeks to purchase the old Tarboro Inn just down the street from us. We thought it would also be a great opportunity to bring awareness to the community about what HOPE is and what we do."

She spoke quickly, but Elijah didn't get the impression it was out of nervousness. He couldn't say for sure. His eyes stayed glued on the boy she introduced as Kollin.

Kollin shrugged off his book bag and pulled out several information pamphlets. He handed one to Sherri and then turned to Elijah and gave him a curious once-over.

"Nice suit. Dior?"

Elijah nodded once and offered a rare, small smile. "Impressive."

Kollin raised his shoulder and gestured toward his own outfit—burnt orange pants, a white hippie shirt, and black suspenders he somehow managed to make look good. "I'm into fashion."

"Ah, I see that," Elijah replied.

He held out another pamphlet. "You want one of these too?"

Elijah took the paper and glanced at the front page. "You look a little young to work for a place like this."

"I'm just helping Kirsten out today. She can't go anywhere by herself apparently." Kollin raised his voice enough to catch Kirsten's attention, making her hip-check him in the middle of her conversation with Sherri but not slowing her down at all. "But I'm also one of the impressionable young minds who benefits from everything HOPE has to offer." He rolled his eyes, but the warmth of his smile told Elijah the kid was grateful for the center.

"You are, huh?" Elijah waved the pamphlet around. "So, what's the plan for the Tarboro Inn?"

"Adam wants to renovate all the rooms and set up some kind of system so homeless youth can have a safe place to stay. He wants to help them find work and all that. Give 'em a chance to get back on their feet."

Elijah nodded, once again impressed. What Kollin described was no small undertaking, but if successful… well, his life would've been a lot different if something like that had been around seventeen years earlier. He had no business asking something so personal, but as he glanced back at Kollin's too-familiar face, he couldn't help himself. "And will you be needing the inn?"

Flashing him a bright smile, Kollin shook his head. When he spoke, the sarcastic lilt was back in his voice. "My parents tolerate me well enough, as long as I don't wear the suspenders in the house."

Elijah huffed out a laugh.

"Ready, kiddo?" Kirsten asked, grabbing the back of his shirt.

"Yes, ma'am. Nice meeting you, sir."

Elijah shook Kollin's hand and thanked him, purposely not introducing himself. Even if Kollin hadn't reminded him of Brian, Elijah would have found him to be a breath of fresh air—once he got over the initial shock of staring his past in the face, that is. Kollin was comfortable in his own skin and didn't seem to give two shits what anyone else thought of him. Elijah didn't want the kid to know he'd just made one of the most influential men in Cary nearly speechless.

"Mr. Langley, sir?" Sherri stared at him, a questioning look on her face as Kollin and Kirsten left his building. "Would you like me to run down to Etman's and get you that sandwich? Your meeting starts soon."

Elijah's gaze strayed to the clock on the wall. He'd spent over half of his break talking to Kollin. "No thank you. I'll find something in my office."

Elijah tapped the pamphlet on Sherri's desk and went back to his office to review its contents. He showed up at his final meeting of the day almost ten minutes late and still hungry.

IF ELIJAH'S parents noticed how distracted he was at dinner that night, they didn't mention it. They also didn't question why he wanted to go through his old room when he excused himself after dinner. His parents had redecorated immediately after he moved out of the house, so it looked nothing like the room he'd grown up in. He found the box he was looking for shoved into the very back corner of his old closet, and briefly considered grabbing the other two as well, but he childishly decided he liked the idea of inconveniencing his parents.

Elijah placed a kiss on his mother's cheek and assured his father he'd prepared for the quarterly board meeting the following day. He dropped the box in the passenger seat of his Lexus and spent the short drive home wondering what in the hell he was doing. He'd quickly learned that the only way to move past Brian's death was to pretend he'd never existed. It had been over fifteen years since Elijah locked his past away in his childhood bedroom closet and metaphorically thrown away the key. He knew leaving his past in the past was the smartest thing he could do, but he couldn't stop himself from plowing forward when he had that old box within arm's reach.

At home, Elijah poured himself two fingers of scotch from his fully stocked bar and stared at the black and red Air Jordan shoebox on his coffee table. He took a healthy swig of his drink, topped it off again, and sank into the couch. Steepling his fingers, Elijah eyed the top warily and wondered what fresh hell awaited him. As he gently removed the lid, he immediately regretted his decision to take a trip down memory lane.

Staring up at him was the seventeen-year-old version of himself. His smile was huge, and he had a basketball tucked under one arm, but all Elijah could see was the boy tucked under his other arm. Instead of looking at the camera, Brian was grinning up at Elijah, the smile on his face betraying how utterly smitten he'd been. Elijah had always loved that picture. While he'd never considered himself closeted—more like careful—that particular picture told the truth about what he and Brian really were to one another.

The alcohol in Elijah's stomach swirled around, and he shoved the top back on the box, unable to look into those trusting blue eyes any longer. He pushed it farther away, stood, and ran his hands through his hair. What the fuck was he thinking when he grabbed that box? He hadn't been able to deal with Brian's death when he was seventeen, and he sure as hell hadn't done anything since to change that.

Clearly time didn't heal all wounds.

Elijah stripped off his suit as he climbed the stairs to his bedroom and carelessly tossed the discarded clothes into a pile outside his closet door. Kollin's flippant comment about his parents merely tolerating him popped into his mind. Elijah didn't know the kid from Joe Blow on the street, but he couldn't help wondering how much truth lurked behind his facetious words. His heart twisted at the thought of Kollin ending up like Brian. Had anything improved? Were there more places like The Center for HOPE? Was it easier to be a gay teenager today than it was fifteen years before? Elijah had no idea, but he was damn sure going to find out.

CHAPTER 2

ELIJAH'S DATE, Katie, grazed one perfectly manicured finger over his knuckles, and Elijah had to refrain from jerking his hand away. She seemed nice enough, but Elijah was entirely too anxious to deal with her as he drove to The Center for HOPE fundraiser. He'd been to dozens of benefits, and while he didn't particularly enjoy schmoozing with people he'd never see again, he understood it was a necessary evil.

If it were up to him, he'd write a check and skip all the mingling, but Elijah would never hear the end of it if his father found out he'd missed a chance for a face-time return on his investment. Normally Elijah plastered a fake smile on his face, made his rounds—being sure to talk up Langley with the most prominent attendees—and left before the dancing started. He could do it in his sleep.

The HOPE benefit was different. No matter how hard he tried, he couldn't forget this was not just any old fundraiser—not since he'd taken the top off that box. He was already regretting inviting Katie.

Shit. Or was her name Kelly?

Lately his mom seemed more determined than ever for him to settle down, and his date that night was her most recent attempt at finding him a wife. Elijah would have to avoid introducing her to anyone until he had a spare moment to check the e-mail his mother sent with the girl's name.

Elijah grabbed his date's roaming hand and gave it a squeeze. He rested their joined hands in her lap and then tugged his hand back to downshift.

"So, what kind of event is this?" she asked, unsuccessfully trying to cross her legs in Elijah's tiny front seat.

He glanced over and delivered the same line he'd given his father. "It's a fundraiser hosted by The Center for HOPE. They're looking to renovate the old Tarboro Inn so they can pull homeless youth off the streets."

"Oh. I know about that place. My little sister used to go there after school when she first came out. She still volunteers on occasion."

Irrational fear zipped through Elijah, forcing him to take a deep breath. What did it matter if his date—whose name he couldn't even remember— had a small tie to the center? After that night, he'd never see her again, and his business with the center would be complete. Besides, even though North

Carolina wasn't exactly known for being gay friendly, Katie/Kelly hadn't seemed shocked or repulsed.

"Right. Well, Langley makes a point of contributing to as many local charities as possible. We're happy to help at-risk youth any way we can."

"Mmm. I hope they serve chicken," she replied, touching up her makeup in the mirror.

Elijah grunted his response and was saved from further small talk when they pulled into the hotel parking lot. Foregoing his overcoat despite the chilly January weather, Elijah draped a long blue scarf around his neck, helped his date from the car, and hurried her inside. While he'd planned to arrive just in time for dinner, they were actually running a few minutes late even for that. Elijah hated tardiness.

Katie/Kelly's heels clicked furiously across the shiny tile of the hotel floor as they crossed through the lobby. Soon enough they found the ballroom, where a petite brunette stood on the stage asking everyone to find their seat. They received instructions from a gentleman at the door and Elijah quickly ushered his date to their table. The woman on stage, whom Elijah recognized as the one who'd shown up at his office a few weeks prior—Kristen, he thought her name was—swept her arm to the side and finished her introduction.

"...the founder of The Center for HOPE, the man I still call my brother, Adam Lancaster."

The room filled with raucous applause. Elijah even heard a few wolf whistles as Adam walked onto the stage. Dressed in a black suit with a black shirt and black tie, his red-orange hair stood out, and the square frames he wore looked almost too big on his slender face. His lips were full but complemented his strong jaw. Elijah's table was close enough that he could see Adam's two front teeth were slightly crooked, making them overlap just a bit. Elijah's stomach did a little flip-flop as he stared Adam down, taking in every surprisingly sexy inch of him. If just the sight of Adam made him react, it'd been far too long since he'd been with another man.

"As always... first I have to thank Matthew and Amelia Wright for being the best parents I've ever known. Theirs was the eighth home foster care placed me with in just under five years. Between the ages of eleven and fifteen, I felt nothing but hatred and disappointment from my parents, my family, my friends—practically the whole world, it felt like at the time.

"If it weren't for Matthew's and Amelia's selfless, unconditional love, I wouldn't have survived much longer. They fought *with* me. They fought *for* me. And they insisted I was deserving of their love. Then they proved it by never once letting me think I wasn't as smart, or as good, or as *normal* as everyone else. Simply by being themselves, they made me want to be the very best version of myself and instilled in me a deep desire to help other struggling LGBT youth. Without Matthew and Amelia, The Center for HOPE wouldn't exist."

Adam lowered his head and smiled. He waited for the smattering of applause to die down before he spoke again. Elijah listened as Adam rattled off the depressing statistics about homelessness and LGBT youth. Elijah had first-hand experience with how bad life could be for a gay teenager whose parents didn't want him. He wondered, for the first time in years, how Brian had managed to survive as long as he had on the streets. Elijah didn't care for the way the most probable answers made his chest tighten with guilt and regret.

Closing his eyes, Elijah shoved unwelcome thoughts of Brian into the dark recesses of his mind. When he opened them again, he zeroed in on Adam and paid attention to the way he tapped the tips of his long fingers together every time he drove his point home. And though stumbling over a word during a professional speech normally irked Elijah, he found it endearing when Adam did so and then cocked his head to the side and shook off the mishap. He sounded desperate as he implored his audience to understand how imperative it is for queer youth to know they aren't alone. Already more than willing to throw his entire checking account at the center to assuage his guilt, Elijah wondered if he shouldn't dip into his savings as well.

Adam paused to look down at the podium he stood behind. He closed his eyes for a moment, and Elijah could see his jaw twitch. He recognized that look. Adam would most likely start ad-libbing words from his heart. "I used to think having more than two emergency beds for my kids to sleep in was a pipe dream, but the recent progress being made in our country, along with support from the general community, has given me hope. Hope that I'll never have to turn away another teen who's traveled hundreds of miles to find us. Hope that one day I'll be out of a job because being gay won't be shameful. And hope that, instead of turning their children away, parents will cling to them, smother them with love and acceptance, and be proud of them for being themselves. So thank you again so much for supporting my dream and helping to make it a reality. After tonight, we'll be one step closer to buying and renovating the old Tarboro Inn to help keep our youth off the street."

Adam walked off stage to more applause and whistles. He paused briefly to hug an older woman—his foster mother maybe?—and several people stopped him as he made his way toward the center of the room where Elijah was sitting.

"I think he's at our table," Katie/Kelly whispered in his ear. Between Adam's speech and thoughts of cornering the guy in the bathroom, Elijah had forgotten she was even with him, much less remembered to look up her name. He at least had enough decency to feel guilty, but it wasn't like their relationship was going anywhere. Maybe it was better if he just came off as a pompous asshole who ignored his dates.

Right. As opposed to a pompous asshole who merely forgot his date's name.

Adam finally reached the table, and the man sitting on the other side of the empty seat next to Elijah stood to greet Adam with a quick kiss on the cheek.

"You were amazing."

"You really think so? I felt like I rambled and then was too boring," Adam hedged.

"Not at all. Adding the personal touch was really…. I had no idea."

Elijah watched as Adam's friend—date?—gripped his hand, but Adam quickly shook him off, removed his suit jacket, and hung it on the back of his chair. Rolling up the cuffs of his shirt, Adam revealed what appeared to be a full sleeve tattoo on each arm. Elijah shifted uncomfortably in his seat, unable to take his eyes off him. "Well, thank you. And thanks for coming tonight, Bruce. I know I'm totally ignoring you."

If Bruce was upset about being shrugged off, he didn't show it. The two men sat, but before they could continue their conversation, Elijah cleared his throat impatiently. He was already smiling when Adam offered his hand.

"Elijah Langley, right? I'm Adam Lancaster."

ADAM GAVE himself a quick pep talk and returned Elijah's smile. In a town as small as theirs, almost everyone knew of Elijah Langley. He'd recently taken over his father's most lucrative business, making him one of the wealthiest men in a fairly well-to-do area. Drinking in his dirty blond hair, blue eyes, and cock-hardening smile reminded Adam that Elijah was also Cary's most sought-after bachelor. Unfortunately for Adam, if the man's date was any indication, Elijah seemed to have a thing for gorgeous blondes with fake tits, which really was a pity. Even Elijah's tux couldn't hide the strength in his massive shoulders. On a scale of one to ten, his in-person hotness factor had to be at least a thirty-seven. Adam squelched that line of thinking and reminded himself to be professional.

"Impressive speech," Elijah said, trailing one finger against Adam's palm as he pulled away from their handshake. Adam's eyes nearly popped out of his head, but Elijah's face remained impassive. Adam chalked the inappropriate touch up to wishful thinking and an overactive imagination. Fuckity, fuck, fuck, but the man was hot. "I was just as touched as your friend."

Shit. Bruce. Adam had forgotten about him while drooling over Elijah's five o'clock shadow and cocky smile. He cleared his throat and leaned back in his seat. "Elijah, this is Bruce. He agreed to accompany me tonight, even though I'm forced to ignore him most of the time."

Adam winked, making Bruce preen as he offered his hand.

"Pleasure to meet you," Bruce said.

Adam waited for Elijah to introduce his date, but it quickly became awkwardly obvious he had no intention of following through, so he plowed ahead. "I was thrilled when I found out Langley L&C was interested in our cause. It's always exciting to find new support within our own community."

"We're happy to help wherever we can. I wasn't aware the center existed before I met Kollin." Elijah smiled again, this one smaller but more genuine. "He made quite an impression when he stopped by my office."

Adam barked out a laugh. Figured Kollin would be responsible for attracting one of the most prominent men in Cary to the fundraiser without even realizing he'd done so. "Kollin is something else. Best basketball player we have too. I've been trying to convince him I'm letting him win for the past two months, but I don't think he's buying it, since I limp off the court after every game."

Elijah sat back in his seat as one of the waiters interrupted to deliver his food. "It sounds like you really have a passion for those kids, but I'm wondering how much you actually know about the business side of it."

Adam stiffened. He was used to explaining his business plan, but Elijah's choice of words didn't sit well with him. Adam had to do whatever it took to win over the guests, and Elijah's pockets were deeper than Mary Poppins's magic carpetbag. Scoring a donation from him would be huge for HOPE, especially if he became a committed benefactor.

"I received my MBA from the University of Virginia, but honestly, most of my knowledge comes from running HOPE. Founding and sustaining a not-for-profit business, especially one that primarily relies on community donations, is nothing like what they teach in school."

"Indeed. What've you found to be the biggest challenge?"

Elijah's follow-up question surprised Adam as much as his initial one, but the longer they talked, the quicker he forgot that the man who dominated his dinner conversation had acted as if Adam didn't know the difference between an asset and a hole in the wall. Elijah grilled him relentlessly, asking not only detailed questions about the capital project but also about how Adam spent the bulk of his time.

"Sounds like you run a pretty solid foundation." Elijah's praise washed over Adam, turning his insides as warm and soft as the apple pie they were eating. "I just wonder if you couldn't accomplish more if you focused on the business aspect of it rather than playing with those kids all day."

Adam's eyes bulged, his forkful of apples and cinnamon suddenly stuck in his throat as he did a damn good impression of a fish out of water.

Elijah, seemingly oblivious to Adam's new aquatic lifestyle, continued. "I mean, most of your potential donors are open for business when you're out there playing big brother to some of those kids. And you have volunteers, man—people showing up to do what you're doing for *free*. You could make a lot more headway expanding your organization if you left playtime to them."

Adam pushed his dessert plate away. He knew Elijah had a point. It was one Adam turned over in his own head when funding was low and he had to figure out ways to stretch every dollar.

But these were his kids.

His kids.

Adam finally blurted out the obvious. "But they need me."

"They need *someone*. Sure," Elijah said, his tongue swiping a dusting of sugar from his lip. Two minutes earlier that sight would've been fodder for any number of naughty scenarios to play out in Adam's head. Now, with his heart lodged firmly in his stomach, it only made him feel sick. "Doesn't mean it has to be you."

Adam shook his head. "How can I expect the kids to trust our center if I'm not out there, showing them how important they are to *me*?"

Elijah frowned, finally seeming to realize he'd offended Adam. "Then maybe you should consider hiring someone to take over the business part, so you can be free to work with the kids."

Adam clenched his fists, anger roiling inside his gut. Of course that would be Mr. Moneybags' suggestion. Just hire someone else. No matter there was zero budget for additional staff. Adam had always been proud of the way he was able to both manage the business affairs and interact with the kids, but Elijah was doing a bang-up job of making him feel as if he'd fucked it all up from the beginning.

"It's not that simple," Adam argued. "You, of all people, should understand how complicated it is to hire additional staff... and that's assuming we have the funds for it, which we don't."

"Which is why it makes the most sense for you to leave the coddling of the kids to someone else," Elijah insisted. "Look, I'm not saying you have to give up all of your time with them. You have a good business plan, a great one actually, but there's a huge difference between running a gay-friendly shelter that encourages kids to do their homework and running what basically amounts to a halfway house. Plus, you would have more time to devote to your... personal life," he finished, his eyes cutting to Bruce, who was at one of the tables set up for the silent auction, deep in conversation with one of HOPE's therapists.

What the...? Who the fuck did this arrogant asshole think he was, telling him how to run his personal life? Adam counted to ten and willed himself not to sucker punch Elijah right in his fat mouth. Instead, he took a deep breath and focused on Elijah's advice about HOPE. "I won't give up my time with those kids. Feel free to think what you want, but they rely on me to be there for them. It may sound as if all I'm doing is playing a game of catch or helping kids with their homework, but it's more than that. I promise you. And my plan is solid. You can stop by the center anytime, and I'll be happy to give you a tour and address any concerns you may have."

Elijah held up his hands. "We'll have to agree to disagree for now, but you'll definitely be hearing from me."

Baffled by Elijah's hot and cold attitude, Adam slid his business card across the table.

Elijah pocketed the card and stood, apparently done with the conversation. "See you soon, Adam," he said. Then he walked to one of the tables and jotted down a bid, while his nameless date followed behind him like a trained puppy. Elijah, egotistical prick that he was, never even looked back.

"How'd it go?" Bruce asked, appearing beside him out of nowhere. Adam took a deep breath and wished his date had stayed away. He knew Bruce meant well, but he didn't feel right complaining to a guy he was only seeing for the second time. They'd had an amazing night their first time out together, and Bruce didn't deserve Adam's bitchiness just because Elijah Langley had made him feel no bigger than an ant.

"I don't even know." Adam sighed. "I thought it was going really well. I thought he got it... but then he turned into this business shark and told me how I'm doing everything wrong."

Bruce grunted. "That blows."

Adam snorted, pleased his date hadn't offered empty reassurances. Hoping to shake off his bad mood, Adam grabbed Bruce's hand and kissed his knuckles just as Kirsten plowed into him from behind. With a loud *oomph*, she threw her arms around his shoulders. "I don't know what the hell you said to that man, but a-fucking-mazing job."

"Real funny, Kris," Adam grumbled, shrugging out of his sister's arms. "He just trashed the way I run the center. Told me I didn't have my priorities straight."

"He must like gay priorities, then, because he just bid a hundred thousand dollars on a restaurant voucher worth seventy-five bucks."

Adam was in the middle of rolling his eyes at Kirsten's lameass attempt at humor when what she'd said hit him. "Are you serious?"

"Do you really think I'd lie about that?"

"Did he actually write the check? He's already left."

"Fucking hell, Adam," Kirsten exclaimed. "Who gives a shit if he left early? I'll throw on a blonde wig, stuff my bra, and pick up the damn check myself if it's got that many zeroes. Do you really think he'd make that type of commitment and then back out? What's the point?"

Adam's eyes widened as he stared at Kirsten. They'd expected to *maybe* raise that much tonight from the entire crowd. It was unbelievable. Maybe he'd read too much into Elijah's comments. He'd desperately wanted to impress such a wealthy potential benefactor, so it was no wonder he was oversensitive.

"Yeah, I guess. I'm just stunned as hell, though."

Patting his cheek, Kirsten said, "You did good, Adam. Now go do your thing and pull in some more donations."

As much as Adam wanted to stand over Elijah's bid all night to confirm it was real, Kirsten was right. He spent the rest of his evening introducing his alumni to as many guests as possible and did his best to put Elijah Langley out of his mind. By the time everyone had left, Adam was so exhausted that all he wanted to do was go home and crash for the next twelve hours.

Adam fought back a yawn as he pulled into the HOPE parking lot where Bruce had met him before the benefit. "I'm sorry tonight was such a lame date for you."

"Are you kidding? I got a free dinner, drank with some of the most prominent citizens of Cary, and was able to ogle you all night. How's that not exciting?"

Adam laughed and turned to face Bruce. "I guess you have a point there. Maybe next time we can go out, just the two of us, instead of the biggest group date in the history of the world."

"Sounds perfect, especially since I won't have to wait so long this time. Plus, it'll be our third date." Bruce winked, and Adam was smiling when his lips met Bruce's over the console. They lingered over the kiss, but Adam felt a small pang of disappointment that it didn't hold the same promise or excitement as their first kiss two weeks prior. He broke off from the kiss first, unable to keep another yawn from escaping. He was probably so far past the point of total exhaustion that even the most sizzling kiss wouldn't register.

"Thanks for being so understanding. I'm planning on sleeping until at least dinnertime tomorrow, but I'll call you Monday, and we'll set something up for next weekend."

"Sounds good, and congrats on such a great job tonight. You were amazing." Bruce leaned in for a quick good-bye kiss and hopped out of Adam's car. Adam briefly considered going home as Bruce pulled away but knew his mind wouldn't let him rest without double-checking the night's total. He trudged inside instead.

"How'd it go tonight, boss?" Clint, the night volunteer, asked.

"Pretty damn good. We'll make an official announcement tomorrow."

"Good luck, man. And congratulations. I'm sure you're glad it's over."

"'Til next time, at least," Adam said and headed into his office. After adding everything three times, he finally trusted his less-than-desirable math skills enough to confirm the unbelievable total his accountant had already given him. Elation pulsed through him. They'd raised nearly a quarter of a million dollars in one night, bringing them over halfway to their goal.

Adam's mind drifted to the man largely responsible for the night's over-the-top success, and he wondered what had possessed Elijah to donate that much money—not that he'd ever get the chance to ask. He didn't think Elijah would actually contact him, since he'd already committed to a donation. Even though he'd cussed the guy out numerous times in his head throughout the night, Adam found he was disappointed at the thought of not seeing him again. He really enjoyed most of their conversation over dinner. Elijah was smart, intense, and had even shown signs of a sense of humor once or twice. And until Elijah slammed the way Adam ran the center, Adam could have easily pictured Elijah in his bed.

Adam shook his head and pushed that thought right out of his mind. Even if Elijah did contact him, from Adam's experience, men like Elijah Langley tended to leave a trail of destruction in their wake. He hardly needed to be lusting after a straight multimillionaire when he was just starting to figure out if he had more-than-friend feelings toward Bruce.

Adam saw it was creeping up on two a.m. and shut down his computer. He offered Clint a tired wave as he walked out and kept his head down against the chilly night air. He was so out of it, Adam didn't notice anyone in the parking lot until a familiarly gruff voice from behind startled him.

"Told you I'd see you soon."

CHAPTER 3

SOME THINGS in life would always be an enigma. Like crop circles. Or the square root of pi. Or why hot dogs are sold in packages of ten and buns in packages of eight. Elijah wondered where he would rank his inability to put Adam Lancaster out of his mind as he tailed his eco-friendly hybrid after the fundraiser.

Elijah had driven Katie home immediately after jotting down his bid. Then he'd driven around for several hours until he found himself back at the hotel's parking lot, hoping to catch Adam on his way out. When Adam walked out with Bruce by his side, Elijah hadn't given a second thought to following them.

By the time Elijah had hidden his car beside the HOPE parking lot, watched stalker-style while Adam kissed his date good night, and then hung around waiting for the guy to come back out, Elijah determined his surprising new obsession was infinitely more confusing than the intricate details of string theory. Not that he had any plans to talk himself out of what he was about to do.

Elijah wanted Adam, and as a general rule, when Elijah wanted something that badly, he made it happen. Even if he was tempted to wonder what the hell he was doing, there's no way he was changing his mind.

When Adam finally walked out the door, his hand thrown over his shoulder in a wave to whoever was still inside, Elijah slid out of his Lexus and jogged across the parking lot.

"Told you I'd see you soon."

Adam jumped and spun around with one arm raised and ready to strike even as recognition dawned in his eyes. Elijah didn't even flinch. He felt fairly confident Adam wouldn't attack him. And if he did? It was the perfect excuse to put his hands on the man.

"Shit. You scared me." Adam bent over at the waist, one hand on his knee and the other covering his heart. "Don't you know it's never okay to sneak up on a gay man in a dark, empty parking lot?"

Elijah snorted and then stepped closer, drinking in Adam's disheveled hair and tired eyes. "It's probably a bad idea to sneak up on anyone in a dark, empty parking lot. I apologize. I didn't mean to startle you."

"It's all right. I'm so tired, I didn't even hear you." Adam sighed and ran a hand through his hair, mussing it up even more. He raked his eyes over Elijah. "So, is there a reason you're stalking me in the parking lot? Change your mind about your bid?"

Elijah took another step forward, dangerously close to invading Adam's personal space. "Of course not. Why would you think I changed my mind about the bid? Or that I'd chase you down in the middle of the night just to do so?"

"Saying I was shocked to receive your *extremely* generous donation would be like saying Brad and Angelina kinda sorta like adopting kids."

"Brad and… wait, what?" Elijah frowned as he replayed their evening in his mind. Had their conversation ended badly? He remembered being intrigued with Adam's passion for his job, offering a few tips to improve efficiency, and then forcing himself to leave as early as possible so he didn't drag Adam into the bathroom. "Our conversation ended badly?"

"You didn't seem very impressed when you left."

Elijah grinned. "Oh, I can assure you I was very impressed." He took another step forward, close enough that Adam had to look up to meet his eyes. Surely Adam knew why he was there.

Adam's tongue peeked out of his mouth, and he swiped it across his lower lip. "Well, in that case, thank you. It was a very generous donation. I can't even begin to thank you enough."

Elijah smiled and dipped his chin, acknowledging Adam's gratitude. He stepped forward again, only inches away from Adam, who took a step back and bumped into the side of his hybrid.

"So, if you're not here because of the bid, why are you here?"

Elijah rested his hand against the car door next to Adam's arm. He'd never had to seduce a man before. Everything between him and Brian had been natural and effortless. Since then, he'd only been with men he'd picked up in gay bars while away on business, and he'd hooked every single one with nothing more than a little eye contact and a jerk of his head. He sure as hell didn't want to force himself on Adam if the guy wasn't interested, but Adam had yet to tell him to stop. Elijah pressed forward.

"I must be off my game if it's not obvious by now." Elijah inched forward again.

Adam's mouth opened and closed, and then opened… and closed again. Elijah wondered if it was a quirk of his. He'd seen him do the same thing over dinner. Figuring Adam would've pushed him away by then if he didn't want him, Elijah leaned forward and pressed his hips, chest, and finally his lips against Adam's. Every inch of him zinged alive as he took Adam's mouth in a hard kiss. It only took a moment for Adam to respond. He slid his arms around Elijah's waist to grab at his ass, and damn, if that didn't turn Elijah on even more.

Elijah thrust against Adam, and even through the layers of clothing, the feel of Adam's cock rubbing against his own was sweet relief. Adam groaned, and Elijah gripped the sides of Adam's neck and pushed himself away. Time to find somewhere to finish this. Elijah had no desire to come in his pants in the middle of a cold parking lot. Adam, however, had other ideas. He grabbed the scarf Elijah had draped around his neck, pulled him down again, and locked their lips together once more. Elijah's eyes rolled back in his head as Adam trailed wet, open-mouthed kisses down his neck, his whiskers scraping against Elijah's sensitive skin.

"Fuck," Elijah sighed.

"Mmnnff," Adam agreed.

"Should we go somewhere more private?" Elijah asked. Without warning, Adam's body went from soft and pliable to stiff and tense. He jerked away.

"Shit. I'm sorry," Adam stuttered, covering his mouth with the back of his hand.

Elijah reached for Adam but ended up wrapping his hand around the back of his own neck when Adam ducked out of the way. "Too much?"

Adam barked out half a laugh. "Yes. I mean, no. I mean, I just… I can't believe I did that."

"There was nothing wrong with that from where I'm standing."

Adam ran a hand over his face, distress in his hazel eyes. "You mean other than the fact that we were both out on dates with other people three hours ago, and you just became HOPE's largest benefactor?"

"What does money have to do with anything? And I wasn't aware you were that hung up on your date, given the amount of attention you gave him tonight."

Adam gaped at him, his eyes wide. "Since you seem to have such a huge problem with the way I manage my social life, you should be glad I ended… whatever that was."

"It was a kiss—a fucking hot kiss at that—and I was fine with the way you ran your social life until it stopped me from getting what I want."

Adam threw his hands up in the air. "What in the hell is that supposed to mean?"

Oh, for fuck's sake. Elijah had never put so much effort into getting laid. "Isn't it obvious? I thought I'd made myself pretty damn clear, considering—"

Adam's eyes widened. "Is that... is that why you made that bid? You thought I'd sleep with you if you threw some money at my center?"

Elijah clenched his jaw and crossed his arms against his chest. "I'm not exactly in the habit of dropping a hundred grand when I have an urge to fuck someone."

"Well, you picked the wrong person to start with," Adam exclaimed.

"I didn't.... Fuck it. This was obviously a mistake." Elijah turned on his heel and stalked back to his car without another word. He would fulfill his promise and sign the check for HOPE Monday morning, and then he would put Adam Lancaster and his conceited assumptions out of his mind for good.

ELIJAH SPENT the rest of the weekend working from home, only stopping for a couple of hours to hit the gym in his basement. First thing Monday morning, he signed a check made out to The Center for HOPE and shot off a quick e-mail to his dad to warn him about the upcoming draft. Technically he had no say, but given the amount was well over what the company normally donated and the fact that his father was... well, his father, Elijah knew he'd be hearing from him if he didn't head off the attack. Once he finished combing through his work e-mail, Elijah set the check on the corner of his desk for Sherri to send to HOPE.

Nine hours later Elijah spotted the check still on his desk and realized he'd completely forgotten to ask Sherri to mail it. After briefly considering leaving the check until the next day, he closed down his computer and grabbed the damn thing on his way out.

Elijah rolled his eyes at his own stupidity as he pulled into HOPE's parking lot and remembered how foolishly he'd acted Saturday night. He hadn't let anyone have even that little amount of power over him since he was a teenager. He'd acted like a damn fool, coming on to Adam like that, but fuck if he didn't push all the right buttons. He was so damn hot, he would've been Elijah's first choice in any crowded gay bar. But if Elijah'd picked him up in some random club, he wouldn't know jack shit about his foster-child-turned-gay-Superman routine, and he wouldn't have let him get under his skin. Lesson learned, at least. He was better off sticking to random hookups where he never even learned the guy's name.

Expecting the place to be nearly deserted at 6:00 p.m., Elijah was surprised to open the front door and find the foyer filled with people he recognized.

"Come on, Adam. I'm practically on your way home. If I take the bus, I have to leave now, but if you drive me, we can get another game in." Though Kollin almost sounded as if he were whining, his entire face was lit up in a smile while he pestered Adam.

"Kris. Control your boy. I thought *you* were on driving-Ms.-Daisy duty since he's been helping you advertise." Adam, who looked completely different dressed in distressed black jeans, a dark gray Henley, and a gray beanie, was munching on something as he spoke—M&Ms maybe. His smile was big enough to rival Kollin's.

"Don't blame me. I offered to drive him home, but I'm leaving now, and apparently that's not a good time for his majesty." Kirsten grabbed the huge bag she'd been shoving shit into and threw it over her shoulder. She finally noticed Elijah and offered him a smile and a wink. "Up to you, kiddo, but this cabbie has a hot date with her hubby tonight. And it looks like my dear brother has some unfinished business to take care of."

Three pairs of eyes turned Elijah's way, and no one spoke for a moment.

"Hey. Mr. Langley, right?" Kollin finally asked. "We met the other week in your office. You coulda told me you owned the place."

Elijah cleared his throat. "Sorry about that. How've you been?"

"I was fantastic until I found out I'd be taking the bus home today," Kollin said, eyeing Adam and Kirsten.

"Oh, stop pouting," Adam said, still throwing food into his mouth. "I'll have you home by seven."

"Sweeeet."

Kirsten patted Adam's arm and kissed his cheek. "Very sweet. I'm out of here. See you guys tomorrow," she said as she flitted past Elijah.

"So, you in for another game of basketball?" Kollin asked Adam.

Adam pushed off the desk he'd been leaning against and playfully shoved Kollin away. "Let me talk to Mr. Langley first, and then we'll see how much time we have. Okay?"

"'Course, man." Kollin was practically dancing on his toes with excitement as he pointed to Elijah. "You should totally join us, though. We can play two on one. Adam needs all the help he can get."

Elijah looked at Adam, hoping for a little help, but Adam only dug his hands into his pockets and smirked. Bastard expected him to watch Elijah squirm out of Kollin's invitation, but he'd be damned if he was going to allow Adam Lancaster to have the last word.

Elijah met Adam's eyes and smiled. "If Adam's up for it, so am I."

CHAPTER 4

"I'M TELLING you, Kris." Adam sat back in his chair and threw the butt end of his sub onto the desk. "You should've seen the look on Kollin's face when Elijah offered to drive him home."

"I'm surprised he didn't squee like a little schoolgirl, or the gay boy we know and love, with front row 1D tickets. Doesn't Elijah drive the new Lexus LFA?"

Adam stared at Kirsten. "How the hell am I supposed to know? I don't know squat about cars. It had that funky looking *V* on the front."

"You mean the *L*? You're kinda pathetic, you know."

"What? How do you know what he drives anyway, Ms. Busybody?"

"I don't for sure, but Kollin and I saw one in the parking lot of LL&C when we were over there a few weeks ago." Kirsten shrugged a shoulder. "Figured it had to be his. They cost more than my house."

"Why do you know more about cars than I do?"

"I don't know. Why do I dress better than you? You're supposed to be gay. Show a little respect for the stereotype. This grunge look you're rockin'… not really working for you."

"It's not grunge. It's hipster, wench. Why are you in my office ridiculing me again?"

"Because I brought you lunch, and you love me."

Adam rolled his eyes and shoved Kirsten's feet off his desk. "*Anyway,* he told me before he left he'd call me sometime today. Said he has a proposition for me and wants an official tour of the center."

"A proposition like the one from Saturday night in the parking lot or a legit one for the center?"

"Didn't say, but I can't imagine it'd be personal after the way things ended between us. I pretty much accused him of trying to pay me for sex. So I have no idea why he'd want to help the center either."

"And could you just quickly remind me again why being with him is such a bad idea?"

"Uh… he's straight."

"Uh…," Kirsten mimicked, "he's obviously not, if he kissed you."

Leaning forward to rest his elbows on his knees, Adam ticked off points on his fingers. "Okay. Even if he's gay or bi, he's clearly still in the closet. We have absolutely nothing in common once his check clears. And besides, I know things kind of fizzled with Bruce Saturday night, but we really had a great time on our first date. I thought you were in his corner anyway."

"Make no mistake, brother mine, I'm on your side. If that means a cushy, safe relationship with Bruce, then I'm all for it. But if it means a torrid, whirlwind romance with Cary's wealthiest, ending in tear-soaked Ben & Jerry's, then pass me a spoon."

Adam grinned at Kirsten. "That doesn't even make sense."

"Fine. Maybe I just want some ice cream."

"You're not very good at this."

"Shut up. I am *so* good at this. You're just not listening. My point is… sometimes going with the option that makes the most sense or gives you the most security isn't always what makes you happiest."

"Okay, Confucius. I hear you. Regardless, getting involved with Elijah Langley is not going to happen."

"Are you at least going to tell me if he's a good kisser?" she pouted.

Adam sighed dramatically as he rolled his eyes, but he knew his grin gave him away.

"Ack! Tell me everything."

"No, you nosy whore. Butohmygodhemademytoescurl," Adam rushed out. "And his body… he's built like fucking Thor."

Kirsten squinted. "I can see the resemblance… though I'm surprised you even know who Thor is."

"Ha-fucking-ha. I know my hot men, thank you very much."

Kirsten threw her wrapper at Adam and laughed as it bounced off his cheek and landed on his desk. "So, you really think this thing with Bruce will work out?"

"I don't know, but we have a lot in common. Aaaand his ass looks amazing in a pair of jeans."

"At least you have your priorities straight," Kirsten deadpanned as she stood and plucked the stray trash off Adam's desk. "I have to get out of here and back to work. If you see Julie, will you tell her I can't make it back over here today? I'll have to catch up with her tomorrow."

"Of course, but I should warn you, she was here yesterday with some suspicious bruising. I asked her about it, but she swore someone had run into her at school. Said some books hit her arm."

The color drained from Kirsten's face as Adam spoke. It wasn't the first time during the three years she'd been coming to HOPE that Julie had shown up with bruises, but they seemed to be popping up more often. State law required Adam to report any suspected parental abuse, but over the seven years he'd been doing this, he'd learned to be discerning in how and when he reported such suspicions. He'd seen too many parents evade charges. Then the kid would never return to the center because Adam ran to the police.

As unfair as it seemed, he'd finally learned to start carefully playing the system. Julie would be eighteen in just six months, and in addition to her inherent kindness and fierce loyalty, she was also insanely stubborn. If she hadn't yet admitted one of her parents was responsible for her injuries, Adam knew it would never happen. Without her cooperation, this close to her eighteenth birthday, it was too risky to pursue legal action without more evidence.

Kirsten fell back onto the old couch Adam kept in his office. "I wish she'd just tell us the truth. She's old enough to be emancipated, and I'd take her in myself if she didn't want to stay here."

"I know," Adam said softly, "but we can't save them all."

A tear slipped down Kirsten's face. "I hate that stupid saying. Does it make me a bad person that I want to save her more?"

Adam shoved himself out of his chair to join Kirsten on the couch and wrap his arms around her shoulders. "No. It makes you human. You saw something in Julie that a lot of people miss, and you fought for her trust and her friendship. I don't, for one minute, think you'd trade her life for someone else's. You just love her a little bit more. And that's okay, because you know what? She needs it."

Kirsten sniffed into Adam's shoulder. "I still hate that saying."

Squeezing her in one last tight hug, Adam whispered, "I do too, but sometimes it's the only thing that gets me through the day."

ELIJAH PULLED into HOPE's parking lot and eyed the bag sitting on his passenger seat. He'd packed gym clothes that morning, hoping Kollin would want to play ball again. In an unusual jolt of insecurity, he felt hesitant to bring the bag inside for fear of appearing presumptuous. He was supposed to be getting an official tour of the center and laying out his idea for Adam. Hanging out with Kollin again would just be a perk.

Aside from wanting to wipe the smug look off Adam's face, Elijah couldn't say why he'd accepted Kollin's offer to play ball the other day.

Kollin looked a lot like Brian, but it wasn't as though Elijah thought he was some miraculous reincarnation. Ignoring their similar looks and love of basketball, Kollin and Brian didn't have anything in common. Brian had been reserved—shy even—while Kollin seemed to have never met a stranger, and his huge personality filled every room he walked into. All Elijah knew was, as soon as Kollin asked him to play, turning him down wasn't an option.

In the end, he was glad he'd accepted Kollin's invitation. Aside from having the most fun he'd had in years, playing with him and Adam had also given Elijah a better idea of what Adam meant when he said the kids needed him. As confident and self-assured as Kollin appeared, it was clear he idolized Adam. The two tossed insults back and forth throughout the game, but Elijah didn't think he'd ever seen someone look as proud as Kollin did when Adam coached him on his technique and praised him on his fade-away jump shot. Elijah could see why the kids needed *Adam*. Knowing how committed the man in charge was to their happiness and well-being sure would provide an extra layer of security for the kids.

Elijah climbed out of his car, leaving the bag, and walked swiftly through the cold January air. The reception area was nearly empty this time. Only an older woman sat behind the welcome desk. She looked up at him and smiled brightly.

"Good afternoon. I'm Chloe Nickols. Thanks for coming by today, Mr. Langley. And right on time too."

Elijah plastered a smile on his face. This woman was far too chipper, but he had to give her points for knowing who he was and when he was supposed to arrive.

"Thank you. Is Adam available?"

Somehow her smile grew larger. "He's here... somewhere. I told him to keep an eye on the time, but once he gets started with those kids, he loses track of everything else."

Elijah forced another smile and remained silent. Thankfully Adam chose that moment to run into the foyer. He wore distressed jeans—again— with a dark green hoodie. His glasses were tucked into a black beanie that showed off a rainbow-colored My Little Pony. Clearly Adam hadn't felt it necessary to dress up, but Elijah's body didn't seem to mind. He shifted uncomfortably as he tore his eyes away from Adam's ridiculous hat and settled them on Adam's ridiculously handsome face.

Perfect.

"Sorry you had to wait. Couple of the guys thought they could school me in Ping-Pong," Adam said with a roll of his eyes and a grin that could rival Mrs. Nickols's.

Two boys, also smiling widely, trotted in behind Adam. The taller of the pair lightly shoved Adam's shoulder. "Thought? I'm pretty sure we kicked your ass."

"It was all Ann's fault. She totally missed that last shot."

"Yeah, the twenty you missed before don't count, right?" the shorter boy teased as they headed toward the door.

"Semantics! I was gearing up for an epic comeback, and she ruined it."

Elijah watched as Adam joked with the boys. He was carefree, happy, and relaxed—just like he'd been the other day playing ball with Kollin.

"Ready?" Adam asked. "I thought I'd show you around, and then we can head back to my office to go over the boring stuff."

"Sounds good."

"Right. Then we'll just start here. We keep someone at that desk twenty-four seven. If Chloe has to step away for even a minute, she calls one of the volunteers or me to take over for her. The last thing we want is someone who needs help to walk through those doors into an empty room," Adam explained as they walked away from the front desk.

"Makes sense." Elijah stopped and shot his hand out to grab Adam's elbow. "Wait, even on Saturday night?"

ADAM LOOKED at Elijah. He couldn't tell where Elijah was heading with his question, and hashing anything out in the middle of the hallway was never a good idea. As close as he was with most of his kids, Adam kept his personal life private and away from the center.

"What about it?"

"Did anyone see us?"

"Possibly… *probably*, actually. But you don't have to worry about Clint saying anything. Most of the volunteers here know a thing or two about secrets," Adam hedged, then tried to lighten the mood. "Chloe, on the other hand…. She won't blab your secrets to anyone, but she'll bug the hell out of you until you spill your life story."

Adam could actually see the relief wash over Elijah's face, and he gestured for Adam to continue the tour.

"So…. Dr. Maggie and Dr. Will share this office. They may as well be volunteering for what we pay them, but you'd be hard-pressed to find two people better suited. They've been with me since the beginning, and I'd be lost without them. They also run their own private practice together, and many of our alumni have continued their counseling with them."

"They aren't full-time staff?"

"No. I wish. We have the budget for one full-time therapist, but we decided early on it was better to have a male and female therapist on hand. If a boy comes in here with a black eye because his father doesn't want a faggot for a son, there's no way I'm forcing him to open up to a male when the one man he was supposed to be able to trust has just let him down. Some people don't care, but some do. I'm grateful we found two wonderful therapists who are willing to work with us."

"Sounds like you were very fortunate." Elijah spoke slowly, seeming to choose his words carefully.

"Very. Ready to move on, or do you have any other questions?" Adam peered at Elijah, wondering what demons of his own he was fighting.

"Nope. I'm good. Lead on."

Adam continued to the multipurpose room, which held two big-screen TVs on opposite ends, a Ping-Pong table, several chairs and couches, a wall full of books, and a couple of round tables. There were a handful of kids in the room, most around the TVs, but there were also two girls working on homework together.

"Nice," Elijah commented as he gazed at the group sprawled in front of the TV. "Not what I was expecting."

Adam shrugged. "My main goals when we opened were to give the kids a place where they could hang out—feel accepted and safe—and provide them with the tools they'd need to succeed as adults. This is where they spend most of their time. We do some organized activities. We've gone to some local plays and museums, and we participate in different community-service projects. We've even taken a couple of mini road trips, but for the most part, this is it."

"Are the workshops held in here too?"

"No. Most of them are held in this room." Adam gestured across the hall to a much smaller room outfitted with tables, chairs, and an enormous whiteboard covering one wall. "We found the most successful workshops center around applying for jobs, filling out applications for college, and transitioning to self-sufficiency—basically, things typical teens would rely on their parents and teachers to help them with. We also hold a couple workshops a month for anyone else interested in helping bridge the gap.

There are a lot of people out there who are ignorant of how difficult it can be for LGBT youth, simply because there's a lack of public awareness."

"And that's part of what you do? You're in charge of drumming up awareness?" Elijah asked.

"I do my best, but some of our volunteers excel at it," Adam acknowledged. "Kirsten in particular. We contact as many businesses as we can, targeting schools and hospitals, in an effort to persuade their HR departments to offer awareness courses to their employees."

Elijah nodded but didn't comment further, so Adam finished the tour by showing him the kitchen and finally the spacious back yard, which Elijah had already seen when they played basketball. The grounds also boasted a small garden and several sitting areas.

They were passing the common room again when Kollin shouted, "Hey. You're back. You guys up for a game? Everyone else is being a drag today." He pointed at Chris, who shoved Kollin's shoulder but didn't take his eyes off the television.

"I have some things to discuss with Adam, but I'm in," Elijah said, a genuine smile on his handsome face. "When do you have to be home?"

"For real? Don't have to be home until seven, so I have to leave here at six, unless someone offers me a ride home…." Kollin looked innocently at Adam and Elijah.

"I can take you," Elijah said. "We'll find you when we're done."

At a loss for words, Adam snapped his jaw shut. He'd seen glimpses of this carefree Elijah when they were playing ball on Monday, but Adam was still amazed at how Elijah's entire body relaxed after the short exchange with Kollin. Adam could actually hear the smile in his voice. After seeing how quickly Kollin took to Elijah, Adam dared to hope Elijah would be a positive influence for him—a mentor even. Seeing Elijah's tension melt away in Kollin's presence made him think the kid would be just as good for Elijah.

"Well, now that *that's* settled, you ready to head back to my office?"

Once situated behind his desk, Adam sucked in a deep breath and looked directly at Elijah.

"I didn't want to get into it in the hallway earlier, but before I start, I want to apologize for my behavior the other night. I'm not sure how everything escalated so quickly. I was just so shocked that it happened at all, and then what I said… well, I didn't want you to think I stopped it because of you. No matter how…" Adam paused, "*attractive* my donors may be, I try to avoid making out with them in our parking lot."

Elijah raised his eyebrows in surprise and leaned forward to rest his elbow on Adam's desk. Maybe he'd end up getting what he wanted after all. "So you did enjoy the kiss. And you think I'm attractive."

"Pfft…. I think we both know the answer to that. Low enjoyment factor was *not* the reason I stopped."

Elijah smiled as Adam's cheeks tinged pink. "Good to know," he said, recalling how Adam had pulled him back for more.

"Right. Well, like I said, it was extremely unprofessional of me, and I won't forget myself like that again."

Elijah rolled his eyes. This man was going to drive him insane. One minute they were almost flirting, and the next he was pulling away. "By all means, don't hold back on my account. I was perfectly clear where I stood on the matter, and we already clarified that money isn't an issue for me. In fact, those were business funds, not personal."

"I'm not sure that makes it any better."

"Listen, contrary to whatever your enormous ego is telling you, I did *not* donate that money to get you into my bed, nor would being rejected by you make me change my mind. I have my own reasons for wanting that inn opened."

"Of course. I'm sorry. Can we just pretend like none of that ever happened?"

Disappointment shot through Elijah, but he shrugged his shoulders. "If that's our only option, then I guess it will have to do."

"Thank you. Now let's move on to whatever it is you want to talk about, before I stick my foot in my mouth again."

Elijah straightened back in his chair and linked his fingers over his stomach. "I'd like to anonymously donate the rest of the funds your center needs to purchase the Tarboro Inn."

Adam stared at Elijah, his eyes wide. "You want to *what*?"

"Do I really need to repeat it?"

Adam nodded. "Yeah, I think you do, because I'm pretty sure there's no way you said what I just heard."

Warmth filled Elijah's chest as he took in Adam's surprised face, and he smiled—a wide, genuine smile. "I said…." Elijah cleared his throat. "I'd like to donate the rest of the funds needed to purchase the Tarboro Inn. I'm also interested in helping to solicit any remaining supplies needed."

Adam looked around the room. "Are we on some kind of prank show?"

"Nope. I can have legal papers drawn up if you don't believe me."

"But… why? You flat out told me I wasn't doing a good job running the center."

Elijah stiffened. He might not be able to get Adam out of his head, but that didn't mean he was going to spill his guts to the guy. "I didn't say that at all. I said there were better ways, which I still believe. However, after being here and meeting some of your youth, I have to agree that they're better off with your direct involvement."

Elijah looked around Adam's cluttered, almost lived-in office and then down at his hands. He took a deep breath. "I thought that if we work well together, and you're interested…. Once the inn is ready, I can help figure out a way where you have plenty of time to spend with the youth coming through here without working fourteen hours a day."

Holy fuck. Elijah felt like a bumbling teenager asking his crush to prom. He didn't often admit he was wrong, mostly because he rarely argued a point unless he was sure he was right, but Elijah had seen the impact Adam had on these kids, not just Kollin. He looked up at Adam, certain he would be rolling his eyes, but instead, he had propped his elbow on the arm of his chair and covered his mouth with his hand. He was staring at his computer screen, though clearly not seeing whatever was on it. Elijah would have to be blind to miss the fat tears threatening to spill from Adam's eyes. Rather than fill the awkward space with more babble, Elijah remained silent and waited for Adam to speak.

"I'm not sure how to thank you," Adam finally responded. "I knew we'd get there eventually, but this is just… really beyond my wildest dreams."

"It's the least I can do."

ADAM STARED at Elijah, his mind reeling. Matthew and Amelia were long-time friends with the former owners of the Tarboro Inn, which shut down just after Adam started The Center for HOPE. When Adam joined the Wright family, they insisted he be a part of the standing family-dinner night they had at the inn's small restaurant every Thursday. The consistency of those weekly dinners—something so simple—had been a turning point in Adam's life.

After being tossed from one home to another, always dismissed when his guardians found out he was gay, he'd lost hope of finding a family who truly accepted him. Adam liked Matthew and Amelia from the beginning and, knowing he was running out of options, made a conscious effort to keep his sexual orientation to himself. He tried his best to downplay his more flamboyant nature, pretending to be someone he wasn't, and hoped this family would stick. It was the first time he'd ever intentionally compromised who he was, and the more he hid that very large part of his life, the angrier he became and the more he acted out.

About three months into his stay with the Wrights, Adam carefully applied some eyeliner, squeezed into his tightest jeans and flashiest pink shirt, and joined his caretakers in the living room to go to what he was sure would be his last Thursday dinner. Amelia merely motioned him forward and fidgeted with his already perfect collar. Then she dropped a kiss on his cheek and told him how handsome he looked. When the owner came by during dinner, Matthew draped his arm around Adam's shoulder and referred to him as his son. It was the first time in a long time that Adam had felt as if he'd belonged somewhere.

Things didn't get better overnight. In fact, it took years for Adam to trust his new family, but he never forgot those family dinners and had even gone so far as to tattoo that date onto his chest, right over his heart.

Even though he'd only begun fundraising a little over a year before, buying the inn had been on Adam's mind since he first heard it was closing its doors. He seriously doubted Elijah understood exactly what it meant to him. On top of creating a safe haven for LGBT young adults, he was saving one of the most precious memories of Adam's youth. It was far from the least Elijah could do.

"No, it's really not. The least you could've done was have Langley sponsor a table. This… this is… I don't even know. Thank you doesn't seem big enough for this."

"Well, I assure you it's plenty," Elijah said, his voice stiff and formal. "Why don't you take a few days and think about how this works best for you. Let the current owners know you'll be buying soon. My only caveat is that I'd like to tour the inn first. Give me a call when you're ready, and we can set something up to get the ball rolling." Elijah avoided Adam's eyes and checked his watch. "Kollin only has about an hour left. Mind if I change in here before we play? I grabbed my bag while you were in the can earlier."

"Of course not. I'll step out and check on things while you get ready." Adam stood and held his hand out to Elijah, still completely befuddled by everything that had transpired over the past few days—not only by Elijah's insane offer, but also by the numerous personalities he'd shown Adam over the handful of times they'd interacted. Every time Adam thought he had a handle on him, Elijah surprised him all over again. "Thank you. So much.

When I get my head wrapped around this, I might be able to say something else. But for now, it's all I have."

Elijah accepted Adam's handshake but offered little to nothing in terms of his emotions. Closing his office door behind him, Adam immediately recognized the frazzled, terrified look of the young man sitting in the reception area. An old, beat-up book bag sat at his feet, and his clothes were dirty and a little too big on his slight frame. Adam glanced at Chloe, who was on the phone. She held one finger up as she wrapped up her conversation and then motioned him over.

"This is Mark," she said, gesturing toward the boy. "I just got off the phone with Dr. Will, who suggested we let Mark get some rest, since it's so late in the day."

Then Chloe spoke directly to Mark. "He said he'd talk with you tomorrow unless you need him tonight."

Mark eyed them warily and shook his head. "Tomorrow's fine."

"Have you had anything to eat or drink yet?" Adam asked.

"Kollin's fixing him something," Chloe said before Mark could answer.

Adam squeezed Chloe's hand, hoping to reassure her. No matter how many times she'd done this, she fretted over every single teen. "Thanks, Chloe."

He turned back to Mark. "My name's Adam Lancaster. Welcome to HOPE." He didn't offer his hand. Without knowing what the guy had been through, it was safer.

Mark continued to stare at Adam and then nodded. "She said if I talk to someone, I can stay more than a couple of days. I don't have anywhere else to go."

"She's right. If you're under eighteen, it's our policy to offer a safe place to stay for up to forty-eight hours before we have to notify the authorities. If you're of age, we have some leeway, but there's still a process to follow."

Raising his chin a notch, Mark looked into Adam's eyes, almost daring Adam to challenge him. "Turned eighteen a couple months ago."

"Okay, then. My office will be free in just a minute, and we can go over some ground rules. It won't take too long, and then we can get you set up with a place to sleep. And here comes Kollin now with some food."

Mark perked up, though Adam couldn't be sure what held his attention more, given the way his eyes raked over Kollin as he grabbed the peanut butter and jelly sandwich. He tried not to make snap judgments, but so far,

Mark made him more than a little nervous. Though clearly in need of help, he held his body as if he had a huge fucking boulder on his shoulder, and that didn't often end with a grateful and cooperative tenant.

Elijah strolled out of Adam's office wearing warm-up pants and a Yale rugby shirt. The dark blue pullover stretched over Elijah's chest almost obscenely, showing off his incredibly muscular shoulders and pecs. Adam had a feeling that if the bottom of the shirt were just as snug, he'd be able to count off a nice, tight six-pack. When he tore his eyes away from Elijah's body, it was too late to pretend as if he hadn't been ogling him.

Elijah stared at Adam with a crooked grin on his face. "You guys ready to play?" he asked, not taking his eyes off Adam.

Adam shook his head. "I have to take a rain check this time. Something came up, but take it easy on the kid. He gets winded pretty quickly."

Kollin scoffed. "You're obviously confusing me with yourself, old man. Let's go, Mr. Langley. Time's a-wastin'."

Elijah glanced from Mark to Kollin to Adam, apparently gauging the situation, and nodded. "Sure thing. I'll be in touch." He walked over to Kollin, ruffled his hair, and threw an arm around his shoulder. "You know you don't have to call me Mr. Langley, right? My name's Elijah."

As they walked down the hallway, Kollin shook his head. "Can I call you Eli?"

Adam smiled and turned back to Mark, who was stuffing the last bite of his sandwich into his mouth. "Come on. I have some water in my office, and then we'll get you settled in with some more food."

Mark watched with an air of distrust as Adam plopped the application down in front of him. "I'm going to be blunt, because I have to be. We only have two emergency beds right now. I don't know what your story is yet, but you're welcome to one of them—provided you follow the rules, of which there are many. If I find out you're not yet eighteen, I'm obligated to contact the appropriate authorities, but I want to help you out as much as possible. To do that, I need honesty from you."

"I swear I'm eighteen. I left my parents' house right after my birthday and was staying at this place in Greensboro. But they figured out I was gay, and I had to leave. One of the people who works there found me on the street a couple days later and told me about this place."

Adam didn't think Mark was lying. He was defensive, sure, but unless he was a very skilled actor, his words rang true. "I'm sorry to hear that, but I'm glad you found us. While you're here, you'll have full access to any programs we offer, and you'll be required to participate in some—including therapy sessions. The safety of everyone here is my main priority. We have plenty of youth who only drop in here once or twice, and we have a core group consisting of about fifteen right now who call the center their second home. I'm not sure how much you know about us, but, more than a safe house, we're a place teens like yourself can come to be themselves and have access to programs you might not feel comfortable participating in under normal circumstances."

Mark struggled—and failed—to hold back a yawn as he listened. Adam wondered how he'd gotten from Greensboro to Cary. It was at least seventy-five miles, and if he walked even part of it, the guy had to be exhausted. Adam tapped the paper on the top of the stack. "Read this over. It's good for forty-eight hours and states that you'll agree to have one session with one of our therapists, one formal meeting with one of our volunteers, and you won't steal from me. We also have a strict no-touching policy. Hands should always be visible. If you agree, sign it, and we'll get you to a shower and a bed. We can go over the long-term stuff tomorrow."

"What happens if I leave as soon as I wake up?"

"No one here will stop you, but if you don't meet with our therapist and a volunteer tomorrow, you won't be sleeping here tomorrow night. I have no idea when someone will come in needing one of those beds, and I'm not going to turn them away if you don't respect me enough to follow my rules."

With wary eyes, Mark leaned forward and signed his name to the top paper.

CHAPTER 5

ELIJAH SMACKED the ball out of Kollin's hands as they walked outside onto the basketball court. "Play to twelve, win by two?"

"How about we just play a game of HORSE?" Kollin asked. "Wouldn't want you to strain something trying to keep up with me."

"I like how you think you got jokes."

Kollin shrugged his shoulder and offered a grin that quickly fell.

"You okay? Everything all right at school?" Elijah hadn't spent a lot of time with Kollin, but he'd never seen the kid abandon a battle of wits so quickly.

"Yeah, just… you know. That guy." Kollin shrugged again.

"He's here now. I'm sure Adam will take good care of him."

Kollin grabbed the ball back from Elijah, dribbled a few times, and took a shot. When the ball swished through the net, he flashed Elijah a smile and stepped aside. "I know… it's just… I mean, sometimes I think it's better to just keep it all quiet if being honest about who you are means you'll be kicked out of your house. Right? Seems like it'd be harder to lose your parents and your *house*, your clothes… food on the regular, than it would to just pretend for a few more years."

Elijah took a deep breath and dribbled the ball. He was in no way prepared to have this conversation. "I don't know, man. I'm not sure there's an Easy button here. I can tell you I admire the hell out of anyone who owns who they are regardless of the consequences. Doesn't mean I look down on anyone who does what they have to do to stay safe or stay sane."

"Yeah. I guess."

Elijah took a shot, not really taking the time to aim, and missed.

"Look who's got H," Kollin singsonged.

"Yeah, yeah. Take your next shot."

Kollin grabbed the ball and dribbled to the basket for an easy layup.

"You know, the scary part is… maybe he didn't even come out. Maybe his parents just found out because he wasn't careful enough. So, one day his life is pretty good, and the next he's on the street, feeling grateful his parents let him stuff some shit in his book bag before they threw him out." Kollin tossed the ball to Elijah and stared him right in the eye. "That's what happened to this girl, just a couple weeks after I started coming here. 'Cept she was only sixteen. So Adam had to call the cops eventually, but she took off before they got here. She told me she'd rather be on the streets than go in the system if she couldn't stay here. That's when I started helping Kirsten pass out stuff about our fundraisers. If we'd already had that inn, she might've had another option."

Elijah had no idea what to say or what kind of assurances the kid was looking for, and his natural instinct was to fix whatever problems he encountered. Adam Lancaster needed money to buy an inn. Elijah could write a check. If Langley Lumber lost a big client, Elijah showed up at their door, and nine times out of ten, the client came back. Telling a fifteen-year-old gay boy everything was going to be okay… not really in Elijah's bag of tricks.

"You know what?" Kollin finally said. "Forget it. I didn't mean to be a drag. Seeing that guy wolf down that sandwich like he hadn't eaten in days—and smelling like that… it was just a lot, you know?"

Elijah walked over to Kollin and placed a hand on his shoulder. He looked so small right then. Even though he didn't even come up to Elijah's shoulders, Kollin's larger-than-life personality often made him seem bigger—older. It was too easy to forget Kollin was still very young, and Elijah had no idea what struggles he faced day in and day out. "It *is* a lot, and to be completely honest, I'm probably the last person you should be talking to about this. But I've only been here a couple of times, and I can already see what a great support system you have here. You know Adam would've done everything in his power to help that girl. She just didn't want to be helped. Maybe she wasn't ready. Maybe she'll be back."

"Yeah. I know. I ain't mad at Adam." Kollin rolled his eyes. "As if that's even possible. Everybody loves Adam. It's like his gift or something."

Sensing Kollin was ready to move on—he sure as hell was—Elijah started back to the three-point line to start his layup. "His gift?"

"You know what I mean. Some people are good at numbers. Other people can sing really well, and some are great cooks. Whatever. They're just really good at it. Adam makes people love him. I don't really know how, because he can really be a smartass sometimes. And he's not that great at basketball… or *Call of Duty*. He's a shitty cook too. But don't tell him I said that."

Elijah laughed as he jogged toward the basket and made his easy layup. "Oh, I'm definitely telling him."

Blocking Kollin's next shot, Elijah stole the ball and ran to the hoop, hoping like hell he could pull off a dunk. About halfway up, he felt fairly confident but realized a moment too late he wasn't going to make it. Instead of jamming the ball through the rim, he bounced it off the side. The force of the ricochet knocked him flat on his ass.

His mortification doubled when he heard Adam join in with Kollin's laughter. "You know what this means, right?" Kollin asked as he held out a hand to help Elijah up.

"What's that?" Elijah groaned.

Kollin's smirk was triumphant. "You gotta keep coming back until you can make that dunk."

Elijah glanced at a shrugging Adam. "Yeah. You might want to choose a harder goal, man. I'll be nailing that dunk by this time next week."

"OH, FUCK me." Elijah rested his head against his steering wheel and closed his eyes. He took a deep breath and peeked up again, hoping the rundown shithole he'd just been staring at had changed into something salvageable.

Nope.

In fact, as he caught a glimpse of a tree branch sticking out of the roof on the far side of the inn, he felt pretty certain it was worse. Paint peeled off every visible surface, and the windows—the ones that weren't replaced with huge slabs of wood—were covered in a thick film of grime. Weeds had taken over the outside, and by the looks of it, started their own dictatorship. Their leader was a massive kudzu vine taking over the entire left end of the building.

A shiny red convertible pulled up next to him. Its owner surveyed the building and gave him a huge, fake grin. Not that he could blame her. It would be awfully difficult to find something positive about the disaster Adam called an inn. A moment later Adam tapped on his window, and Elijah nearly groaned when he saw his face lit up in a genuine smile.

How in the hell was he going to convince Adam what a horrible investment this was?

"I know what you're thinking," Adam began as Elijah got out of his car and stepped directly into a pothole.

"I seriously doubt that," Elijah said under his breath.

"You guys ready to go in?" the Realtor chirped.

Elijah swirled his finger around, indicating they should get the show on the road, and they walked toward the main entrance, situated in the center of the inn.

"The outside isn't the greatest," Adam began again. "But most of the rooms are still in great condition. We'd just need to paint and maybe replace the carpet."

"Mmmhmm." Elijah waited as the woman unlocked the door and gestured them inside. Adam grabbed his arm and started tugging him straight through the lobby into a small seating area with an old buffet in the back right corner.

"Isn't it perfect?" Adam asked, not noticing Elijah's reaction. "The kitchen is through here. It's kind of small, but we don't need anything extravagant. I mean, it's better than nothing, right?"

Elijah winced at Adam's subtle reminder. The kids who showed up at this place would be coming from nothing. "Perfect might be a stretch," he conceded. "Can we look at some of the rooms?"

Adam's face fell a little, but he pulled his smile back up quickly enough. "Sure. She has a master key to all the rooms."

Elijah led them back outside and down the aisle toward the end of the inn. He stopped in front of the room with the tree branch sticking out of the roof. Even the walkway in front of the door was more weathered than the surrounding areas—Elijah assumed from where the water leaked in after each rain. The agent unlocked the door and stepped back, clearly not willing to go in. Elijah turned the doorknob, shoved the door open, and discovered why.

The smell hit him first—a mixture of mold and human waste. Peering in, Elijah saw the room had been completely ransacked and stripped of anything remotely valuable. The beds were upturned, and the already shitty dresser had no drawers and was broken into four pieces. The carpet and baseboards had sustained noticeable water damage that Elijah guessed had also leaked into the rooms on either side. There were several stains around the room—he didn't even want to guess what caused them—and from the smell, he could only imagine the state of the bathroom.

"This room is in the worst condition," Adam said.

"I sincerely fucking hope so."

"There are a few other rooms that have been raided, the ones with broken windows. I guess some squatters tore them up."

"Squatters?" Elijah laughed, nearly hysterical. "We should only be so lucky. More like strung-out drug addicts. Is this fucking dump even safe? This is a nightmare, Adam. Does everyone else know exactly what their money is going toward? You'd be better off tearing the place down and starting over."

"I told you this was the worst room. It's not *that* bad."

"Not that bad? I could take a piss on this floor, and it would improve the value of the place."

"Elijah—"

"No. Seriously, Adam, you've got to change your plans. I'll tell the city to torch this place, and we'll figure something else out."

Adam stepped forward, closing the distance between them. "Stop." He pointed a finger in Elijah's face. "This is not under your control, and it is not your decision to make. If you want to rescind your offer to help with the remaining purchase of the inn, that's up to you. But if you think for one fucking second that I haven't done all of the research necessary to determine that *this* is our best bet to open a safe place sooner rather than later, you don't know me at all. Those kids don't need the fucking Taj Mahal—they need a roof and food and some small sense of security. A mattress to sleep on at night is icing on the cake to them."

Elijah stared at Adam, and once again, the seriousness of what Adam dealt with, day in and day out, hit home. Looking down, he pinched the bridge of his nose and sighed. "This place is a dump."

"What'd you expect? I'm buying an entire hotel for a million dollars. Did you really think it would only need a new paint job? I told you there was some roof damage—"

"I thought that meant it leaked—not that there was a fucking forest in room eighteen."

Adam continued as if Elijah hadn't spoken. "I also told you there were plumbing issues in some of the rooms and that some had been broken into. We have volunteers who are willing to put in the manpower to fix this place up. All we need is to buy the materials. If you could get your head out of your ass for five minutes, you could see that not everyone in the world drives a... a Lexus LRA and uses gold-threaded handkerchiefs to wipe his ass."

Adam's voice had risen throughout his entire spiel, and his arms flailed a bit more wildly with each passing statement. When he was finished, he huffed and stared at Elijah with his hands on his hips. If looks could kill, Elijah would've been gone before Adam even started rambling about make-believe cars.

"What the hell is an LRA, and who told you I wipe my ass with a gold handkerchief?"

Elijah watched, fascinated, as Adam's expression morphed into one of utter embarrassment, and then the color drained from his face. "Ohhhmygod. I'm so sorry," he blurted. "That was completely uncalled for. But you're so insufferably shortsighted, I couldn't stop myself."

Elijah laughed—short and loud. He'd never been told off quite like that. Plenty of people had tried to intimidate him, but a take-no-shit reputation came along with his father's name. Most people respected him and his authority, even if they didn't like him very much. In the few days he'd known Adam, he was beginning to think he had no respect for Elijah's position in life, but liked him in spite of it.

"You're kind of shitty at apologies."

"I'll add it to the list of my shortcomings," Adam snapped.

"Man, will you calm down? I'm *trying* to apologize."

"And you say *I'm* shitty at it."

"Look. You're right, okay? I'm not used to these conditions or your world. Money has never been a concern for me, so it's easier for me to start from scratch than work with… this." Elijah waved his arm at the room. "I'll follow your lead on this. I trust your judgment."

Adam sighed. "Thank you. And I really am sorry I said those things. I don't mean them, mostly. I just—"

"Why don't we quit while we're behind, and go find the Realtor. She tittered away when your horns came out."

They took a few steps in silence and Adam looked at Elijah. "Tittered?"

"Shut up. I'm buying you this shithole—and I mean that in the most literal sense of the term. I can use whatever words I want."

Adam tilted his head in acknowledgment. "Fair enough."

CHAPTER 6

THE NEXT two days passed slowly for Elijah. He did his best to immerse himself in his job, but he couldn't focus on anything long enough to complete any real work. When he realized he'd been staring for no less than twenty minutes at a gift someone had given him for Christmas the year before—a stupid flower that danced in the sunlight—he'd thrown the damn thing away. He exhausted every possible combination on his Newton's cradle and shoved it in the far corner of his bottom desk drawer. He even cleaned up his work inbox *and* his personal e-mail, then reorganized everything on his desk. Menial tasks were the only things that kept his mind from revolving around the inn he was about to help purchase and its frustratingly sexy owner. The most annoying part was that Elijah couldn't figure out *why* he was so distracted.

The money leaving his personal bank account wasn't much of a concern. He didn't need it, and he'd make it back soon enough. The Center for HOPE was a solid nonprofit organization, and even though the inn needed considerable work, Elijah trusted Adam. It was a sound investment with a high payoff—not the return on investment he was used to, but a payoff nonetheless.

As Elijah parked his car in the same spot as the previous two times he'd been to HOPE, he resisted the urge to check himself in the mirror. After their blowup at the inn, Adam had started sending Elijah random texts—mostly about the purchase of the inn—but each time they ended up texting back and forth about whatever shit happened to be going on at the time. Elijah even found himself grabbing his phone to tell Adam about a ridiculous e-mail he received from his father.

Of course, he stopped himself before actually going through with it. For one thing, Adam knew nothing about his love-hate relationship with his father, and for another… maybe that's why Elijah was so antsy lately. He wasn't used to sharing personal information with business associates—particularly business associates who looked so fuckhot in a tux or made his dick hard simply by wearing a pair of Levi's. Elijah shook his head and climbed out of the car. No point thinking about that. Adam had drawn the line, and Elijah had promised not to cross it.

Chloe Nickols welcomed him with her too-big smile and offered him a drink. Then she sent him straight to Adam's empty office and promised he would be in momentarily.

Unaccustomed to waiting, but realizing he'd have to get used to it when Adam was involved, Elijah took in his surroundings and attempted to rein in his irritation at the delay. A picture of Adam with his foster parents, his foster sister, and a blond man with his arm around Kirsten—husband probably—sat on Adam's desk. The walls were adorned with several LGBT-friendly posters, but one in particular caught his eye, most likely because Adam's handsome face stood out in the center. He wore a white shirt, and silver duct tape covered his mouth. His family surrounded him, similarly dressed, and everyone wore the somewhat familiar NO H8 logos on their cheeks. Adam held his pointer finger over his mouth, while Matthew, Amelia, and Kirsten's hands formed hearts, surrounding him in love. Elijah shifted in his seat, and an uncomfortable feeling settled in the pit of his stomach.

Before he could analyze his reaction, Adam burst through the door. "I'm so sorry you had to wait. Mark is being difficult, and I wanted to talk to him again before I'm forced to ask him to leave."

"No problem," Elijah said, his anger evaporating at Adam's worried expression. "Mark is the new guy, right?"

"Yes, the one who arrived the other night. He's a bit of a loose cannon. His gratefulness disappeared once his belly was full and he'd gotten a good night's rest. I know they're nothing more than cots that we pull out into the multipurpose room, but it's better than sleeping on the streets. Mark doesn't seem to think they're good enough for him to have to follow our rules."

"You have rules for homeless kids?"

"Of course we have rules," Adam said, shooting Elijah an incredulous look as his fingers clicked the letters on his keyboard. "I'm happy to take anyone in who needs us, but you have to be willing to help yourself. If you're here full time and relying on us for a place to sleep and eat—beyond a snack every now and then—you're damn well going to help out around here. And if you're no longer in school, you'll spend your free time searching for jobs."

Elijah frowned. "That seems a little harsh."

Adam looked at Elijah and narrowed his eyes. "I disagree. When you've done this as long as I have, you'll see a bigger, more accurate picture. But you must understand *now* why we have rules in place if you want to keep helping out. No one knows better than I do how difficult, frustrating, and scary Mark's life is right now. Sitting around here licking his wounds and moping about his problems won't help the kid. The longer he does that, the harder it's going to be for him to accept responsibility for himself.

"I'm not asking the impossible of him, but he can help out with the cleaning and fix his own meals. He can also start using the resources we make available to get his GED, hone his job skills, and figure out his next step. We can't let him sleep here forever, and we're his only option. That's his harsh reality, and he needs to accept it sooner rather than later."

Elijah held his hands up. "Okay, okay."

"I'm sorry. I don't mean to sound defensive, but you sounded just like he did earlier. You'd think I'd be used to it by now."

Not knowing how to respond, Elijah suggested they get started, and they spent the next two and a half hours elbow deep in spreadsheets and planning. Adam was open to most of Elijah's ideas, and the ones he flat out rejected made Elijah suggest hiring a service to clean the inn each week—just so he could see the fire in Adam's eyes when he explained why it was such an asinine notion. For reasons Elijah wasn't willing to explore, he enjoyed getting a rise out of his new business partner.

Holed up inside the tiny HOPE office, Elijah discovered Adam was even more intelligent than he originally had given him credit for. He would've been content to spend the rest of the evening talking with Adam, if not for a sharp rap against the window. Startled, they both looked up to see Kollin wildly swinging his arms around.

Elijah shook his head. "I don't know how you have time for anyone else with him around."

Adam laughed. "The others are just as bad when I'm alone. Kollin just doesn't respect your presence as much as everyone else."

Elijah sat back in his seat and stretched, then waved Kollin inside. "I'm thinking I don't really care. He's a good kid."

Kollin popped his head through the door, and Adam fired off a balled-up piece of paper. It smacked Kollin right in the forehead and rolled under Adam's desk. "Yeah. He's okay, I suppose," he said through his laughter.

"What was that for?" Kollin asked, hanging half in and half out of the doorway.

"Seemed like the thing to do."

"Whatever, weirdo. You guys up for a doubles game of Ping-Pong with me and Ri?"

Before Elijah could accept, Adam shook his head. "Last time I played with you two, I almost broke my hand."

"Not my fault you have a temper," Kollin quipped.

Elijah's eyes widened, and he looked at Adam. "You hit something?"

"No. The little snot convinced me I could take on both of them, two on one, but failed to mention they could beat Forrest Gump. I slammed my hand against the corner of the table trying to hit a shot. Nearly broke it."

"You gotta admit, if you hadn't hurt your hand, it would've eventually been funny, right?"

"I couldn't write for two weeks," Adam pouted.

"I'll play you guys," Elijah said. "I haven't played in years, though. Sure you don't want to join?" he asked Adam. "I promise to take all of the hard shots."

"Funny." Adam sneered. "I'll play, but the second Kollin and Ri start acting like they belong on tour, I'm putting my paddle down. And don't think I don't know this was all Riley's idea."

"Yes." Kollin raised his hand in victory. "Let's roll."

"So, Riley's good at Ping-Pong, huh?" Elijah asked Kollin as they traipsed out of the office and down the hall.

"Yeah, he's like a Ping-Pong genius or something. He's been showing me some stuff, but I'm nowhere near as good as he is." Kollin jumped up to touch the doorframe as he entered the multipurpose room. Then he turned to look back at Elijah. "But I'm damn good at getting Adam riled up during a game."

Laughing, Elijah turned to make fun of Adam but was cut off by a sharp elbow to his rib. Adam pointed toward the Ping-Pong table against the wall. The ball was moving so fast, he could hardly see it, and the guy holding the paddle looked as if he was barely moving. Except... the closer Elijah looked at him, the more the guy looked like a girl.

Her hair wasn't very long, but the cut was feminine, although it looked as if she'd mussed it up as much as possible. Despite appearing several years older than Kollin, her baby-soft face looked very delicate. Elijah continued to stare at Riley while Kollin joined her and announced that Adam and Elijah had agreed to play. Riley turned toward them, and the huge smile on her face fell as she took in the way Elijah gawked at her.

Quickly looking away, Elijah felt his face heat up. He glanced at Adam, hoping to get some help. "I thought he said Riley was a guy," Elijah whispered.

"He identifies as one, but his parents won't let him go for hormone therapy or even talk to anyone about it. He lives in Raleigh and catches a ride out here a couple of times a week. This is the only place people will refer to him with masculine pronouns."

Elijah nodded, still not looking back at Riley. "I fucked that up."

Adam nudged Elijah again. "No big deal. Just apologize. We could've warned you, but I was following Kollin's lead." Adam paused and tilted his head toward Kollin. "He may be testing you right now. I wouldn't put it past him. He's not necessarily what he seems to be. In fact, I suspect he's still hiding things, even from me. He may be perfectly comfortable talking to complete strangers, but it takes a lot for him to trust someone. You're different for him. That instant connection you two have is rare in his world."

Elijah swallowed the lump in his throat. "So just apologize?"

"Yep. And Elijah? If you're going to keep hanging out here—and I hope you do—a good rule of thumb to remember is never to assume anything."

Elijah acknowledged Adam's statement and took a deep breath so he could apologize for the second time that week.

THE BELL above the door to Langley Lumber and Construction jingled when Adam opened it, drawing the attention of an older woman sitting behind a desk.

"Can I help you?" she asked.

"I'm looking for Elijah." Adam held up a black leather folio with LL&C embossed in fancy silver letters on the front. "He left this behind yesterday. I thought I'd drop it off in case he needs it. I never see him without it."

The woman didn't return his smile, though Adam didn't think it was out of rudeness—more like the thought simply didn't occur to her. Everything about her screamed überprofessional, and Adam wasn't surprised Elijah had chosen her to guard his front doors. "And you are?"

"Adam Lancaster." He started to add where he worked, but stopped when he remembered Elijah's specific request to remain anonymous.

"Did Mr. Langley know you were coming?" she asked as she started punching numbers into her phone.

Adam shook his head and wondered if visiting Elijah at work was such a great idea after all. Surely he knew his folio was missing and where to find it if he needed it.

Too late now.

The receptionist spoke into her headset, announcing Adam's surprise visit. Moments later Elijah walked down the short hall on the left. As usual his broad chest and shoulders perfectly filled out his suit. His short blond hair, which was normally in a state of disarray by the time Adam saw him, looked nearly flawless. The darker curls framing his ears—evidence of how much he needed a haircut—were the only strands of hair not perfectly coiffed. Elijah complained about the ringlets incessantly, but Adam not-so-secretly thought they looked cute.

Elijah stood tall, looking a bit uncomfortable as he greeted Adam, but his smile appeared genuine. "Adam, how are you?"

"Not bad. Just thought I'd bring this by. Hope that's okay," Adam tacked on and glanced at the stern receptionist to his right.

"Of course. Thank you. Want to talk in my office?"

"Hell yeah, man. I came all the way out here. Lemme see where the magic happens."

Elijah looked like he wanted to laugh, but when stern receptionist lady glared at Adam, he squared his shoulders, dipped his head, and motioned for Adam to follow.

Elijah's office was fairly large—bigger than Adam's, for sure. It was nearly empty, aside from a large corner desk and a filing cabinet. The walls were bare, and his desk was devoid of any personal pictures or knickknacks.

"So," Adam began, "your receptionist is a real people person. Think she could give Chloe a tip or two?"

Elijah laughed and threw a paper clip at Adam. "Shut up, you ass. She's been with us longer than I've been alive. If she ever tried to take over the company, she'd probably do a better job of it than I am."

"Ah, so that's where you got your winning personality."

Elijah leaned forward and whispered. "Dude, I don't think I've ever seen her truly smile. It's kind of scary."

"I'm sayin'," Adam whisper-shouted. "She's scarier than some of the worst ladies at the group home I stayed at."

"I didn't know you were in a group home."

Adam sat back in his seat and shrugged his shoulders. "At first for a few months, and then for a stint between each foster home. It's standard for most foster kids. More often than not, I would have preferred to stay there rather than go to another home."

"I'm sorry."

"It was better than the streets." Adam shrugged again like it was no big deal. And it wasn't. Now anyway.

"Shit, man."

Adam flashed a grin. "Blah, blah, blah. Poor me. Poor you. Everyone has a sob story."

"Yeah, but maybe everyone's doesn't involve a fucking group home and eight foster homes."

"Aww, you remembered," Adam teased. He was genuinely touched Elijah recalled at least part of his story from the first night they met, but he also wanted to lighten the mood—and change the subject. He didn't mind talking about his past, but this wasn't the time or place. "So, you ready to do this thing tomorrow?"

"Tomorrow's easy. We're just transferring the money. The real work begins in a couple weeks." Adam nodded. Of course he knew that, but still, transferring almost half a million dollars was a pretty big fucking deal to him. Elijah didn't seem concerned at all, but when he spoke again, he sounded almost hesitant. "I had a thought for the name of the inn."

"Oh yeah?" Adam raised his eyebrows. They'd tossed a few names back and forth, but nothing had stuck. "Let's hear it."

"I was thinking, since the kids will actually be living there, we could call it Home for Hope. Not HOPE like the center, but the real hope. That way they're tied together but not exactly the same. And I thought using 'home' would make it feel more permanent than using 'inn.'"

Adam grinned. "I like it. It'll make a good acronym, too, which is nice for advertising and whatnot. Good thinking, man."

"Yeah?" Elijah's eyes were bright and betrayed how pleased he was with himself. Adam didn't know why. It certainly wasn't the first time he'd made a suggestion that Adam loved, but Elijah seemed to be extra proud.

It was cute.

"Okay, Daddy Warbucks, I guess I need to get back. I'll be sure to schedule an appointment next time I drop by so as not to enrage the bull out front."

"She's not that bad," Elijah said. "Usually if someone comes by unannounced for me, it's bad news, and I end up taking it out on everyone here. She was probably scared you were here to piss me off, and then she'd have to pay for it by helping fix whatever problem you were dumping on me."

Adam grinned and stood. "Can't beat the life of the rich and glamorous—shoving all of their dirty work off on other poor souls."

"Damn straight. And once we get this inn running, I'm going to figure out how to get you the same setup. We'll see what tune you're singing then."

Holding up his hands, Adam backed away. "I give. You win. You are all-knowing and always right."

Elijah narrowed his eyes at Adam. "Get out of my office, Annie," he finally said, though Adam could hear the smile in his voice.

Sure enough, as Adam rounded the corner and offered the receptionist a two-fingered wave, Elijah's soft laugh echoed down the hall.

CHAPTER 7

ELIJAH TOOK the first bite of his sandwich and groaned in approval as he chewed the tender buffalo chicken with ranch dressing. Adam bit his bottom lip and held back his own groan as he watched Elijah's face transform into what had to be one good tug away from his O-face.

"This is amazing," Elijah said.

"I can't believe you've never been here before. It's one of my favorite restaurants." Adam snatched a fry off Elijah's plate, pleased Elijah was enjoying his dinner.

"Guess it was just never on my radar."

Fairly confident that any restaurant below a five-star rating never made Elijah's radar, Adam laughed. "So glad I could be the one to introduce you, then," he said, bumping his elbow against Elijah's.

Elijah jerked away so violently his arm bumped into his glass and splashed iced tea onto the table. Surprise and disappointment shot through Adam, but he schooled his features to make sure his face showed nothing and made a mental note not to touch Elijah in public. They often joked around at the center, hitting each other or even doling out the occasional friendly hug, but apparently touching in public was a no-no.

Elijah slowly relaxed his body and asked, "You know this means you have to take me to your other favorite places, right?"

"Is that a shameless ploy for another date?" Adam teased, keeping his voice low.

Elijah smiled and rolled his eyes, and Adam was glad the awkward moment had passed so easily. "Trust me. If we were on a date, you'd know."

"Why, Elijah Langley," he said, pitching his voice into a higher range, "I do believe—"

"Fucking faggots," a man walking by their table sneered as he flipped them off. "Can't you just stay home?"

Elijah's fork clattered to the table, and his seat flew back. He was on his feet, fists balled up before Adam had even fully registered the remark. The asshole didn't even glance back. He only laughed as he walked away. Adam laid a tentative hand on Elijah's forearm, urging him to sit, and Elijah gradually uncurled his fists and took his seat again.

Elijah's sexuality remained an untouched subject, and that wasn't the best place to get into it. Unsure of how to calm him down, Adam went with the truth. "Ignore him. He's not worth it."

Elijah remained silent for several long moments and then finally asked, "Why'd he even think we're together? I've had countless business meetings over dinner, and this has never happened."

Disappointment shot through Adam and, like an arrow killing its prey, landed right in the middle of his heart. It wasn't uncommon for strangers to throw around words that would slice through the souls of the youth Adam, and now Elijah himself, fought so hard to protect. He'd hoped, after spending so much time at the center, Elijah would be more disgusted by that insensitivity, rather than upset that someone thought he might be gay.

Adam cleared his throat. "Well, I'm not exactly in the closet. In fact, I'm about as far out of the closet as I could possibly be. The NO H8 poster my family did together to promote HOPE is all over the place. It's not a huge leap."

Not taking his eyes off of his plate, Elijah nodded. "Right. You're right. That guy was stupid. Let's just forget about it." Back to all-business mode, Elijah pushed his half-eaten sandwich away.

If any doubts about ending that kiss with Elijah lingered in Adam's mind, they'd just been erased. Adam had promised himself that he'd never lie about who he was, and starting something up with someone like Elijah was as good as stepping back into his own closet. Adam was about to suggest they finish up their work another day when Elijah finally spoke so quietly that Adam had to lean forward to hear him.

"What did you say?"

"Don't you get tired of that shit?" Elijah picked up a french fry, broke it in half, and then tossed it back on his plate.

A small seed of hope planted itself inside Adam's chest—maybe Elijah's anger wasn't as misplaced as he'd thought. Adam contemplated his answer, not wanting to undermine the importance of the moment or cheat Elijah out of an honest answer.

"Sometimes," he nodded. "Some days a guy like that pretty much guarantees I'm eating a pint of Ben & Jerry's before bed. Other days I can just let it roll off my back." He paused. "I'd be more disappointed in myself if I let them get to me every time—if I let them keep me down or change who I'm meant to be."

When Elijah spoke again, his voice was barely audible. "That's good. The world needs more people like you."

Elijah's words reverberated through Adam as if he'd just taken a swing at a huge gong. "Thank you."

"So, does anything piss you off?" Elijah injected an air of levity into his tone as he pulled his plate close again and dipped a fry in his ranch dressing.

"What're you talking about?" Adam laughed. "Of course I get pissed. Particularly at you."

Elijah lifted his eyes off his plate and smirked. "Getting pissed at me doesn't count. I've spent more time with you in the past three weeks than I ever have with someone outside of my family, and I haven't even seen you so much as raise your voice at those kids. It's a fair question."

Eager to keep the twinkle he so rarely saw in Elijah's ocean-blue eyes, Adam leaned forward. "Okay. There is one thing I get quite a lot that really pisses me off. Ready?" Elijah nodded. "'You don't *look* gay.' I mean, what the hell is that, right? I can't like other men because I don't dress well enough or hold my hand a certain way?"

"Okay, so you get pissed, but you never act on it."

Adam's smile faltered. No way was he going there tonight. "Not violently, no. My past is too fucked up for that shit. But this one girl, she was in my econ class junior year, she kept asking me out. After three weeks, I finally—gently—told her I appreciated her offer, but I didn't swing that way."

Elijah grinned. "And?"

"And… she didn't believe me. She thought I was lying because I didn't want to hurt her feelings. Kept telling me I didn't look gay. After two more weeks of her bugging the ever-loving hell out of me about why I wouldn't go out with her, I'd had enough. I showed up to class dressed as I would to go clubbing on a night I was feeling a little femme—eyeliner, eye shadow, nails painted, tight shirt, and tighter pants. I sat down right next to her before class, and with my best *gay*"—Adam's fingers made quotes in the air, "voice said, 'Do I look queer now, girl?'"

Elijah snorted and choked on his fry. "She take the hint?"

"I guess. She never spoke to me again after that." Adam shook his head. "Most people aren't as obvious about their ignorance, but it still pisses me off. Every. Damn. Time. Like I really need to have makeup on to think you're hot."

ELIJAH DIDN'T miss the not-so-Freudian slip but let it slide without comment. No way was he touching the subject of their obvious physical attraction to each other right then. Still, Adam had shared so many pieces of himself with Elijah….

"How about people who don't think it's possible to be bi?" He didn't have the guts to look at Adam, but Elijah sure as hell did his best to take in Adam's reaction from the corner of his eye. As soon as he saw Adam's warm smile of acceptance, the knot in Elijah's chest slowly unfurled, and he took a deep breath. It was the first time since losing Brian that he'd said the words out loud—even if he did say them in a roundabout way.

Adam leaned forward, closer to Elijah, nearly knocking over his glass of water in his excitement. "Yeah. But you know the truth. At some point, you have to chalk it up to ignorance and do your best to educate the people around you. Anyone can look at HOPE and see what's important to me. We offer kids a safe place to hang out where they don't have to worry about someone else judging them, and we do our best to educate the community. Sure, there are a lot of different ways we go about that, but in the end, all we're looking for is acceptance—not to be in the fun gay club or make straight people feel better by allowing them to say we're BFFs. Like me or don't like me for who I am, not who I want to be with. Besides, what makes a man 'manly' anyway? Power and prestige? Or strength and compassion?" Adam ticked off his fingers and paused, making sure Elijah was looking at him before he continued. "Doesn't really matter, Elijah—you've got 'em all."

As usual, Adam dug to the core of the issue and ferreted out the perfect thing to say. Elijah had seen him do it with the kids at HOPE and had recognized it as another of those reasons people loved Adam. As Kollin claimed, it was Adam's gift. However, having that uncanny knack turned on him was as disconcerting as it was comforting. Deciding it was best to get home before he opened his big mouth again and blurted out something embarrassing, Elijah suggested they head out. Adam quickly agreed while glancing at his watch.

"Somewhere else to be?" Elijah asked.

Sighing, Adam nodded. "I'm meeting Bruce for drinks at nine. I'm going to have to fly to get across town in time."

Elijah's heart leaped into his throat and stuck there. "I'm sorry. I didn't realize I was keeping you."

"No. You're fine," Adam said. "I'm not really looking forward to it, to be honest. I have to end things with him tonight. I'm too distracted with everything else going on right now."

Elijah nodded, unsure of what to say. Finally he came out with a lame "Sorry, man."

Adam waved off his apology and quickly grabbed the check as soon as the waiter laid it on the table. "My treat."

Elijah's eyes widened. "Thanks."

"Don't get used to it." Adam grinned. "Next time we're mistaken for being on a date when we're really discussing how to spend the half a million dollars you're giving me, you're totally paying."

Elijah snorted and shook his head. "You're such an ass."

"Man," Adam quipped. "I'm an ass *man*."

"That's good for me, then." Elijah balked at his own words, surprised he'd actually uttered them aloud. He floundered for something else to say—a way to take it back without being a total jackass.

Thankfully Adam saved him with one of his I-put-everyone-at-ease smiles and a wink. "Ready to go?"

As they stepped out into the cool night air, Elijah took a deep breath and did his best to clear his mind. He hadn't decided how he felt about the events of the night. The asshole stranger had pissed him off, no doubt about that. But he wasn't quite sure what his anger stemmed from—outrage at the foul word in general, or outrage because someone had pegged him for what he was. His talk with Adam had helped, but the intimate discussion and peek into Adam's life roiled in Elijah's stomach like a gallon of spoiled milk. Unaccustomed to caring about anyone's personal life, he found the feeling didn't sit so well.

And what the hell was that at the end? They'd definitely been flirting.

Elijah nudged Adam with his elbow and cleared his throat. "Thanks for the talk. I know I'm not very forthcoming about personal shit, but there're a lot of people depending on me, and some private things are just better left private."

Adam's steps faltered, but he didn't press for more details. "Don't mention it. And seriously, anytime you want to talk, you know how to reach me."

Elijah barked out a laugh. "Okay, let's not play the psych game. Go do whatever you have to do with Bruce."

Groaning, Adam opened the door to his car. "I can't imagine he'll take it too hard. We've barely seen each other. You coming by the center tomorrow?"

"Yeah, man. Usual time."

"Sounds good." Adam held his fist out, received an awkward fist bump good-bye, and climbed into his car.

CHAPTER 8

BRUCE WAS already at Macados, beer bottle in hand and chatting animatedly with the bartender, when Adam arrived. Adam smiled as he watched Bruce's arms flail around, and he remembered why he'd put this off for so long. The guy had a passion for life and loved to talk to people. Not for the first time, Adam wished he had stronger feelings for him. He'd been so hopeful after their first date. They had an instant connection and hogged their dinner table so long their waiter was shooting them evil looks. But they'd barely talked over the following two weeks. Adam had spent every waking moment preparing for the fundraiser, and by the time he dropped Bruce off that night, the spark had already dimmed. Adam had seen him just once and talked with him a handful of times over the past two weeks, too immersed in his work with Elijah to give him a second thought. If Adam hadn't made Bruce a priority by then, it was never going to happen.

Bruce turned midsentence as Adam approached, obviously keeping an eye out for him, and waved him over. "Hey. I was just telling Charlie about the mastiff that got loose today while one of the assistants was walking her. It was like a scene right out of a comedy! The poor girl was dragged fifteen feet before she finally let go of the leash."

"Did you ever get the dog back?" the bartender asked, clearly amused by the story.

"Oh yeah. The dog has no clue how big she is, but she's a sweetheart. She only wanted to play, but she's enormous, so very few people take her out. As soon as she saw me, though, she came bounding over. Knocked me flat on my ass, but at least she couldn't drag me around."

Adam laughed along with the bartender, who poured Adam's drink and slunk away quietly.

"So," Bruce began, "you and Elijah get a lot done?"

"Enough, I guess." Adam bit back the urge to dissect his and Elijah's conversation with Bruce. Besides the fact that he was about to kind of sort of break up with him, it would've felt like he was betraying Elijah. "I can't believe we're closing next week. It's still a little surreal."

"Well, congratulations. I'm really proud of you. You've worked so hard over the past few weeks." Bruce smiled and patted Adam's knee. He left his hand there as he took a sip of his drink. The look on Bruce's face betrayed his complete faith in Adam. Bruce truly was proud of him.

Adam smiled weakly and looked down into his mug, shifting slightly toward the bar and out of Bruce's reach. He thought it was subtle enough, but Bruce's shoulders dropped immediately.

"Okay," he sighed. "I'd kinda hoped you were telling me the truth all of those times you canceled on me."

"What?" Adam looked at Bruce, eyes narrowed. "What's that supposed to mean?"

"I assume we're breaking up… or whatever it's called when you're never really together to begin with. It just would've been nice if you'd been honest and told me you had feelings for someone else."

"Someone else?"

"I'm not stupid. Please don't treat me like I am. You've seen him almost every day since you met and canceled twice on me for him. I wanted to give you the benefit of the doubt because I understood—since he donated a shitload of money to the center—but obviously I was wrong." Bruce signaled for the bartender and pulled out his wallet.

"Elijah?" Adam's mouth gaped. "You think this is about Elijah?"

"You think it's not?" Bruce countered.

"He's straight." Obviously, Adam knew that wasn't the case, but Bruce didn't.

"Oh, I think we both know that's not entirely true. And if you don't know, you better figure it out fast, or you're in for a world of hurt." Bruce threw down a twenty. His business card lay on top. "Thanks, Charlie. If you're really interested in adopting that mastiff, let me know. She doesn't have much longer, and she's too sweet to be put down. Keep the change."

Charlie nodded and pocketed the card as Bruce turned to go. Before he could walk out and leave Adam standing there feeling like an idiot, Adam grabbed his arm. "Can you hold on for one damn second, please? I get you're upset with me, but can I at least apologize?"

"What's there to apologize for, exactly?"

"Nothing. I just…." Adam struggled to find the right words. How could he explain his feelings to Bruce when he didn't even understand them himself? He sighed. "Look, I didn't mean to hurt your feelings. I really did enjoy our first date, and I hoped we'd work out, but I'm too busy and too emotionally drained to invest in a relationship right now. I swear to you, nothing happened between Elijah and me after tha—"

Bruce's eyes widened just as Adam realized that he was about to confess a transgression he'd technically never committed. "Exactly. Like I said, good luck with the inn, Adam. I really do think what you're doing is amazing."

Adam's shoulders drooped as he watched Bruce walk out of the bar. He slouched down on his stool and stared at the door. He couldn't remember being this confused since he was nine and asked his birth mom why everyone kept asking him if he had a girlfriend yet when all he wanted was Tommy Johansen to be his boyfriend. Of course Adam thought Elijah was hot—he doubted many people would disagree. And he admired the hell out of him for many reasons, but that didn't make him incapable of having a relationship with someone else.

He wasn't sure how long he sat there, but when the bartender not-so-casually cleared his throat behind him, Adam turned and paid his tab. Then he wandered back to his car, wanting nothing more than to collapse in bed and sleep through the next day.

"THANKS FOR reminding me about these, Chloe." Adam yawned as he slid a stack of resumes across the welcome desk.

"Anytime, sweetie. Last thing I want is to have that inn ready for occupancy and no staff to run it."

"Aw, come on. I wouldn't have waited that long." Adam couldn't help laughing when Chloe cut her eyes toward him and huffed. "Okay, maybe I would have. So thank you again. Can you call the three on top to come in for an interview?"

She nodded and tsked at Adam when he yawned again. "Late night?"

Groaning, Adam nodded. "Just couldn't sleep. Probably too excited about the idea of a completely free weekend."

"You best enjoy it. I suspect once you close on that inn Monday, you'll be eating, sleeping, and drinking this place."

Adam's smile grew. "For a while, yeah. But it'll be worth it when it finally comes together. I still can't believe it's actually happening."

The bell above the door jingled, interrupting their conversation. Kirsten stomped into the lobby, Prada bag on her shoulder, eyes narrowed, and mouth pinched together. She managed to unfreeze her sour face long enough to spare Chloe a small smile. Then she pointed to Adam's office without saying a word. With a soft groan, Adam dropped his forehead to the tip of the reception desk.

"Good luck with that one," Chloe whispered. "I don't know what you did, but you may want to remind her the walls are thin."

Adam scrunched up his face and followed his sister. Gently closing the door behind him, he plastered on a fake smile and said, "Let me guess. Bruce called Sue, and Sue called you?"

Kirsten and her friend Sue had originally set Adam and Bruce up on a blind date, and Adam hadn't warned his sister ahead of time that he was ending things.

"What the hell, Adam?"

"What?"

"She said you cheated on Bruce with Elijah."

"What?" he asked again.

"You tell me."

Adam plopped down on the old couch in his office, flung his head back, and rubbed his face with his hands. "Kris, I slept like shit last night, and I'm really tired. Can you please tell me what's going on? You know I didn't cheat on Bruce. Hell, we weren't even really together."

"Sue said you ended things with Bruce last night after you admitted something was going on with Elijah." Adam opened his eyes and studied his sister. He could tell by the tone in her voice that she was more hurt at being left out than angry with him for whatever crime he'd supposedly committed. There was no one in the world he was closer to than Kirsten. She'd been his first real friend and had never shown him anything but love, even when he was struggling to find his way and acting like a little shit. They told each other everything.

"Nothing has happened between Elijah and me since that first night. And if you could please remind Sue that Elijah is straight, I'd appreciate it. The last thing I need is Elijah thinking I'm outing him to strangers. As far as last night goes, we did have dinner, but we discussed work most of the evening. At least until some asshole decided to try to take us down a notch by calling us faggots, and I thought Elijah was going to have a coronary. There is no way that man is looking for anything more than a one-night fuck from a man—and you know that is not my scene."

Kirsten's eyes were wide. "Well, what the hell was Sue talking about?"

Closing his eyes again, Adam sighed. "I don't know. I mean, I did meet Bruce last night with the intention of ending things. You know I wasn't really feeling it with him anymore. I must've been acting weird, because he figured it out right away, before I even said a word. He accused me of having feelings for Elijah, but when I tried to tell him Elijah had nothing to do with it, I ended up blurting out something about that stupid kiss a few weeks back. He was halfway out the door the second he realized I wanted to break it off between us anyway. He never gave me a chance to explain."

The couch shifted next to Adam, and Kirsten wrapped her arms around his shoulders. "I'm sorry," she murmured. "I shouldn't have assumed, but I had no idea you were planning to break up with him. I knew it wasn't all peaches and cream, but your first date went so well. I thought once you weren't so busy, you'd get excited about him again."

"We both know I would've made time for him if I'd wanted to."

Kirsten adjusted herself until she was sitting beside her brother and then circled Adam's arm with both of hers and laid her head on his shoulder. They sat like that for several long, quiet moments until she finally broke the silence. "What'd Elijah do after that douche nugget called you out?"

Adam groaned. "Acted like he was going to fight the guy right in the middle of Chili's, then wondered why the douche even thought he was gay."

Kirsten waited a few beats, then said, "Maybe he just finds the term offensive. He's been spending so much time over here, I don't know how he'd remain indifferent to the word."

Adam swallowed. He'd wondered the same thing as he replayed the night's events over and over in his head. Had he jumped to a conclusion too quickly? Elijah had all but admitted to his bisexuality, but telling Kirsten about Elijah's confession would break his trust.

Adam wasn't dumb. He knew he and Elijah had enough sexual energy between them to power all of Cary, but that didn't mean it was a good idea to jump into bed. Thoughts of their kiss, right outside in the dark parking lot, rolled freely through his mind. But because life was too cruel, he remembered the anger written all over Elijah's face when he stood up to retaliate against that idiot.

Adam shook his head and looked at his sister. "I don't know what to think anymore, and honestly, I'm too tired to care, at this point."

CHAPTER 9

THE FINE city of Cary had exactly zero gay bars. Anyone who wanted to go to a legit gay club had to travel to nearby Raleigh, but there were a few local restaurants the gay boys and girls tended to frequent. Since Adam and Bruce had caused somewhat of a scene at one of them two nights before, Adam wasn't keen to return there anytime soon. So when his friend José called and invited Adam out for drinks with him and his husband, Alex, Adam asked if they could go to The Pub, for a change of scenery. The place was huge, with three separate dining rooms, two dance floors, and two rooms to play pool or darts. It even boasted a rooftop patio, complete with a bar.

After several hours of drinking and laughing with his friends, Adam felt relaxed and more than a little buzzed. Needing to use the bathroom, he excused himself from their corner booth. When he turned around, he was surprised to see that the restaurant was full. The bar was packed, and nearly every table was occupied. Passing by the hallway leading to one of the rooms reserved for dancing, Adam saw it was brimming with bodies moving in time to the music.

Adam took care of business, checked himself over in the mirror, and wondered if he could have one more drink before switching to water. José had picked him up, so he didn't have to worry about driving home, but this was his last free weekend for who knew how long, and he didn't want to spend the next day nursing a hangover.

Deciding one more wouldn't hurt, Adam tossed his paper towel in the trash and began to weave his way back through the crowded restaurant. He would've missed seeing Elijah completely if he hadn't heard a hushed "Isn't that the guy from the fundraiser we went to last month?"

He snapped his head to the left, and his eyes widened as he saw Elijah sitting next to the pretty blonde he'd brought to the HOPE benefit. Elijah's arm rested on the back of the booth behind his date, and she was pressed up against him so closely, Adam doubted a piece of paper would've fit between them. Across from them, looking as uptight and out of place as possible in their expensive designer suits, sat an older couple Adam immediately recognized as Elijah's parents.

Completely avoiding eye contact, Elijah offered Adam a curt nod. Then he picked up his highball glass and took a swig of the dark liquor inside. Not one to miss a hint that he wasn't wanted, Adam nodded back dumbly and tried not to trip over his own feet as he started back toward his table.

"Fundraiser?"

The senior Langley's voice and the good manners Amelia had eventually managed to ingrain in Adam forced him back toward their table.

"Yes, sir," he said, offering the man a smile and holding out his hand. "I'm Adam Lancaster."

"You're the one my son donated so much of our money to a while back, right? What's your charity again?"

Righto. No need to introduce himself. It's not like everyone in Cary didn't know who he was.

"The Center for HOPE, sir. We're a nonprofit organization that—"

"Helps at-risk youth."

Adam snapped his mouth shut and stared at Elijah. Granted, what Elijah said wasn't a lie, but the main focus of HOPE was to serve *LGBT* at-risk youth.

"Ah, that's right. Elijah spoke very highly of you and your organization. I'm glad we ran into you. It takes a lot to impress my son."

Elijah's eyes remained on his highball glass, studiously ignoring Adam's stare and acting as if making the amber liquid in his glass swirl in perfect, concentric circles was the answer to world peace.

"I'm so glad to hear that," Adam said, dragging his eyes back to Mr. Langley. "I can't tell how you thrilled HOPE was to receive such a generous donation from Langley Lumber."

Mr. Langley laughed. "Generous indeed. I must admit, I was surprised to learn the amount, but Elijah assured me you were a sound investment. And of course, now that you've reminded me, we're always happy to help our youth."

"Well, thank you again. I should probably get back to my friends, but it was a pleasure to meet you, Mr. and Mrs. Langley. And, of course, it was nice to see you again," Adam said, addressing Elijah and his still-nameless date.

Adam's stomach churned as he made his way back to his own table. He suspected Elijah's father was in the dark about Elijah's personal donation to HOPE, but he had no idea the man didn't even know where the business funds had gone. Granted, it was none of Adam's business how they ran Langley L&C, but he'd been under the impression that, while Elijah had officially taken over the business, his father kept his fingers in most of the pots. He couldn't believe Elijah had straight-washed HOPE. Of course, Elijah didn't answer to him and owed him no explanations on his personal life, but the entire conversation left Adam feeling hurt, betrayed, and even embarrassed. Deciding his night was over, Adam stopped by the bar and asked for a water. Then he returned to his booth.

"Were you just talking to the Langleys?" Alex asked before Adam's ass even touched the seat. His eyes were wide, and he looked a little awestruck. Not that Adam blamed him—the Langleys had employed half the residents of Cary at one time or another and were never seen at lowly establishments like The Pub.

"Yeah." Adam dragged out the word. "Why?"

"I didn't realize you knew them. No wonder we haven't seen you in months," José joked.

Adam took a sip of his water and shifted in his seat. The memory of Elijah's offer to help purchase the inn almost a month earlier rushed back. He hadn't been surprised when Elijah asked to remain anonymous as a condition of donating the remaining funds, but he also hadn't expected him to become a semipermanent fixture at HOPE. Elijah's actions within those four walls had fooled Adam into believing that he wanted to remain anonymous simply to be selfless. Now… now it felt dirty and shameful. He couldn't even tell two of his closest friends how he ended up accomplishing the single most exciting goal of his life. And was he supposed to keep the fact that Elijah volunteered at HOPE quiet too?

Forcing a smile on his face, Adam answered. "I met Elijah at the HOPE fundraiser last month. He made a sizeable donation on behalf of Langley Lumber and Construction. Can't say I really know them."

"Wow. Wonder what the hell they're doing here, though," José mused, peering around Adam.

"I wouldn't know." Adam drained his water and looked at his friends. "I think I'm about ready to head home. If you guys want to stay, I'll just call a cab."

Alex shook his head as he signaled their waitress. "Nah. We were just saying we were ready to go too."

Adam kept his head down as they headed toward the door, not even daring to look toward the Langleys' table and risk being ignored by someone he'd considered a friend. As he walked to the car, Adam thought of the coming week with diminished enthusiasm. Elijah had taken the week off to deal with the closing, help interview applicants, and finalize the remodeling plans. With one conversation, the days Adam had been looking forward to more than anything had turned awkward and uncomfortable, at best.

TWO DAYS after almost completely ignoring Adam in public, Elijah still hadn't heard from him. He'd sent Adam one text the morning after, asking if they could talk, but his phone remained silent. Elijah couldn't blame him for being pissed, but he figured Adam would at least give him a chance to explain. It was the longest they'd gone without speaking to one another, and the silence spoke volumes to Elijah about how much he'd betrayed Adam.

Elijah stepped into the bank's waiting area five minutes early, wondering if he was even welcome in the process anymore. Elijah spotted Adam immediately, and his shoulders drooped when he didn't even greet him with a smile. Resigned to an uncomfortable meeting, Elijah sat down in the chair next to Adam.

"You ready?" Elijah asked.

"Yep," Adam chirped. "Not much could make this day better."

Elijah cringed. He didn't miss the subtle dig or the falseness in Adam's tone.

"Listen… about the other night—"

Adam held up his hand and finally raised his eyes to meet Elijah's. "You don't owe me anything. You don't want your father to know how you spend your time and money. It's none of my business."

"It's not as simple as that—"

"It never is, Elijah. Best not to forget what I do for a living. I've heard it all."

Elijah opened his mouth to argue again but couldn't find the right words. Adam was right. There'd been plenty of instances over the past several weeks when Elijah could've let Adam in and told him about his past…. Brian… his guilt. Instead of sharing something real about himself with someone who would actually get it, someone who would actually care, he'd stuck to business as usual. He'd let his guard down enough to consider Adam a friend, but he hadn't treated him like one. Why should Adam give him a chance to explain? He heard far worse stories than Elijah's all the time. The last thing he expected Adam to do was to coddle and coax Elijah's fucked-up past out of him.

"Look," Adam sighed. "I don't mean to be callous, but maybe this isn't the best time for this, okay? Right now, I need you to do what you do best, and be the business guy. Make sure the bank hasn't screwed us and we didn't miss anything. Can you do that?"

"Yeah," Elijah nodded. "No problem."

Adam took a deep breath and closed his eyes. "Thank you."

Kirsten's husband, Derek, acting as HOPE's financial advisor, walked in with their lawyer a moment later, saving them from any further awkward conversation. Within minutes, they were called into the office to start the long and arduous process.

Reviewing all of the paperwork and watching Adam sign his name about a hundred times lasted over an hour, but everything checked out perfectly. The keys were finally pushed across the table, and Elijah had never seen Adam's smile so huge. After a round of handshakes, they headed to the parking lot, where Matthew, Amelia, and Kirsten were waiting for them, each holding a balloon. Kirsten wasted no time. She bounded up to her brother and threw her arms around him in what could only be called a massive tackle-hug. Adam laughed as he caught her midflight and squeezed her tight. Then he set her down and turned her over to her husband.

Amelia was next. Tears were brimming in her eyes as Adam wrapped his arms around her waist and buried his face in her hair. The moment was so intimate, Elijah felt guilty watching—but found he couldn't turn away. Adam must have whispered something to her because every few moments, Amelia would nod her head or laugh through her tears. She finally released her grip on Adam and handed him off to Matthew. This time, when he saw Adam wipe his tears away as his foster father embraced him. Elijah forced himself to look away.

Taking a deep breath to steady his emotions, Elijah turned toward his car. A small hand landed on his arm and forced him to stop in his tracks.

"Oh no," Kirsten chided. "You're not getting away that easily." Before he could protest, Kirsten circled Elijah's waist with her arms pressed her head against his chest. "Thank you. I realize we've only said like ten words to each other, and this is probably really uncomfortable for you, but this is a dream come true for our family—for Adam. We'd still be a long way off from making this happen if it weren't for you. So you have to endure me invading your personal space for the next five seconds."

Elijah wrapped his arms around Kirsten and smiled. "I think I can handle that… for the next five seconds."

Laughing, Kirsten pulled back. "Well, look at that. You do have a sense of humor. I was starting to believe my brother was making it up."

Elijah looked down at the ground and hoped she didn't notice the blush he felt creeping up his cheeks. "Yeah. Well, I guess I better get out of here."

"Nope." Kirsten grabbed his hand, stopping him. "We're surprising Adam with a little shindig back at the center, and you're going to be there. He'd be upset if you weren't, so I refuse to take no for an answer."

Clearly Adam hadn't told his sister what happened Saturday night, which was more than a little surprising. He knew how close they were. But Kirsten pulled him toward the rest of the group before he could protest further. Elijah met Adam's red-rimmed eyes as they walked up, and he cringed when Adam offered him a small smile that fell flat as quickly as it appeared. One thing was for sure—it was going to be one hell of a surprise party.

CHAPTER 10

KOLLIN SWEPT his blue-streaked bangs out of the way, and his dark chocolate eyes darted back and forth as he slipped through the gym's back door and slunk across the school parking lot. He'd been skipping PE for months—ever since Brad *fucking* Winston had seen him with Chris behind the bleachers. Kollin had grinned that day, even bounced a little, when he finally agreed to go with Chris to The Center for HOPE—a place he could be himself and still be accepted. He never asked how Chris knew, and at the time, he really didn't give a damn. He was just relieved *someone* knew and didn't care.

When Kollin finally gave in, Chris tugged him closer and planted a swift kiss, right on his mouth. It was Kollin's first kiss ever—with a boy anyway. He'd tried kissing Ashley Sherman the year before, just to be sure, but the moment her squishy chest pressed up against his, he was forced to fight back an honest-to-God grimace. There was no doubt left in his mind that he preferred a guy's flat, hard chest to… *boobs.* Kollin shuddered. *Gross.*

With a quick glance back at the school, Kollin darted out from behind a car at the edge of the lot. Then he crossed the road and disappeared into the woods. He'd spent three weeks perfecting his path so he knew he'd show up at HOPE as though he hadn't skipped his final class of the day. Jumping over a fallen tree, Kollin recalled Brad's smug face the day after his first kiss, when he was still reeling from the high of feeling Chris's plump lips against his, even if only for a moment. Brad told everyone in the boy's locker room to cover their junk before the fag caught a woody. The entire locker room turned to stare at Kollin, and the crimson flush that spread all the way down to his chest was the only proof needed.

Until that moment, Kollin *thought* he'd been able to cover up the fact that he liked guys. He'd always been active in sports, pretty much excelling at any game that involved a ball—except football. He was much too small to play that, though he still enjoyed watching—for obvious reasons. He thought playing in various sports would keep people from noticing the trill in his voice when he became too excited, his abnormal interest in the latest fashion trends, and the fact that he was the only guy in his group of friends who didn't ramble on forever about jacking off to pictures of naked girls on Tumblr. When everyone immediately turned toward Kollin at the word "fag," though, he knew he'd only been fooling himself.

The real teasing didn't start until the next day, and as each day passed, it grew progressively worse. Kollin considered going to one of the gym teachers. But he knew it was pointless when Coach Turner walked by one day and turned the other way as Brad shoved Kollin against the lockers and Kain grabbed his junk—checking to see if the perv fag was hard. The first time he skipped gym class, he waited for one of the teachers to say something to him, but no one ever did. After skipping every day for two weeks straight, he was terrified to receive his report card. When he saw a *B* next to Physical Education with no further comments, he figured there was no reason to go back.

With Dr. Will's help and Adam's support, Kollin had slowly stepped into his own identity. He still didn't flaunt his sexuality at school, and he remained downright reserved at home. His colorful hair was the only thing he couldn't hide from his parents, and he brushed it off as something everyone was doing. The minute satisfaction he had for holding on to that one piece of himself was enough for him to ignore his dad's disbelieving looks every time he chose a new color.

HOPE became his safe haven. No one blinked an eye if he flicked his wrist while deciding what top best matched his new pair of jeans, and when he was tired of gabbing with the girls, he always managed to con Adam, and now Eli, into a game of basketball. The center was the only place he ever let his guard down, the only place he ever truly felt safe, and the only place he felt real, unconditional love.

Kollin ducked under a pine tree and checked his watch. He was a few minutes early, so he stayed hidden and leaned against the huge tree. If Adam found out he was skipping, he'd force him to attend PE or not let him come back to HOPE—and that just couldn't happen. Even more upsetting would be the look on Adam's face when he realized Kollin had been lying for months, pretending everything at school and home was just peachy. Kollin pushed those thoughts out of his mind and forced himself to smile. He shoved off the tree and sauntered into the open, toward the one place that gave him hope for his future.

ADAM TOOK his time driving back to HOPE. He knew Kirsten and Chloe were planning some kind of party to celebrate finalizing the purchase of the inn. He also knew it was supposed to be a surprise, but asking Chloe Nickols to keep anything a surprise was like sitting a two-year-old in front of chocolate cake and telling him not to eat it. While Adam appreciated the gesture, all he really wanted to do was drive to the inn and start looking around. After his shitty "weekend off" and subsequent awkward conversation with Elijah earlier in the day, he didn't feel like celebrating at all.

He pulled into the parking lot and was surprised to see Elijah's car. He figured Elijah would make a quiet escape, and to be honest, he'd been a little relieved. Elijah's presence in his life had become so fucking big over the past several weeks, and Adam hadn't even realized it. More than just the pretty face and deep pockets, Elijah was funny, crazy smart, and had a heart as large as his wallet—when he let go of whatever baggage he carried around. No matter what Elijah had done, Adam wasn't ready to let their friendship go. Since he couldn't see himself forgiving Elijah right then either, he'd settle for a childish in-between until he absolutely had to face the music.

He could see everyone gathered in the foyer before he opened the door, and even though Adam didn't want to be there … he couldn't help but smile—because he kinda sorta did want to be here. As much as he wanted to get to the inn and bask in the feeling of owning the place, it felt amazing to just enjoy the victory.

Kollin was the first to reach him. He gave Adam a one-armed hug and proudly presented him with an ice cream cake. "Dude. You did it!"

Adam shrugged. "I had some help."

"Whatever. You're takin' over the world. We all know it."

Kirsten was next, even though she'd already had her turn, and everyone lined up behind her to congratulate Adam. Elijah remained off to the side, his arms crossed over his massive chest. His eyes never left Adam. Elijah didn't make a move to approach him, so Adam followed the rest of the crowd into the multipurpose room to get some cake.

Nearly all of his regulars had shown up for the party, along with several volunteers and alumni. Adam mingled for a while, making sure he spoke to everyone. Then he excused himself to grab his laptop from his office, so he could head to the inn. When he opened the door, Adam was surprised to see Elijah sitting behind his desk, papers spread out before him as he studied something on the computer. He'd obviously been in there a while. His hair was sticking up on top, creating a rather eccentric fauxhawk down the center—a sure sign he'd been scrunching it through his fingers as he studied their plans. His dark purple tie was loose, the top button of his rich lavender shirt unbuttoned, and his sleeves were rolled up to his elbows. A Rolex costing more than Adam's annual salary jangled on Elijah's wrist as his hand returned to his hair.

"This isn't going to work."

"Huh?" Adam asked, snapping out of his gawking.

"These numbers. We're going to have to charge some of these kids to stay at the inn."

Adam stared at him. "Charge the homeless kids?"

"Yes," Elijah said, not taking his eyes off of the computer to notice the flabbergasted look on Adam's face. "Maybe just the oldest ones, though."

"You realize how absurd you sound right now, don't you?"

"It's not absurd. They need to learn the value of a dollar. We've already decided they'll need to volunteer until they find a paying job. Once they do, there's no reason a portion of their paychecks shouldn't go back into the place giving them food and shelter."

Adam's eyes widened, and he thrust out his chin in disbelief.

"Are you fucking shitting me with this? We're supposed to be helping them through the lowest point of their lives, not extorting them."

THE DISBELIEF on Adam's face would be comical if it weren't a sign of exactly how badly Elijah had fucked up. He couldn't believe Adam actually thought he'd charge anyone to stay at the inn.

"Of course I'm shitting you, but at least you're talking to me."

Adam plopped down on his couch. "Fuck you, asshole."

Elijah sighed and scrubbed his face with his hands. "Look, I'm sorry I blew you off the other night. I know it was rude, but nothing good can come from my dad finding out I'm associated with an LGBT center."

Silence filled the room until Adam raised his eyebrows and shrugged with his hands palms-up in helplessness. "You want me to do a song and dance to find out more, or is this the big revelation?"

Elijah narrowed his eyes at Adam. "You really suck ass at your job if you treat the kids like this."

"Yeah. Well, those kids smile and wave at me when they see me in public… even when they're with their parents."

Elijah sat up, clenching his fists. "Fuck you. We were only there because my dad is thinking of buying the place. I never thought I'd see anyone I knew, and I was caught off guard. I handled it poorly, and I've already apologized for it. What else do you want?"

Adam buried his face in his hands. "You're right. I don't know why I can't let this go." He shook his head and looked up. "Okay. That's a lie. You're... *you*. And I almost dry-humped your leg in the middle of the parking lot the first time we met. I keep trying to figure out what your damn story is, and it's driving me fucking crazy that every time I think I have a grasp on who you are, something happens to prove me wrong."

Well, fuck. That was the last thing Elijah expected to hear. He knew his relationship with Adam felt different on his end, but he chalked it up to his small obsession with him. Staring down at his fingers, silently tap, tap, tapping on his leg, Elijah decided it was time to man up and share his past with Adam—or at least the parts that wouldn't leave his heart ripped open and splayed on the floor.

"When I was in high school, my dad walked in on me and my best friend, only he didn't know the guy was actually my boyfriend and that I liked to suck his cock whenever we were alone. Dad wasn't exactly supportive when he caught us."

When Adam looked up, his face gave away nothing, so Elijah took a deep breath and continued. "My dad... he's not a bad guy. And he doesn't have anything against gay people in general, but that doesn't mean he wants the heir to Langley Lumber to be one. After...." Elijah shook his head. "After a while, he even told me he didn't care if I hooked up with guys, as long as I was discreet. But I was expected to settle down once I was out of college and ready to start taking over the business. The guy—my boyfriend—wasn't in the picture anymore. I really do find women attractive, so it didn't seem like a big deal. It seemed easiest to just go along with his plan. We never spoke of it again."

Elijah felt his throat clench as he raised his eyes to meet Adam's. He could feel the bile churning in his stomach at the nonchalant way he'd explained Brian out of his life, as if they'd just had a fight and broken up rather than the ugly, violent truth.

"Elijah, man, I don't know what to tell you." Adam nudged his glasses up his nose and tugged his beanie off with one practiced swipe of his arm. He pulled at the matted hair on top of his head, and Elijah recognized the smooth motion for what it really was—Adam organizing his thoughts. "I'm gonna be real honest here. It sucked huge, hairy balls for me the other night. It's been a really long time since I've had to hide this part of me from someone. And frankly, I'm pretty damn proud of everything we've accomplished here, and you should be too. I'm glad you told me what happened. I really am, but the thing is...." Adam sighed. "The thing is, you don't owe *me* anything, and I should've been able to live with that. You've more than fulfilled any obligations you had to the center, and there's no way I'll ever be able to repay you for what you've done for me. I'm telling you, though, if you see Kollin in public, and you treat him like that…."

"I would never."

"Are you sure about that? You only have to look at Kollin anymore to tell he's gay. How would you explain to your father that the twink is all buddy-buddy with you?"

"He's not just some twink."

"*I* know that, and *you* know that, but if he's out with people from the center, and he bounces up to you in public and sticks his hip out too far while tossing his pink or blue or 'whatever the fuck color it is that day' hair out of his eyes, that's all anyone around you is going to see. Shit on me all you want, but you need to think twice before you ingratiate yourself even further into these kids' lives if you're not willing to tell your dad where you're spending your time and your money these days."

The bile in Elijah's stomach jumped, threatening to escape as he pictured Kollin's dejected face. "I wouldn't do that to him," he insisted.

Adam relaxed a little. "Good. Then we're cool."

"Are we?"

"Yeah, Elijah. We're fine. My feelings were hurt, but I get it. I'm sorry I didn't handle the situation better. I never claimed to be perfect."

Elijah nodded and stared at Adam. He was slouched down on his couch with his head resting on the back and he looked exhausted. At some point during the party, probably within the first five minutes, if Elijah were to hazard a guess, Adam had loosened his tie. It hung haphazardly around his neck and the top button of his shirt was undone. Tearing his eyes away from the tufts of curly red chest hair peeking out of Adam's shirt, Elijah focused on the computer. It wasn't the time to start fantasizing about all the things he could do with that tie.

Worried Adam was going to fall asleep, Elijah spoke up. "Want to head over to the inn?"

Without opening his eyes, Adam smiled. "Yes. I really, really do."

"Let's go, then, before you pass out."

"Ugh… I had three pieces of that damn ice cream cake. I think I might puke. Can we please walk, so I don't feel like such a fatty?" Adam finally opened his eyes and smirked at Elijah. "That is, if you don't mind being seen with me on the street and all."

Elijah rolled his eyes at Adam, trying—and failing—not to smile. He held out his hand and helped pull Adam off the couch. "Only if you fix your tie. Sometimes I find it hard to believe you're a respectable gay man."

"Ass," Adam muttered as his hands flew up to tighten his tie.

Elijah laughed and batted down Adam's hands. "Stop it. I was kidding. Let's go. Is anyone else coming?"

"I'm pretty sure my family wants to go, but everyone else can wait until we actually start working over there." Adam bumped Elijah's elbow with his own. "Thanks, by the way. I would have never brought up the other night if you hadn't apologized. I appreciate it."

Elijah shrugged off Adam's apology and waved him toward the door. "After you, boss."

CHAPTER 11

"ELIJAH SEEMS nice," Amelia commented as she dragged a rag through the dust coating the stainless steel countertop.

"He is. Surprised the hell out of me more than once since we met." Adam shuffled through the pots and pans he'd found in the cabinets, hoping some of them might be salvageable. It wasn't looking good.

"I can imagine. He's a very well-mannered young man. His parents obviously raised him right."

Adam snorted. Elijah was full of charm, and though he'd exchanged only a few words with his foster parents, he'd obviously won Amelia over. Adam knew the feeling all too well, but he'd never say Elijah's father raised him right—more like trained him well.

"You two seem very close," Amelia persisted.

Adam found an enormous soup pot still in decent condition and pulled it out. He grinned. "We can save this one, at least."

"Are you very close?"

She was rinsing the rag in the sink when Adam looked at her. They weren't even supposed to be cleaning yet. When they arrived at the inn, they split into three groups to inventory each room and determine exactly what needed to be done. Since Adam, Elijah, and Kirsten knew what to look for, Amelia had stayed with Adam, Matthew had gone with Elijah, and Derek had stuck with Kirsten. Amelia knew better than anybody that Adam didn't actually want help—she'd only get in his way—so she immediately took to dusting.

"Okay… what're you getting at?"

"Nothing. Just chatting with my boy."

"Out with it, woman."

Amelia threw her rag down and turned to look at him. "Honestly, Adam. I was just wondering, because he seems so much more relaxed around you than everyone else. There's a familiarity there that simply doesn't exist whenever I've seen him with other people, so I was wondering *how* familiar you are. That's all."

"Mo-*ther*," Adam teased. "Are you asking me if Cary's wealthiest bachelor is *queer* and if lil' ol' me has caught his attention?"

"Now, you know I don't give two shits about how much money he has." She perched one hand on her hip, pointed a finger at him, and blew an errant strand of hair out of her eyes. "And you know I'm not one for gossip, but he'd be damn lucky to have you—not the other way around. If you're going to act like the little brat I didn't raise you to be, you can just forget I asked."

Adam laughed. He loved riling Amelia. She never involved herself in gossip and rarely interfered or asked Adam personal questions. She must've been very curious to bring it up. Adam set down the laptop he'd been using to take inventory and threw an arm around her shoulder to hug her close. "In that case, no, ma'am. As far as the world knows, Elijah Langley is straight as an arrow, and even if someone suspected that not to be entirely true, I'm not stepping back into the closet for anyone."

"Honey, please," she laughed, grabbing Adam's arm to expose the equality tattoo on his wrist. "I don't know who you thought you were fooling, but you were never in the closet. The gay shines out of you as if you're trying to light up the whole East Coast."

"Ha-ha. You're so damn funny. I meant back in the day, before—"

"I know, but I like to pretend there was no before."

Adam smiled and squeezed her tighter. They'd had that exact conversation countless times, and it never failed to warm his heart. "I know, but if I'd known love like you gave me my entire life, I don't know if I ever would've opened the center. So it all worked out, in the end."

"Stop being all noble, and get back to work before you make me cry," Amelia chided and pushed him away.

Adam pulled her back and dropped a light kiss on top of her head. "Yes, ma'am."

A few minutes later, Elijah and Matthew found them in the kitchen. Amelia was still wiping down the counters, and Adam had separated the kitchenware into throwaway and keep piles.

"What's all this?" Elijah asked.

"I found them in the cabinets. Awesome, right? Most of them should just be trashed really, but there's a few we can use."

"No. Absolutely not." Elijah shook his head to punctuate his point.

Adam's head popped up from his computer. "What do you mean, no? I'm throwing away the ones that are all rusted. I thought you'd be good with that. I considered using vinegar to clean them up."

"I will either personally buy new kitchenware or find someone willing to restock the kitchen. You cannot possibly be considering cooking food for these kids in pots and pans that have been sitting here for at least seven years and have God knows what growing in them."

"I'm gonna clean them first. Obviously." Adam rolled his eyes. "And you've donated enough."

"I trusted you when you told me buying this dump was our best option. Please let me have this one," Elijah muttered through gritted teeth.

Adam huffed. "Fine. But there's nothing wrong with these that some hot water and a strong Brillo Pad couldn't fix."

Sighing, Elijah pinched the bridge of his nose and only looked up again when Amelia clapped once and said, "Okay. I think it's time we get out of here. Don't you boys work too hard tonight."

Elijah's eyes widened, and he looked at Amelia in pure horror. He must've become so consumed in his rage against used pots that he'd forgotten there were other people in the room. "Sorry about the outburst, ma'am. Thanks for your help tonight, sir." He held out a hand to Matthew, who shook it with a smile on his face.

"Glad I could help, and I enjoyed your ideas. I look forward to seeing them play out once the inn is open."

Elijah dipped his chin once, and Adam rolled his eyes at how quickly Elijah slipped in and out of his armor.

LEANING AGAINST the counter, Elijah watched Adam say his good-byes. He was still riding high from the relief of clearing the air with Adam. He knew it could've gone either way. Adam had every right in the world to stay angry with him, and Elijah was thankful as fuck Adam wasn't the kind of guy to hold grudges. Before he'd seen those ridiculously disgusting pots sitting on the counter, Elijah had planned to go along with most of Adam's ideas in an effort to help smooth things over, but one glance at the botulism-waiting-to-happen soup pot, and that intention had flown right out the window.

"You were serious about these pots, weren't you?" Elijah asked when Adam rejoined him.

"Yeah… they aren't rusted or anything."

"I'm starting to think I need to inspect your house so I can make sure you don't have some hodgepodge collection of furniture you found in the dumpster."

"Oh, not our Adam," Kirsten said, waltzing into the kitchen with her arm threaded through her husband's. "He likes to find his furniture at antique sales."

Adam groaned, but Elijah just laughed. "Of course he does. That's like one step up from a dumpster."

"Thank you. That's what I've been trying to tell him, but he insists the weathered look adds character. I have a key to his place. Now that I have you on my side, we'll go over one day and redecorate for him."

"I will smother both of you in your sleep. Leave my armoire and kitchen table alone, Kris. They are *not* junk."

"Settle down, Adam. They're just trying to rile you up." Derek spoke quietly, same as he had during the closing. Elijah had been surprised by Derek's meek nature after meeting Kirsten in all of her exuberance, but anyone could see they meshed together perfectly.

"Yeah. Well, it worked." Adam pouted. "You guys finish up your rooms?"

"Yep. All except eighteen. I think you need to get a hazmat team in there before you take inventory—or rope it off with yellow tape until the end of time. What the hell is that smell?" Kirsten asked.

"You don't want to know," Elijah said.

"I'll take care of eighteen," Adam said, shooting Elijah a nasty look. "Thanks for your help tonight. I would've been here all night otherwise."

"Any time. We're going to grab some dinner. You guys want in?"

Startled by the question, Elijah looked to Adam for help. He was pretty hungry, but he didn't know how Adam would feel about him tagging along on a family dinner after everything that had happened.

"I'm in. All I've had today is that ice cream cake from the party," Adam said.

All eyes turned toward Elijah, and when he hesitated, Adam shoved his hands in his pockets and offered Elijah a lazy smile. Elijah smiled back.

"Sounds good. If you're sure you don't mind."

"'Course not. Now let's roll, boys. I'm ready for some Mexican."

CHAPTER 12

ADAM HOPPED out of his car, twirled his keys around his finger, and shoved them in his pocket. Nothing could ruin his mood. According to Elijah's schedule, the first two rooms would be ready for occupancy by the weekend. They'd been working nonstop for the past three weeks, taking advantage of the abundance of volunteers while interest remained fresh.

Adam hadn't spent as much time working at the inn—or H4H as he'd started calling it—as he originally hoped. Since he was needed at the center most afternoons, when the majority of their volunteers were available, Elijah had rearranged his schedule to work nights so he could be on hand to oversee the workers. Without Elijah, Adam wouldn't be anywhere near ready to open the home.

While it would take several months to finish renovating the remainder of the inn, Adam planned to open each room as it became available. He filed all of the necessary paperwork with social services and hoped to hear back from them any day. As soon as he had the green light, he'd send messages to the national LGBT websites, advertising the shelter for at-risk youth.

Glancing at the whiteboard Elijah used to assign tasks, Adam saw it was fairly empty. Wednesdays were usually light on volunteers, and that day was no different. There were only two names listed, and they were both cleaning the same room. It was the first time that week Adam had been able to stop by the inn, so he decided to take a quick look around before tracking Elijah down. He opened the door to what would be the main office and immediately pulled up short.

An ass he'd recognize anywhere, clad in dark denim, was on full display. Bent over a can of newly opened paint, Elijah had one arm propped on his knee, the other hand was continuously stirring the contents of the can. Before Elijah could even look over his shoulder to see who'd come in, Adam was sporting a semi.

"What's up, man?" Elijah greeted, oblivious to Adam's predicament. "I didn't expect you here this early. I'd hoped to finish the trim before you got here."

Too busy willing his eyes—and his dick—to behave, Adam remained silent. When Elijah turned again, presumably to see why he had yet to say anything, Adam finally snapped out of his ass-coma. But not before Elijah caught him staring.

Grinning, Elijah wiggled his butt. "I forgot you're an ass man."

Adam swallowed and then cleared his throat. "Yeah. Well, yours is quite spectacular, especially in those jeans."

"You like, huh? Ri was giving me shit yesterday for always wearing a suit, so I brought a change of clothes today."

"Hmmph," Adam grunted as he looked Elijah up and down. "He just got excused from bathroom duty this week." *Holy shit.* Adam thought Elijah was sexy in his never-ending supply of suits, but he was positively drool-worthy in jeans paired with a long-sleeved Yale T-shirt that had the words "Born to Ruck" splashed across the back. Elijah pulled off casual-sexy like a pro. The shirt stretched across his shoulders, showing off the strength in his back and his muscles flexing as he continued to stir the paint.

Elijah had nearly transformed into a new person since the day they'd had it out in Adam's office. His smiles came easier, he laughed more often, and he flirted with Adam at every opportunity. He'd remained professional—if not a little condescending—with any social worker or potential donor he ran into. But he had loosened up significantly around Adam's family and most of the volunteers.

"So, you gonna stand there ogling my ass all day, or you planning on helping me at some point?"

"Seriously thinking about standing here all night, now that you mention it. I really am digging this view." Despite his words, Adam crossed the room to grab a brush, and within a few minutes, they were painting sure, slow strokes around the edges of the room.

"I didn't know you like rugby. Did you play?" Adam asked.

"Little bit. Not for the team or anything. But in college, some of the guys would play pick-up games during the week."

"You any good?"

"Eh. Decent, I guess. I usually played forward because of my size. You know rugby?"

Adam shrugged and blushed a little. "Not enough to brag about, but you know, any sport where men wear pants that tight and grab each other's junk is sure to interest a gay teenage boy. Once I realized the scrums were never going to turn into a big gay orgy, my interest waned a bit."

Elijah laughed. "Of course, it's always about the ass."

"What can I say? I know what I like."

"Then I'll have to start taking the stairs at work to keep your attention." Elijah winked.

"Pretty sure that won't be a problem."

"So you say now, but will you still want me in ten years when you can't bounce a quarter off my ass?"

Adam's eyebrows rose. "I can bounce a quarter off your ass now?"

Elijah dipped his brush in the can again. "Guess you'll just have to find out for yourself."

Adam glanced at Elijah, completely content and happy, and wondered what had happened to the man from a few weeks ago. Adam struggled to remember why he'd ever turned Elijah down. Well, that wasn't true—he remembered exactly why, but maybe he'd been too rash. Should he have at least given Elijah a chance? He clearly had his baggage, but once he dug through a few of its contents, Adam could honestly say Elijah was one of the best people he'd ever met.

Elijah interrupted Adam's train of thought before he could dig too far into the "what if" game. "Walls aren't going to paint themselves, Adam."

"Fuck you," Adam replied, grinning. "Just so you know, when we finish remodeling this damn inn, I'm bouncing a quarter off your ass to celebrate."

"WHAT'S THE deal, Eli? Do you not have a job anymore?" Kollin grunted as he scrubbed through the dirt, grime, and lime build-up in the bathtub of room six.

Elijah laughed from beneath the sink where he was replacing the plumbing. He'd learned a lot about home improvement over the past few weeks. Ever cognizant of Adam's insistence on "not just paying someone when you can do it yourself," he found he didn't mind the work so much. He was just as proud of learning to replace a broken toilet as he was of closing a multimillion-dollar deal. "Why? You getting tired of me?"

"Not a chance, man. You still haven't made that dunk."

"You keep blocking me. That wasn't part of the deal."

"Not my fault you weren't specific in your terms."

"Whatever. Like I'd stop coming by anyway. Ri would hunt me down and murder me if I stopped bringing him sundaes."

Laughing, Kollin sat back on his haunches and threw the scouring pad into the tub. "You're probably right. He's scary when he's hungry."

Elijah finished tightening the last bolt and scooted out from beneath the sink. He eyed Kollin from behind and nudged his shoe with his own. "I could maybe think of another reason to keep coming by too."

"I know, I know. I'm faaabulous," Kollin sang. "But seriously, don't you work for your dad? He lets you get away with it?"

"Sorta. I'm the CEO, so he can't really tell me not to take the time off. But he's still on the board and stays involved. That place is his baby. My grandfather may have started it, but my dad is the one who turned it into a billion-dollar company. I get all of my work done, if that's what you're wondering."

Kollin turned and leaned against the bathroom wall so they were facing one another. "Is being CEO what you always wanted?"

Having no idea where Kollin was going with his line of questioning, Elijah furrowed his brows. While the two of them never ran short of conversation, it usually revolved around inconsequential matters, such as sports, music, or which actors were still in the closet. Kollin asking about Elijah's personal life was new.

"You thinking of owning your own business one day?"

Kollin looked down and shook his head. "I barely know who I am yet, much less what I want to do, but running a company isn't in my future."

Elijah took a deep breath and let it out slowly, weighing his words carefully. "Seems to me you know exactly who you are, but maybe you're still working on coming to terms with it."

"You don't think it's weird I like playing ball as much as I like shopping?" Kollin's voice was small.

"I don't. Not everyone fits into some predefined box, Kollin. You definitely weren't made to fit in one, but it doesn't mean there's anything wrong with you."

"Your dad know about you?"

Fucking hell. Where did that come from? The kid was giving him whiplash. "Know about me?"

"Yeah. That you're into guys." Elijah gaped at Kollin, trying to figure out how and what Kollin knew. Surely Adam wouldn't have told him, but that was the only explanation he could come up with. Kollin rolled his eyes. "I've seen you checking out Adam's ass. Several times. So, if it's supposed to be a secret, you might wanna work on hiding that shit better."

Heat crept up Elijah's neck, and he dropped his head between his knees for a moment. "It's complicated," he said.

"Usually is."

Ignoring the need to defend himself—this wasn't about him—Elijah gripped Kollin's ankle, making him jump. "Your dad giving you problems?"

"No more than usual, I guess…. He doesn't exactly know about me."

"Seriously?" Elijah cringed, hearing his own disbelief. He'd never prided himself on his gaydar, but it wasn't too hard to pick up on Kollin's orientation. His dad would have to be in some serious denial not to suspect.

Picking at an invisible string on his shirt, Kollin shrugged. "I tone it down a lot at home. My dad probably suspects, but doesn't want to admit it—or thinks he can bully the gay out of me. Everyone at school already knows. Someone outed me a few months ago, but no one bothers me much, as long as I keep quiet… act normal."

"Normal?"

"Yeah, like before I started coming to HOPE. Chris, you know the one with short, spiky hair?" Elijah nodded. "He was the only one who knew about me. We'd been kinda flirting, I guess. Nothing ever really came of it because we have absolutely nothing in common, but he bugged me for weeks about coming to the center with him. I didn't want anyone to know about me, but I eventually gave in. When I walked through those doors the first time, it was like I could be exactly who I wanted to be, for once. Like I could finally breathe. And I like who I am when I'm there—I do—but I don't know if it's really me or just another facade to cover up how shitty the rest of my life is."

Shifting closer to Kollin, Elijah asked, "Have you told Dr. Will any of this?"

"Not really. They know my dad gives me a hard time, but they all think I'm out to him."

Elijah cupped the back of Kollin's neck. "You know I'm always here to listen, but you should probably talk to someone other than me. I'm not trained and can't help you like Dr. Will or even Adam can. I promise you though, Kollin, there's nothing wrong with who you are. I know safety is an issue when you're flamboyant, so I get toning it down. But don't ever let anyone else make you think that who you are is anything less than fucking amazing."

KOLLIN NODDED and fought back tears, wishing—not for the first time—his dad could be someone like Elijah. Someone who cared more about Kollin than about what other people thought of him. Someone who didn't let society browbeat him into turning a blind eye to the clues his son had given him. Or even someone who took thirty minutes out of his week to play ball.

Kollin didn't know what Elijah's "complicated" meant, but it wasn't an outright *no*, so he figured Elijah's dad knew and wasn't signing up at PFLAG anytime soon. He half wished Elijah had shared a story about a conservative father who accepted him with open arms. At the same time, he was mostly relieved that wasn't the case—better to never have hope that everything would work out than to have it squashed when he confronted his own father and everything went to shit.

"I think I've really screwed things up with Adam," Kollin finally whispered.

Elijah scoffed. "Impossible, and trust me, I would know."

"He thinks everything is fine at school and that I'm out to my parents, Eli. He's going to hate me when he finds out I've been lying all this time."

When Elijah's arms circled his shoulders, pulling him into a warm hug, Kollin finally lost it. A sob he'd been holding in for the past four months tore free from his chest, but Elijah's shirt soaked up his tears before they had a chance to fall. He felt ashamed for breaking down, but the relief of finally confessing consumed him, wracking his body with heaving, uncontrollable shudders. He hadn't meant to say anything, but once he started talking, everything just came tumbling out. Kollin cried on Elijah's shoulder for what felt like hours while Elijah held him, and when he finally calmed down, he made no effort to move, not quite ready to relinquish the comfort from someone who gave a damn.

"Thank you," he whispered.

"Anytime." Elijah patted the back of Kollin's head and sat back against the wall again. "You know you need to tell Adam, right?"

"Yeah. I guess. Can you give me a few days, though?"

"Of course. And I mean it. I'm always here for you, but I can't help you like a professional can."

"You really think he won't be mad at me?" Kollin wrung his hands in his lap, pissed at himself for screwing everything up so badly.

"Not a chance. I'm not gonna lie to you. He'll worry his left nut off about you now. But he gets it and he'll be happy you're asking for the support you need."

Kollin nodded and finally looked Elijah in the eye. "Thanks again, Eli."

"Don't mention it. Wanna knock off early and get one of those nasty cheeseburgers you like so much?"

Grateful for the swift change of subject, he grinned. "Can you spring for cookies today too?"

CHAPTER 13

ADAM DIDN'T bother hiding his stare when Elijah fell back on the newly made bed in room thirteen, threw his arms over his head, and revealed a small patch of pale skin with just a hint of a happy trail. They'd been working all day, and Adam knew Elijah was past exhausted, but he was determined to finish the first two rooms that day. Thanks to a generous donation from Matthew and Amelia, the pantry would be stocked the next day, and they'd be able to call the place open.

"We did it," Adam said softly. He grabbed Elijah's knee and wiggled it. He wanted to scream and shout and jump up and down, but he thought that would ruin the moment—lessen it. Besides, Elijah hadn't been himself the past couple of days, and Adam had yet to figure out why. He worried more than he cared to admit, but he avoided bringing it up for fear of interfering in something that was none of his business. Elijah tried to cover it up, but Adam hadn't missed the strain around his eyes or the way he avoided Adam's gaze.

"Yeah, thanks to you." Elijah yawned, but kept his eyes closed. His voice sounded weary when hc continued. "You were like a ninja on crack today. I'm going to have to sleep all day tomorrow to recover."

"You've earned it. I owe you, man."

Elijah grunted, and Adam stared at him. He decided he might as well ask. "You okay? You've been a little off lately."

Elijah grimaced and then sighed. "Yeah, I'm fine. Just a lot on my mind."

"Wanna talk about it?"

Elijah looked at Adam. "I wish I could, man, but I promised I wouldn't."

Adam nodded. "I get it. Just know I'm here if you need me."

"I know. I appreciate it, and you'll know soon enough."

Adam's eyes widened. "It's one of our kids?"

He winced. "Yeah."

Adam fell silent. He was glad whoever it was—most likely Kollin—felt comfortable enough to talk to Elijah. He really was. But he couldn't help the small pang of jealousy he felt either. Even more unsettling was the very small part of Adam that still worried Elijah would bolt at the first sign of protest from his father. They hadn't spoken of him since Elijah's confession, and Adam had no idea where the two stood now. He often wondered if the change in Elijah's demeanor had anything to do with his dad, but he didn't dare ask. Images of Elijah goofing around with Kollin, throwing his arm over Ri's shoulders, even playing ball with Chris flashed through his mind, and guilt for not trusting Elijah crept in.

"That's great, man. Really. They need someone else they trust, and honestly, they'd have a hard time finding someone better. You're so good for these kids, and not because of the money. You're here almost every day, showing them how important they are to someone who they think probably shouldn't give a damn. That's way more valuable than the money."

ELIJAH BLINKED.

Dammit. Why did everything that came out of Adam's mouth make Elijah want to grab him and never let go? Whether they were flirting, fighting, or sharing overwhelming moments, Elijah found it more and more difficult to stop himself from begging Adam to give him a chance. He just wasn't sure what he'd be asking for. A chance for a one-night stand? Adam had made it perfectly clear that would never happen, and Elijah knew Adam deserved better than that anyway. A chance to be fuck buddies? That didn't sit well with Elijah either, but the only other alternative was a full-blown relationship.

The scary part? He was beginning to think he actually wanted that.

Elijah had lost track of the number of times he caught Adam making a complete fool of himself just to make one of his kids smile, or how often he had canceled plans with Elijah because someone at the center needed a shoulder to cry on. Those moments interrupted his every thought and danced around in his head, always reminding him that Adam was good down to his very core.

Adam's sacrifices for those kids and his commitment to the center made Elijah think being with a man—with Adam—wouldn't be as far-fetched as he'd always thought. How could his father disapprove of someone as worthy as Adam? Not that any of it mattered—he promised Adam he wouldn't make another move, and he valued Adam's friendship far too much to ruin it for physical gratification.

Elijah forced himself upright. He gripped his shoulder as he stared at the floor. No matter what Elijah felt for Adam, his words hadn't been meant to do anything more than compliment Elijah's commitment to the kids at HOPE. That didn't automatically mean he wanted anything more than friendship. "Dangerous territory, Lancaster. You keep saying shit like that, and one day I'll believe it."

Grabbing Elijah's hand as he started toward the door, Adam stopped him. "You need to believe it, Elijah. You think we'd be here today without you? There's no way I would've had this place ready without your help. You're so fucking generous with your money and your time and your huge heart. You blow me away every damn day. I don't know how it happened, but you barged into my life, turned it upside down, and I don't think you've looked back since. And the kicker is, you don't even seem to realize how amazing you are or what you do to me. Do you know how terrifying that is?"

Stunned, Elijah watched Adam pace the room, tugging at his hair with each step. He knew Adam respected him—admired him even—and it apparently wasn't a secret that they were flirting more often than not. Hell, there were a few times when Elijah was sure one of them was a wink and a nod away from finding the next available flat surface. But Adam had never spoken like this—like he felt anything more for Elijah than a flirtatious friendship. He knew the sexual tension between them was palpable, but wanting to fuck the living daylights out of someone often had nothing to do with actual feelings.

Elijah's mind drifted to thoughts of Adam and him together, and he allowed the dream to play out in his mind. His nerves zinged, starting in his chest and traveling outward. His breath hitched, and his arms tingled—something physical seemed like a real possibility.

Confused and a little hopeful, Elijah stepped forward, but he stopped when Adam's eyes met his. Adam's brows were drawn together, and Elijah fleetingly wondered if Adam might hit him.

Instead, Adam took three steps forward, covered Elijah's mouth with his own, and grasped Elijah's arms. The kiss was rough, as if Adam had something to prove, and his touch consumed Elijah, taking over every part of his body.

Feeling helpless to do anything other than soak up everything Adam offered, Elijah slipped his arms around Adam's slim waist and surrendered.

Adam slid his hands beneath Elijah's shirt and jerked it over his head. He ran his fingers over Elijah's chest and nuzzled the small patch of dark blond hair between his pecs. The shirt hit the floor, and Adam's mouth closed around Elijah's nipple. He swirled his tongue around the pebbled tip and then pulled away with his teeth clamped around the sensitive skin.

Elijah's wince was quickly swallowed with a low grunt when Adam trailed his lips up Elijah's chest and neck until he could look in Elijah's eyes. He grinned and stepped forward. Elijah walked backward until his knees hit the side of the bed, then tumbled down and pulled Adam with him.

Their heads bumped together, and Adam let out a frustrated growl as he rested his forehead on Elijah's bare chest. "Fuck."

Adam's breaths were so heavy, Elijah wasn't completely sure he actually heard the curse until Adam's eyes met his again.

"I'm sorry."

"I'm not," Elijah said. He cupped the back of Adam's head to drag him up to his lips.

Elijah was far less demanding as he kissed Adam. He peppered soft kisses along Adam's mouth between slow, sensual explorations with his tongue.

"Are you sure?" he asked between kisses, insecurity heavy in each word.

Hell, yes. Elijah was sure. He'd wanted Adam since the first night they met, and the feeling had only grown.

"More than anything." Elijah glommed onto Adam's neck. He sucked the salty flesh into his mouth and slowly pulled away. "Are you? I thought you didn't want me like this."

"Always. I always wanted you like this." Adam slipped both hands beneath Elijah's pants and boxer briefs and bared the other side of his neck—a clear invitation for Elijah to continue. Adam kneaded Elijah's ass and pulled their hips closer together while he rubbed his groin against Elijah's, practically dry humping his leg.

Elijah wasn't sure that he and Adam were talking about the same thing. He couldn't find the will to care when Adam thrust his hips again and finally rubbed their cocks together. A low growl rumbled deep in Elijah's chest, and he spun Adam around and threw him on the bed. Adam scrambled back toward the headboard, stripping down to his underwear along the way.

Elijah's cock swelled as Adam spread out his heavily tattooed body before him. He'd only ever seen Adam's forearms, but now he saw that both of Adam's arms were covered in full sleeves that extended over his shoulders and across at least part of his back. His chest was mostly bare, except for one small date tattooed directly over his heart. Elijah wanted to crawl next to Adam and study each one, find out every instance in Adam's life that made him want to mark his body so permanently, but then Adam's lips curved up into a smile, and he tucked his hand beneath the waistline of Elijah's black boxer briefs and grabbed his cock.

Elijah shucked his own pants and crawled over Adam. He swatted his hand out of the way and lined up their bulges. Planting his hands on either side of Adam's head, Elijah watched as he slid his black briefs against Adam's teal ones.

"Mmm," Adam mumbled against Elijah's shoulder. He groped Elijah's back and tugged his ass closer. Skimming his fingers lightly up Elijah's ribs, Adam panted. "God, that feels good."

Elijah groaned. He'd hooked up with plenty of men since he'd firmly shut his closet door, but it was never anything more than a perfunctory fuck, a convenient way to satisfy an itch when he wasn't in the mood for female company. There was never any hanging around, no lingering touches—not even kissing most of the time—and he hadn't realized how much he missed the intimacy.

Elijah tore his eyes away from their cocks and attacked Adam's mouth. He kissed him roughly, grateful he didn't have to hide how much he craved the affection. His teeth scraped across Adam's nipple as he made his way down and gently bit the side of Adam's belly while he pulled the sexy-as-fuck briefs down Adam's legs and engulfed his cock without warning.

"Hnnng." Adam moaned, grasping at Elijah's short hair.

Elijah was out of practice and gagged as soon as Adam's cock hit the back of his throat, but Adam didn't seem to mind. He sucked Adam back down, flattened out his tongue, and ran it along the curved vein in Adam's dick. Then he buried his nose in Adam's balls and nuzzled into his sweaty scent. Elijah gripped Adam's cock and slowly stroked it while dragging his tongue farther down but stopped when his tongue neared Adam's hole.

Elijah squeezed his eyes shut for just a moment and glanced up at Adam. He was fucking gorgeous. His hair was a complete mess, his face twisted, and every muscle in his body seemed tense.

"Too far?"

"No," Adam panted. "I… wasn't expecting any of this. I, um, don't have anything. Do you?"

Relieved, Elijah licked up the crease between Adam's leg and pelvis and slowly stroked Adam's cock again. "Yeah. Gimme a second." Unable to resist—because fuck if he still couldn't believe this was happening—he crawled up Adam's body and kissed him again. He thrust his tongue in Adam's mouth and clashed their teeth together. Then he leaned over the side of the bed and dug into his pockets. He'd never been more thankful that he was always prepared.

Elijah slid his boxer briefs off and climbed on top of Adam again. He kneeled between Adam's knees and licked Adam from his balls to the tip of his penis. Then he sucked him in again and slipped a slicked finger into him. Elijah spent several long minutes stretching Adam, enjoying the way he squirmed whenever Elijah tugged on his balls and how his fists tightened in Elijah's hair whenever he hummed around Adam's cock. His responsiveness was as big a turn-on as anything else. He always found foreplay—with a man or a woman—far more intimate than having sex. He had never been interested in intimacy, but when Adam's low moans became breathy whimpers, Elijah struggled to remember why.

Elijah made quick work of the condom and added more lube. He leaned down and rested his forehead against Adam's.

"Ready?"

Adam pulled Elijah closer, his hazel eyes bright with lust, and stilled for a moment. Then he threw his head back and laughed. "Stop being so nervous."

Elijah grimaced and buried his face in Adam's neck. "Shut up. It's been a while since this has meant something." His chest tightened at his confession, but he couldn't help laughing too.

Adam nudged Elijah's neck until their eyes met. "I'm glad it means something," he whispered and pulled him closer. Then he kissed him hard, with a loud smack of his lips. "And yes. Fuck me already!"

Elijah snickered and then swallowed Adam's own laugh with his mouth. With a low hum, he positioned his dick against Adam's hole and pushed inside. He didn't want to hurt Adam, so he slowly slid in and enjoyed the warmth of Adam's body taking him. When his groin hit Adam's ass, he circled his hips and half-kissed, half-dragged his tongue across Adam's collarbone.

"Holy fuck. You feel good in me."

"I can't believe this is happening." Elijah panted, pulling out so slowly that Adam grunted and bucked his hips.

Elijah flexed forward and lost himself in the hard muscle beneath his fingers, the squeeze of Adam's strong thighs around his hips, and the tight pressure of Adam's ass around his cock. Setting a languid pace, Elijah closed his eyes and enjoyed feeling consumed by Adam. He savored the slow build until Adam groaned again.

"Shit. Faster. Please, Elijah."

Hearing his name roll out of Adam's mouth, husky and dripping with want, Elijah relented and pushed forward—hard. He leaned back and slipped his arms beneath Adam's legs. Then he thrust again… and again….

"Oh God, yes," Adam moaned, reaching for his cock. He stroked quickly, and Elijah did his best to match Adam's rhythm. The sound of his balls slapping against Adam's ass mixed with their grunts and groans of pleasure, filling the room with the oldest, most primal song known to man. Adam writhed beneath him, on the cusp of his climax, with his hand jacking his cock and his body covered in a light sheen of sweat.

"Fuck. Fuck, fuck," Elijah gasped.

"Don't stop," Adam gasped. "Almost." His hand sped up, but Elijah barely noticed as Adam's ass clenched tighter around his cock.

Elijah dropped onto Adam's chest and let Adam's legs fall as he slipped his arms beneath Adam's armpits. His balls tightened, and he desperately fought his orgasm, hoping he could hold off long enough for Adam to finish first. Tightening his grip around Adam's shoulders, Elijah buried his head into Adam's neck and sunk his teeth into the flesh as he humped Adam's ass hard and fast. Finally, hand flying, Adam shouted as his hot, sticky release spurted between their stomachs. Several uneven thrusts later, Elijah buried himself one final time and filled his condom. He could feel every nerve in his body scream in exhausted pleasure.

Elijah closed his eyes and melted into Adam, panting into his neck. Along with the usual serene, relaxed feeling in his muscles, Elijah felt a sense of comfort all the way down to his bones. He smiled and kissed along the edge of Adam's ink until he finally pulled out and rolled away to dispose of the condom in the trash can next to the bed. Adam rolled right along with him and settled into the crook of Elijah's arm as he trailed his fingers through Elijah's chest hair. Content and happy, Elijah sighed and kissed the top of Adam's head. He couldn't figure out how in the hell he deserved to have Adam Lancaster naked in his arms.

No sooner had the feeling settled than the same feeling began to unnerve him. Whispers of doubt swirled around inside him, surrounding his veins like a destructive vine and slowly squeezing the peace right out of him. He was too damaged for someone as good as Adam—too scared of his father, too burdened with ghosts of his past. Elijah steeled himself and tried not to let his inner turmoil show. Adam deserved so much better than him—someone stronger, someone unafraid to be himself, someone who wasn't fighting past demons.

Earlier he was confident about facing his dad and accepting his own role in Brian's death. That confidence was gone. He wanted nothing more than to flee the room as quickly as possible, but he was too much of a chickenshit even to be honest about that. Instead, when Adam threw his leg over Elijah's and sighed, "We're so doing that again," into his chest, Elijah tightened his arm and gave a noncommittal grunt, already hating himself for what the next day would bring.

CHAPTER 14

KIRSTEN KNOCKED twice on Adam's office door and entered without waiting for an answer. "Have you seen Julie today?" she asked as she perched herself on the edge of Adam's desk.

"I think she's in the multipurpose room. She walked by a little bit ago, but I haven't seen her since."

Kirsten noticed the shit-eating grin on Adam's face as he sat back in his chair and linked his fingers together, but she was too worried to dig for info and tucked her questions away for later. "I know that, but have you *seen* her? Really looked at her?"

Adam sat up straight. "No, why?"

"She's keeping to herself more than usual. She swears she's fine, but I'm really worried. She's been crying off and on, trying to cover that up too. I can't be positive, because her face is so red and puffy, but it looks like she might have a black eye."

"Shit. Are you sure?"

Kirsten threw her arms up. "No, I'm not sure. I just said that."

"Calm down. We'll figure it out. She'll be eighteen soon, and if someone in her family is abusing her, we have the inn ready for her."

Kirsten wanted to scream. "We've been saying that for months, but it keeps getting worse. How far will they go to make sure they have the last word?"

Adam sighed and rubbed his face, and for the millionth time, Kirsten didn't envy him his job. "I'll talk to Dr. Will today, see if we can get her to talk. If she won't tell the truth about how she got the bruise, then I'm backed into a really shitty corner. If we send a social worker to her house against her wishes, she'll never trust us again. And if the social worker finds nothing, everyone loses except whoever is doing this to Julie. Keep on her, but don't push too hard. She loves you, Kris, but she's probably embarrassed and doesn't want to admit what's going on."

"That's ridiculous."

"Doesn't make it any less true."

Kirsten huffed back into the couch and voiced her earlier thoughts. "Oh God. It's been so long since one of our regulars went through this. I forgot how hard it is."

Adam joined Kirsten on the couch and wrapped an arm around her shoulders. Enveloped in the comfort of his embrace, she turned into his shoulder and squeezed her eyes shut, willing herself not to cry. Julie had been so quiet when she first started coming to HOPE—shy and expecting no one to like her. Kirsten never could understand why. Julie had the biggest and most selfless heart she'd ever encountered and was always willing to lend an ear and offer comfort when someone was having a bad day. She never wanted to share her own burdens with anyone else because, in her mind, everyone else's problems were so much more severe than hers. She soaked up everyone else's tears and never asked for anything beyond common decency in return. She was one of the strongest people Kirsten had ever met, and the thought of someone hurting her made Kirsten rage.

They didn't move for a while. Adam allowed Kirsten her meltdown in private and without judgment. When she eventually pulled her head away from Adam's shirt, she dropped a quick kiss on his shoulder.

"Thank you," she whispered.

"Anytime. I couldn't run this place without you, you know. You can always have my shoulder to cry on."

Kirsten wiped under her eye one more time and punched Adam's shoulder. "Okay, so tell me what that grin was about earlier."

Adam balked, but Kirsten still caught the tug at the corner of his mouth as he tried to school his features.

"Do I have any chance of getting out of this?" Adam raised his eyebrows and drew them together, doing his best impression of a wounded puppy, even though he knew it never worked on her.

Kirsten smirked. "Nope. Not a chance. Tell me what's going on. I need good news."

Adam leaned back against the couch and covered his face with both hands. His voice came out muffled, but Kirsten understood every word he said. "I swear if this leaves this room, I will disown you. Not even Derek."

Kirsten gasped. "You hooked up," she shrieked.

Clamping his hand over her mouth, Adam whisper-shouted, "Will you shut *up*? I said keep it in this room, not shout it to the whole damn state."

"Sorry," she whispered. "But, oh my god… *finally*. Elijah, right? How the hell did it happen?"

As Adam recounted the events of the previous night, Kirsten could actually feel her heart swell. She had started to think Adam and Elijah would never give in to what everyone around them could see. Elijah's feelings for Adam couldn't be more obvious if he'd been caught scribbling their names together on the back of a notebook. While she thought Adam did a better job of hiding his attraction, she knew all the excuses he'd made to end his relationship with Bruce wouldn't have even crossed his mind if he'd been dating Elijah.

"I haven't talked to him yet today, though. It was a little awkward after. We kinda dozed for a while, or at least I did. We barely talked while we were getting ready to leave, but he kissed me before we left the room."

"Oh geez. Remind me to change the sheets before we open."

"Please." Adam rolled his eyes. "I stopped by on my way into work this morning to change them. Give me a little credit."

Kirsten smirked. "How was I to know? You were kinda gross when we lived together."

"I was a teenage boy."

"Whatever you say. When do you think you'll talk to him?"

"I don't know. He's been busting his ass at the inn every day for the past three weeks. I know he wanted to sleep, so I'm not going to bother him today."

"Good choice. Don't be pathetic." Kirsten patted his arm and stood.

"Your concern warms me," Adam returned dryly.

Kirsten held out a hand and pulled Adam up to give him a quick hug. "Thank you for letting me fall apart. I'm going to talk to Julie again before I go home, but let me know if something happens. And good luck with Elijah. He's a great guy. I think this could be good for both of you."

"Thanks, Kris. We'll keep her safe, okay?"

Kirsten turned and gave Adam what she probably hoped was a reassuring thumbs-up, but amounted to a halfhearted gesture made more pitiful by a sad smile. "Counting on it, brother."

YOU AT HOPE? Swinging by in ten.

Yep. See you then.

Adam grinned as he set his phone down and tugged off his hat to scratch his head. Elijah's timing couldn't have been more perfect. Adam's day had gotten even shittier after Kirsten left his office, and he really needed the comfort Elijah brought by just being in the same room. Julie had refused to admit anything to Kirsten, but once her crying subsided, her shiner was obvious. She agreed to speak with Dr. Will the following day, but Adam knew from the set of her jaw and the look in her eyes that she wouldn't be forthcoming.

He had spent the rest of the day wracking his brain over what he could possibly do to change her mind and slowly muddling through yet another stack of neglected paperwork. He hoped he'd only have to work a few hours, but dealing with Julie had taken a while—not that he minded. He would gladly give up more time for her—he just wished someone would do the damn paperwork for him. Maybe Elijah was right. He should hire an office manager when the inn was finished. Even part time would be better than nothing.

Adam didn't hear Elijah walk in until he was standing in front of his desk, hands shoved awkwardly in his pockets.

"Hey," Adam said with what he hoped was an easy smile. He reined in the urge to stand and greet him with a kiss. Even if Elijah was receptive, there was a big-ass glass window that anyone walking by could look into. Well, if anyone was still there at this stupid late hour, that is.

"Hey, got a minute?" Elijah shifted, took his hand out of his pocket to wipe his mouth, and then folded his arms across his chest.

Adam tensed and his heart bottomed out in his stomach. Elijah was never nervous, never fidgeted. Even when he was clueless about something, he exuded more confidence than a tiger chasing a wounded deer.

"Sure. What's up?"

"I, uh…." Elijah blew out a deep breath. "Listen. I wouldn't even normally say anything, but I didn't want to blow you off—since we have to see each other every day."

Adam clenched and asked, "So, why do I get the feeling that's exactly what you're doing?"

Elijah had been looking at the ground, but he snapped his eyes to Adam's and set his jaw in a fierce line. "I'm here, aren't I?"

Adam resisted the urge to hit his desk. He was a damn idiot to believe Elijah had changed—for him. He'd known what Elijah was like from the very beginning and never should've let his intense sexual attraction cloud his judgment.

"You know what, Elijah?" Adam shook his head in a vain attempt to pretend like his heart wasn't shattering into a million pieces. "Fuck you. You're not even going to *try* to talk to me about this first?"

Elijah threw his hands up and smacked them back against his legs. "That's what I'm doing here now."

"No." Adam stood and stepped around his desk. "No, you're not here to tell me you're scared and ask for help to get through this. You're here to tell me why it's never going to happen again. Huge fucking difference."

"Fuck you, Adam. If I remember correctly, you kissed me first. I was getting along just fine having you as my friend, respecting your wishes and shit. I didn't make any promises last night, and you sure as hell never stopped to ask for any."

Elijah had a point, but Adam's entire day had been one huge clusterfuck, and this was the last thing he needed. He was too pissed, too tired, and too close to being heartbroken to be rational.

"Of course I didn't fucking ask for any. I thought we were on the same page. You said you wanted me." Adam tried to keep the pleading tone out of his voice but knew he failed when Elijah winced.

Adam needed him out. Now.

He didn't care if Elijah never came back, but Adam didn't want the asshole in his office anymore. He couldn't take any more humiliation or heartache. Pointing to the door, he clenched his jaw as he ground out, "Just get out. Show up whenever you want. Work at the inn. Become best friends with the kids here. Build them a fucking Disneyland next to the inn for all I care, but I think it's best you stay out of my personal life from now on. No more dinners… or touching… or joking around. Business only."

"Adam—"

"Damn it, Elijah. Can you please just fucking leave?" Adam's voice was even, controlled. He refused to give in to the urge to scream.

"Fine. I'll be at the inn after school tomorrow, same as usual," Elijah promised and walked out.

Adam stood where he was for a long minute. Anger, hurt, shame, resentment, and sadness coursed through his veins, to the point that he felt like his insides were going to explode. He couldn't believe he'd not only slept with Elijah but deluded himself into thinking he would actually give him more than a quick fuck. Frustrated, he tugged his hat back on and returned to his desk so he could finish his paperwork and get the hell home. He shoved his chair back and caught a glimpse of the black and gold Langley Lumber stress ball Elijah had given him the week before. Without another thought, he picked it up and threw it as hard as he could. He released a strangled cry as it hit the wall and fell to the floor with a quiet thud.

CHAPTER 15

ELIJAH TRUDGED to his car half-numb, though the frigid air had nothing to do with how he felt. He couldn't believe how quickly everything had gone downhill. Adam was right—Elijah had every intention of telling him that being together was a one-time deal. But Adam wasn't stupid either. It had to be obvious to anyone with a brain that Elijah was not good enough for Adam, so why was he so upset?

Disappointed for failing so spectacularly, Elijah pulled into the street and turned his wipers on. He hoped he could get home before the light drizzle turned into a freezing downpour. Lost in his own misery, he nearly missed the figure stumbling down the road toward HOPE's parking lot. The individual was limping, clearly injured, and far too small to be an adult.

Elijah pulled his car into the other lane and off the road, saying a silent prayer of thanks that they'd just finished the first two rooms in the inn, but hoping they wouldn't be needed. He threw his car in park and hopped out.

"Hey. Do you need some help? Are you trying to get to The Center for HOPE?"

The figure raised his head, and Elijah's entire world stopped.

"Kollin?"

"Adam?" Kollin mumbled. He clutched his sides and stumbled into Elijah's arms.

Bending down to sweep Kollin off the ground, Elijah left his car idling on the side of the road as he jogged back to the center. "I got you, buddy. We're going to take care of you. Everything's going to be fine, okay? Just stay with me."

Kollin winced and tightened his arm around his stomach, so Elijah slowed his jog to a swift walk. He was nearly to the front door when Kollin said Adam's name again and fell limp in Elijah's arms, his head lolling backward.

"No! No, no, no, buddy. I got you. You're gonna be okay. Adam's going to know what to do. Hang on, Kollin."

Elijah did his best to turn the knob as he shoved his shoulder against the door without dropping Kollin. He pushed the door open and shouted, "Adam."

"I told—" Adam yelled, already walking into the foyer.

"Fuck, Adam. I don't know what happened. I found him stumbling toward the center like this." *Please, please, please know what to do.*

"Kollin," Adam whispered. Panic settled in Elijah's chest as Adam stood there, wide-eyed and frozen. Adam wasn't supposed to freak out. Adam was supposed to tell Elijah everything would be fine—that this wasn't a big deal, and Kollin would be okay in a day or two. Looking down at Kollin's bruised face, Elijah knew no amount of confidence from Adam could make him believe that. Finally Adam cursed and waved Elijah forward. "Bring him in my office. Is he conscious?"

"Barely. He's mumbled your name a few times, but other than that, he's dead weight." Elijah laid Kollin on the couch as gently as he could, taking care not to jostle him too much. He had a feeling Kollin's ribs were most likely bruised, if not cracked or broken. Elijah stepped across the room and crossed one arm over his chest. He covered his mouth as he watched Adam look Kollin over. When Adam raised Kollin's shirt, they gasped at the shoe-shaped bruise on his ribcage. Elijah squeezed his eyes shut and blocked out images he'd long ago hidden away.

Kollin is here.

Kollin is now.

Kollin is going to be okay.

Adam mumbled to himself, and Elijah remained silent until Adam mentioned taking him to the ER.

"You can't," Elijah said. "If you take him to the hospital, they'll contact his parents."

"What am I supposed to do? I can't let him stay here, and he needs medical care. Social workers have been dropping by every other day since we started renovating the inn. They'll shut the entire place down if they find an underage kid in here overnight—especially one looking like this."

Adam paced the room, and Elijah worried his lower lip with his teeth. *Fuck.* He'd already screwed up so many times—with Brian, with his dad, with Kollin, and so many times with Adam that he'd lost count. He stared down at Kollin's face again and grimaced at his right eye. It was so swollen, Kollin wouldn't be able to open it even if he were awake.

Elijah dropped his gaze to Kollin's chest. Then he closed his eyes and said a silent thank you for Kollin's chest continuing to rise and fall.

Kollin was still breathing.

Kollin was still alive.

He could help save Kollin.

Elijah didn't know a damn thing about head injuries, but he'd been in enough rugby matches to know how to treat cracked ribs and contusions—even ones as bad as these. As long as Kollin wasn't in immediate danger, Elijah knew there was really only one option he could live with. "Call the nurse. If she clears him, I'll take him home with me."

Disbelieving eyes met his. "What?"

Elijah stared down at the black and blue face of a fifteen-year-old boy who had more courage in his little finger than Elijah had in his entire body.

"He can stay with me. For as long as he needs."

"Eli—"

"You know I'll care for him as well as anyone at the hospital and better than some random foster family," Elijah argued.

"We don't even know who did this to him," Adam nearly shouted, frustration pouring off of him in waves as he threw his hands up in the air. "What if his parents come looking for him?"

Elijah huffed. "I'd bet my last dime that his dad is the one responsible for this."

"What do you mean? What do you know?"

Elijah kneaded his eyes with his fingers and looked down at the floor. "Kollin came to me a few days ago, said no one in his family knew about him. He was too scared to tell his dad. I didn't know how to handle it, but I told him to come clean with you, or that I would. He promised he'd talk to you. He just wanted a few days to figure out what to say. He was so scared you were going to be disappointed in him, Adam," Elijah said. He finally looked up and gestured down at Kollin's battered body, "I won't let him go back there."

"*Fuck*," Adam shouted, making Elijah jump. He watched helplessly as Adam crumbled to his knees and grabbed Kollin's hand. He buried his head in the couch next to Kollin's arm. "Damn it, Kollin," he whimpered.

Elijah's thoughts echoed Adam's, but there was nothing he could do to change the past. If he'd learned nothing else, he'd learned that.

A moment later Adam pulled himself together and grabbed his cell. "I'll call Nancy."

Aside from the steady rise and fall of Kollin's chest, he didn't move during the fifteen minutes it took for HOPE's volunteer nurse to show up. Elijah had only seen her a handful of times. She was young but had a no-nonsense air about her that reminded him of his receptionist. She cared immensely about the youth, though, and from everything he'd heard, she was damn good at her job. She examined Kollin with a critical eye and thankfully found no signs of head trauma.

"Adam?" Kollin asked again as Nancy lifted his shirt to examine his ribs.

"Yeah, buddy. I'm here with Elijah and Nancy. We're gonna take care of you, okay?"

"Can't… g'home."

Elijah growled low in his chest, and Kollin sat up. He looked around Adam's office with terrified eyes.

"I need you to stay calm. Okay, Kollin?" Nancy instructed. She took the opportunity to shine her light in Kollin's eyes. "It doesn't look like you have a concussion, but do you remember if you hit your head at all?"

Kollin slowly focused his gaze on Nancy. "Please," he whispered. "Don't make me go to the doctor. He'll call them."

"Don't worry about that right now. We're going to take care of you. But first I need to know if you hit your head. Can you tell me that?" Nancy's voice was patient and calm—the exact opposite of everything Elijah felt.

"S'hard to breathe," Kollin complained and lay back down.

Nancy lifted his shirt again and ran her fingers over the angry bruise covering Kollin's ribs. Kollin winced. "I think you have a cracked rib. I can give you something to make that feel better, but I need to know if you hit your head."

"No," Kollin said. "Covered my head."

"Good. That's good, Kollin. We don't want anything bad to happen to that noggin." Nancy dug in her bag, pulled out a bottle of ibuprofen, and turned to Elijah. "Can you get me some ice and a bottle of water?"

Elijah ran to the kitchen and procured both items. He returned in less than a minute and opened the door just as Nancy was saying, "… too risky, but if you're sure you can trust him…."

Adam's eyes met Elijah's, and he nodded. "I'm sure."

Elijah let out a deep breath, relieved he'd be able to take Kollin home with him and grateful Adam saw fit to give him a chance he hadn't earned. Nancy grabbed the ice from Elijah and gently placed it on Kollin's side while Adam fished out two ibuprofen. She stared down at Elijah as she recited her instructions. "You're going to need to stay up tonight and most of tomorrow to keep an eye on him. Since he doesn't have a head wound, there's no risk of concussion. So he can sleep, and he needs it badly. The cracked rib makes it difficult to breathe, and if he walked most of the way here, it's no wonder he can hardly keep his eyes open. Rotate the ice between his injuries to keep the swelling down. If he can stand it, make him lie on his side. He needs to take deep breaths or cough at least once an hour to reduce the risk of pneumonia, so don't plan on getting much sleep tonight. Don't wrap his ribs. That might decrease the pain some, but it also increases his chances of pneumonia, and that means hospital. I won't budge on that one."

Elijah gave Nancy a small nod. "I'll call you if anything changes. Promise."

"I'll be by in the morning to check on him. Better plan on taking off work for a couple of days and figuring out what you two are going to tell his school. He's going to be out for at least three days, if not all week. The more he rests, the quicker he'll heal."

"I'll take the week off," Elijah said. He looked at Adam. "And we'll figure out his school tomorrow."

Nancy sighed. "Well then, I'll leave you to it. I mean it—the slightest change and I want to know about it," she said, pointing at Elijah.

Adam gestured toward Kollin. "C'mon. I'll drive you guys home in my car. There's more room in the back than in your car, and he needs someone to hold him still. Just let me call Kirsten in. Alec won't be here for another hour, and we can't leave the place empty."

Nancy stepped out of Adam's office with a small wave, but Elijah grabbed Adam's wrist when he made to follow her. Adam paused and cocked his head to the side as he looked at Elijah.

Knowing he needed to say something, but not quite sure what, Elijah fought back the wave of emotion threatening to drown him and simply said, "Thank you. I won't let him down."

Adam nodded and looked down at Elijah's hand on his wrist. He gently twisted away. "I know you won't," he said quietly and walked out of the room.

CHAPTER 16

EXHAUSTED, ADAM pulled out of Elijah's gated community and turned his car toward HOPE. He had stopped by Elijah's house on his way to work to check on Kollin. He was still asleep, but seeing him again had eased some of Adam's anxiety.

Adam worried his bottom lip as he drove through town. He was more than a little concerned about Elijah, who looked as if he'd gotten even less sleep than Adam. If not for the dark circles under Elijah's eyes, his disheveled appearance—from his old sweatpants to his mussed-up hair—Adam would've suspected he spent a wild night in bed. His voice, scratchy and rougher than normal, broke several times as he told Adam that Kollin had slept most of the night, rousing only briefly whenever Elijah forced him awake to cough or down more pain pills. There wasn't much Adam could do to ease Elijah's struggles, though, especially given the sharp left turn their relationship had taken the night before.

Adam pulled into the Dunkin' Donuts drive-through, ordered himself, Kirsten, and Chloe the largest cups of coffee they had, and tacked on fifty doughnut holes at the last minute. If ever there was a day to indulge….

Chloe's usual, sunny smile was absent when Adam walked through the front doors of HOPE ten minutes later. In its place was a grim frown, along with worry in her eyes. The obvious concern on her face made the severity and reality of the situation sink in all over again, and Adam had to swallow hard as he blinked back tears.

He shook his head and set his goodies on her desk.

"He's going to be fine. No reason to worry, okay?" he said, passing her a cup of coffee. He filled the two empty spaces in the drink carrier with doughnut holes and slid the rest across the desk to her. "Would you mind taking these to the kitchen when you get a chance?"

"Of course, and thank you. I guess you know Kirsten is in your office."

Adam nodded and offered her a small smile, grateful she hadn't pushed—not that he expected her to. As much as Chloe Nickols loved to meddle in everyone's business, she never crossed any boundaries and knew exactly how to toe the line between obnoxious busybody and compassionate friend.

"Adam?" He turned back to look at Chloe, and her eyes were watering as she sniffed. "I'm saying extra prayers for you boys today." She swiped an escaped tear from her cheek and turned back to face her desk.

Adam didn't know how he felt about God and prayers. For a long time, he'd resisted anything having to do with Christianity. He saw it as the main reason he couldn't be himself and still live in the same house as his biological family. But as he grew older, he met a lot of Christians who didn't hesitate to tell him he'd surely be let in the pearly gates long before his heathen parents. Adam may not have believed in prayer, like Chloe did, but he respected her beliefs and he appreciated her meaning. Besides, if prayers helped them get through this shitwagon, with Kollin alive and no one in jail, he'd take all he could get.

He whispered a quiet thanks to Chloe, and with a flick of her wrist, she waved him away.

The moment he walked through his doorway, Kirsten wrapped herself around him and buried her head in his chest. Adam struggled to balance the drink holder and still curl one arm around her. "Is he okay? What are we going to do? He's too young for the inn until the permits come through, but we can't let him go into the system. There's no guarantee he'd stay around here."

Strangely enough, her panic calmed him. For the first time since Elijah walked into his office the night before, Adam felt like he could breathe, and his debilitating fear eased just a little. He held on to her for a minute longer, taking a moment to lean on someone else.

"I brought sugar and caffeine." He nudged the drink tray in her direction.

"Blueberry!" Kirsten jerked the tray out of Adam's hands, offering some levity to the moment. She took two doughnut holes and wrangled her coffee out of the holder while Adam set everything else on his desk and sank into his seat. "So, what's the plan?"

Adam tilted his head to the side and studied Kirsten. He had no idea how she would react to Elijah's idea. "Shit, Kris. I have no fucking clue what to do. I know what I'm supposed to—"

"You can't. Who knows where—"

"Kirsten. Just listen for a minute, okay?" Adam continued without waiting for an answer. "Elijah has an idea, but there are about a million ways it could go wrong." Surprisingly Kirsten stayed silent and gestured for Adam to go on, her forgotten doughnut clutched between her fingers. "He wants to take HOPE completely out of the equation, call the school to tell them Kollin was in a car accident so they don't raise a fuss, and keep him at his house until… well, until whenever."

Kirsten slowly sat back against the couch, eyes wide as she stared at Adam. "What about the police?"

"He doesn't want to get them involved."

"What about Kollin's parents? What if they call the police?"

"He's betting they won't, since his dad is the one who abused him."

"But what if they do?"

Adam shrugged. What Elijah had suggested was completely illegal. Everyone knew HOPE was required to contact the police within forty-eight hours of a runaway minor's arrival. While it didn't happen often, they'd had a handful of teens under seventeen needing to crash overnight at the center. A few just wanted to get away for the night, not necessarily in danger but needing a temporary escape. Adam and his staff did their best to convince them to return to their families but still continue to visit the center and learn ways to cope with being an LGBT teen.

The others weren't as easy. They looked like Kollin when they showed up—though not nearly as bad. They each stayed two nights and allowed HOPE's therapists to help them adjust to their new reality. When Adam contacted the police, both went into foster care, one about a thirty-minute drive away and the other more than two hours. Only one teen had ever vanished in the middle of the night when she found out Adam would eventually contact the authorities. Adam still thought about her and wondered where she ended up.

Scratching at some powdered sugar on his jeans, Adam whispered, "Elijah's prepared to take responsibility."

"Adam, no. You can't let him do that. If we don't tell the police and Kollin's parents report him missing, Elijah'll be in deep shit. They could even accuse him of kidnapping."

"I told him that. It's up to him."

"Up to him?" Kirsten asked, her voice starting to reach unnaturally high levels. "Not if you come forward and tell the truth."

"And then what? You said yourself they'll take him away."

"Well, his parents get away with this shit if you don't! Did you think about that?"

"Of course, I fucking thought about it. There's no clean solution. Either we follow the rules, charge his parents, and risk losing him in the oh-so-perfect system. Or we say fuck the rules and keep him somewhere we *know* is safe, but his parents get away with child abuse. How am I supposed to make that decision? I don't get to wrap this one up in a pretty bow and move on with life, Kris."

Adam knew he was shouting, but he couldn't stop himself. Gripping his hair with his fingers, he buried his face in his hands and waited for Chloe to come knocking on his door and remind him to keep it down.

"I'm sorry," Kirsten finally whispered. "I'm so bad at this. I'm not even making sense. I just argued against both sides."

Slumping in his seat, Adam threw his head back and stared at the ceiling. Frustration rolled around inside of him, so strong he thought it might burst out of his skin and splatter all over the walls of his office. He knew what he was supposed to do—knew what he *would* do if it were anyone other than Kollin. While he cared about, even loved, every teen who came through his doors, with every smile or snarky comment, Kollin had burrowed a little deeper into his heart than most of the others.

Who the hell was he kidding? He knew Elijah was a huge factor. Adam had seen Elijah transform right before his eyes whenever Kollin entered the room. He didn't know why Elijah smiled more freely or why his eyes looked a little less vacant when Kollin was around, but he knew that change in Elijah was the driving force behind their kiss the other night. And he knew he'd never be able to betray Elijah's trust and call the police behind his back.

"I can't let them take him," he finally conceded. "If Kollin decides to stay with Elijah, how can I not go along with it?"

ELIJAH PROPPED his palms against the shower wall and let the hot water sluice down his back. Even though it burned to the point of discomfort, he felt better standing in the scalding heat. He wanted to stay there until the water ran cold, but Adam would arrive soon, and Elijah needed to at least have clothes on. With a heavy sigh, he turned the water off and opened the shower door to grab his towel. He was pulling his jeans up when Kollin's faint and staticky voice came through the intercom.

"Hey, Eli? Adam called. He's coming through the gates."

Elijah crossed the room to the wall intercom and pressed the button. "Thanks, bud. I'll be down in a minute. Don't get up."

"Yeah, yeah. I'm not an invalid."

Elijah shook his head and grinned as he pulled a long-sleeved Henley over his head. He'd worn the shirt only once before. It was a gift from one of the women he'd dated several years before who insisted the blue in the shirt would bring out the blue in his eyes. He'd thrown it on one night to placate her, but their relationship hadn't last more than a few weeks, and the shirt had gone into his closet behind his many dress shirts. As he snapped his watch on, he wondered when he'd gotten so uptight that he only wore high end, stuffy dress suits.

Before he'd donated all that money to HOPE, he'd thought about upgrading his house. Now, he couldn't figure out why. True, he had no particular attachment to it, but the four-bedroom, three-bathroom house was plenty big enough. The spare bedrooms sat untouched. He never used the formal dining room, and he very rarely used the kitchen. His bedroom, in-home gym, and TV room—complete with a wet bar—were the only rooms that saw regular use. Even if Kollin were to become a permanent fixture, as Elijah hoped, he'd still be left with several unused rooms.

The doorbell rang, and Elijah pushed those thoughts from his mind as he jogged down the steps. He could barely hear the sound of his bare feet echoing through the house over the canned voices that filtered out of the living room. Elijah ran a hand through his damp hair, shook out a few beads of water, and opened the door.

"Hey," Adam said, walking in. "How is he?"

"Better. Still in a lot of pain. Keeps trying to make jokes like it's not a big deal his dad used him as a punching bag. Nancy didn't see any immediate danger when she came by this morning. Said she'd stop back by Wednesday to let me know if she thinks he can handle school on Thursday or if he should take the whole week off." Elijah rambled off the facts, keeping his head down while Adam shifted from foot to foot.

"Yeah. I talked to her after she left here. She seemed surprised at how well he was doing."

"Well, his attitude is all bullshit. He's covering. And he looks awful—lip's all busted, eye still swollen shut. So I don't know what the hell she's talking about. I've been keeping ibuprofen and Tylenol in him, so it doesn't wear off. Made him move the ice pack to a different bruise every twenty minutes, and I had some groceries delivered so we'd have something to eat this week." Had he missed anything? He didn't think so, but he was so worn out he couldn't be sure. Squeezing the bridge of his nose with his thumb and forefinger, Elijah finally looked up at Adam.

"How about you? Are you okay?" Adam asked.

Elijah's eyes widened. He hadn't expected Adam to ask about him, but then again, he wasn't surprised by anything Adam did anymore, especially when it involved showing kindness or compassion to someone else. "Yeah, I'm fine," he croaked. "Just a little tired."

"I'll hang out for a while, let you get some sleep." Adam patted Elijah's bicep and turned toward the living room. "Kollin back here?"

"Uh, yeah. Yeah, sorry. He's in the living room, right through here."

Kollin sat on the couch under a pile of blankets, his ice pack lying on the floor and a glass of ginger ale beside him.

"Hey, man." Adam spoke softly, though there wasn't a hint of pity in his voice.

Even with his face battered, Elijah didn't miss the way Kollin perked up at Adam's presence.

"You came by."

Adam dropped to his knees by the couch and grabbed Kollin's hand.

"Of course I did. Where else would I be?"

Kollin's smile faded immediately. He turned away and raised his free hand to cover his eyes. Unsure of what to do or how to help, Elijah stepped forward.

"Hey, what's wrong? You want me to leave?" Adam asked.

"No, I just...." Kollin choked out a sob. "I thought maybe you'd be too mad at me to visit. I let you down."

Anger surged through Elijah. Where the fuck did Kollin's family get off letting him have so little faith in people? Grinding his teeth together, Elijah walked to the bar to fix himself a drink.

"That's not true at all. You've never once let me down." Adam shook his head. "I wish you'd felt like you could tell us the truth, Kollin, but I would never be mad at you for not wanting to share something. I'm so sorry we let you think that."

Tears streamed down Kollin's face as he hiccupped and sniffed. He nodded while Adam spoke, but Elijah knew him well enough by then to know he didn't really believe Adam's words. He was simply trying to get through the moment.

"You hear me, Kollin? We're here for you, no matter what. Not just Elijah. Not just me. Kirsten, Mrs. Nickols, Amelia... everyone. I know it's hard after everything you've been through, but you've gotta trust us. We're going to make sure you're not hurt again."

"Are they going to send me away?" Kollin's voice sounded small as he spoke the heavy words. He was still sniffling occasionally, but he hadn't let go of Adam's hand. Elijah thought he may've even pulled Adam closer.

"Not gonna lie to you, buddy. I don't know what they'll do if we turn your dad in. I thought maybe you could help Elijah and me figure it out."

"What do you mean *if* we turn him in? I thought we had to."

Adam glanced over his shoulder at him, so Elijah left his untouched glass of whiskey on the bar and sat on the floor next to Adam. He leaned against the couch, propped his elbows on his knees, and looked at Kollin. "You know how I told you that you can stay here for as long as you want?" Kollin nodded. "That's still true. I promise you'll always have a safe place here to stay, live, watch a movie, whatever. The thing is… if we turn your dad in, there's no guarantee I can keep you with me. We're not related. Aside from a shitload of money, I have absolutely nothing going for me in the way of taking care of a teenager, and we just met a couple months ago."

"But aren't I old enough to make that decision myself? I'm not a kid."

"Of course you're not a kid, but that might not mean anything in the eyes of the state," Adam said, his voice calm and even.

Kollin's breathing sped up. Distress, anger, and shame were written all over his face. Elijah would've given anything in that moment to meet Kollin's dad in a dark alley so he could wrap his hands around his throat.

"So, what? What does that mean? I have to go away? Can I stay if we don't turn him in? And what about my mom? She didn't hit me, but I don't know why she…." Kollin's voice broke. "Why didn't she stop him?"

Elijah shook his head. "You're not going back there," he said, his voice low and barely controlled, even to his own ears. When Adam grabbed Elijah's ankle and gave it a small squeeze, he dialed back his anger. The last thing Kollin needed to see was Elijah lose control of his emotions. "I promise. We'll figure it out."

"Why don't you tell us what happened, and we'll figure the rest out later."

Kollin shifted on the couch and covered his eyes with the crook of his elbow. He took a deep breath. "He heard I was at the park with someone, this guy who goes to Killington. We weren't doing much, just holding hands and stuff. We kissed before I left, but it was super brief, and I thought we were mostly hidden. I guess some guy Dad works with was there with his kid. He saw us and called Dad."

Kollin stopped, pressing his arm closer against his face as grief overtook him. He cried into his elbow, hiding his bruised face from the world.

"He was pissed when I got home," Kollin choked out. "I didn't even see it coming. He backhanded me as soon as I walked through the door, and he never let up. Mom was crying in the corner, but she just watched. I don't know if she was upset because he was hurting me or upset because I'm such a disappointment. He told me to get out. Said I wasn't his son because there's no way he made a faggot baby." Kollin's laugh was strangled and sad. "That doesn't even make sense."

Elijah glanced at Adam, desperately hoping he knew how to respond. He'd been so sure keeping Kollin with him was the right thing to do, even if it meant his dad went free. After hearing Kollin's story, even the watered-down version, he felt more conflicted than ever. That man didn't deserve to get off scot-free, but Kollin didn't deserve to be taken away from the people he loved and trusted, only to be thrown into an unstable and possibly violent environment. He dropped his head when it was clear Adam had no more answers than he did.

God. He was so tired.

Adam eventually nudged his arm, and when Elijah looked up, Adam tilted his head toward a sleeping Kollin.

"Why don't you go rest for a while? I'll make sure Kollin eats, and when you're awake and not in la-la land anymore, we can figure everything out."

Elijah nodded. He glanced at Kollin and then at his watch. "He gets more ibuprofen in about an hour, but don't wake him up for it."

Adam offered him a small smile, clearly placating him. "Sounds good. I'll just rummage around in the kitchen for dinner or get Kirsten to drop something off."

"Wake me up if you want, and I can go get something. Or you can always have it delivered. Let me find some menus for you... just call the gate and let—"

Adam cut him off. "Elijah, go get some rest, man. I can handle this for a few hours."

Elijah nodded again. He was being ridiculous. All he'd wanted to do since last night was sleep, and now that he finally had the chance, he was scared to. What if something happened while he was asleep? What if Kollin's dad figured out where he was and came after him, or worse yet, went to HOPE and started attacking people there? Elijah didn't know how that would solve anything, but the man was clearly unstable.

"I promise I'll wake you if anything happens, okay? Get some rest."

"Yeah, okay. Thank you. And seriously, anything at all... just wake me up. Bedroom's at the top of the stairs on the right, or you can use the intercom," he said with a wave toward the button on the wall.

Adam shooed Elijah away. "See you in a few hours. And Elijah.... Kollin's going to be okay, and so are you. We're going to figure this out."

"Right," Elijah whispered. He turned and headed upstairs. He couldn't see how anything would be okay. None of their options gave them a solution close to what Kollin deserved. It was a mistake to let Kollin decide what to do. Kollin needed someone to make the difficult decisions for him. He needed to feel safe and secure and loved and taken care of, not as if he were on the verge of becoming an adult. Elijah didn't know how they were going to fix things, but he did know if anyone could, it was Adam. With the comfort of that thought in mind and still fully clothed, Elijah fell into his bed and passed out.

CHAPTER 17

ADAM STARTLED awake when the doorbell rang and nearly fell off Elijah's couch as he tried to get his bearings. Kollin made a sound between a chuckle and a snort, but Adam only raised one eyebrow and pointed at him as he went to answer the door. He'd fall off the couch a hundred more times if it made Kollin smile.

Kollin had begged Adam to order Chinese, claiming chicken lo mein would surely make him feel better. After calling in the order, Adam lay down on the couch opposite Kollin and apparently fell asleep in the thirty minutes it took for the food to arrive. He shouldn't be too surprised, considering how draining the past two days had been.

Adam paid for their food and dropped it off in the kitchen. Then he returned to the TV room to help Kollin get up. When he found Kollin struggling to stand, he rushed to his side. "Whoa. Hold up, killa'. Wait for some help next time, okay?"

"I don't need help." Kollin eased himself away from Adam. "I can do it by myself, and I need to get used to not having anyone around."

Sidling next to Kollin, Adam wrapped his arm around his waist anyway and helped him shuffle to the bathroom. Kollin's statement didn't surprise him. In fact, he'd be more surprised if Kollin *didn't* leap from one extreme emotion to the next over the coming days. He faced far too much uncertainty for one trip off the couch to fix everything.

Adam waited until Kollin was finished in the bathroom. "You know that's not true. We're not abandoning you, and we're going to find a way to keep you here, if that's what you want."

Kollin shrugged off Adam's help and limped into the kitchen. He paused at the island to take a deep breath as he clutched his side. Without looking at Adam, he said, "How long do you think that's going to last, Adam? My parents used to gossip about Elijah. I know he was always out with a different girl and would never settle down. I know what his life was like before HOPE, and I've talked with him enough to know his dad isn't exactly kosher about having a bi son. You really think he's going to ruin his life for someone he's only known a few months? How long 'til he gets tired of playing daddy, and I'm out on the street?"

Adam bristled. He knew Kollin had every right to distrust the world—to have issues with any father figure in general, to be scared, angry, and to rant about everything from the price of sugar to world peace—but Adam still had to clamp down his knee-jerk reaction to defend Elijah. Kollin's outburst wasn't about Elijah… not really.

"Not gonna happen, Kollin." Elijah's voice was strong and sure as he walked into the kitchen, making both of them jump. He still looked worn and haggard, but the conviction in his voice and the determination written all over his face would've convinced Adam he could sprout wings and fly if he'd made the claim. "You hear me? I made that mistake once and lost. I'm not going to do it again."

Kollin didn't answer, but his shoulders shook. He gave a tiny nod and leaned forward into Elijah's chest. Elijah wrapped his arms around Kollin's shoulders and rested his cheek on top of his head. Adam backed out of the room, leaving them to console each other in private, and pulled his phone out to text Kirsten again.

Any word from Derek's guy?

He'd texted her while Elijah took a nap to see if she could find a lawyer to help Elijah legally keep Kollin. HOPE had a lawyer on hand, but Adam didn't want to even hypothetically pose their situation to her. He wanted to keep the whole predicament as far away from the center as possible.

He asked, but the guy had no idea. He's looking into it and will let us know tomorrow.

Adam sighed and sank into Elijah's plush leather couch. He yanked his glasses off, tossed them next to him, and buried his head in his hands. Everything was falling apart. Until recently his life had been damn near perfection. They were almost finished with the first two rooms of the inn. All of the kids at HOPE were thriving, and he'd found an unexpected but welcome friend and possible lover in Elijah. Two days later not one but two of his regulars were being abused. He had no fucking clue what the hell was going on with Elijah, and the renovation at the inn was at a standstill. His phone buzzed again in his hand, and he checked it quickly, hoping Kirsten had news.

Tell Kollin we love him. Take care of yourself too. <3

Adam quickly texted back, then slumped against the couch and closed his eyes. He almost drifted off, but clattering dishes roused him enough to make him return to the kitchen. Kollin, sitting at the bar, looking stiff and uncomfortable, gave Adam a sheepish look as he walked in.

"Sorry about that," he muttered.

Adam shook his head. "No worries. I've heard worse before and will again. Besides, you need to get it all out. Don't keep anything bottled up. If we can't get Dr. Will over here in the next couple days, we'll find someone else."

Kollin nodded and Adam began helping Elijah dish out the food. He was mildly surprised when, with a small glance up and a quick smile, Elijah split the cashew chicken and the General Tso's chicken and put half on his plate and half on Adam's. When they first started working on the inn together, they quickly discovered they shared a love for all things Chinese-food related and always ended up splitting their dishes. Adam tried not to read too much into the gesture. Elijah had made his choice, and it wasn't Adam. Sharing food while they helped Kollin wasn't going to change that.

Adam settled into the seat next to Kollin and tucked into his dinner. Kollin appeared to be feeling better, as he was actually eating his lo mein with some gusto.

"So," Elijah began. "I told Kollin I'd tell him my story… help reassure him that I won't be going anywhere." Elijah swallowed and looked at Adam. His voice was soft when he continued. "I'd like you to hear it too. If you're still interested, that is."

Adam froze, fork midair as he stared at Elijah. He offered a curt nod.

"Uh, oh," Kollin mumbled around a mouthful of chicken. "Are Daddy and Daddy fighting?"

Shocked, Adam gaped at Kollin, who grinned back and wagged his eyebrows.

Elijah tossed a piece of broccoli across the bar, hitting Kollin in the face. Elijah pointed his fork at him. "Cool it, or you'll be watching C-SPAN with me the rest of the week."

Kollin only smirked and shoved more noodles in his mouth. They finished the rest of their meal in relative silence and finally made their way back to the TV room. Kollin settled back on his couch, while Adam sat on the other couch with Elijah.

After several long moments of watching Elijah fidget in his seat and clear his throat Kollin finally said, "Look, I don't need to hear this, Eli. I don't really think you're going to abandon me. It's just… it's hard to trust *anyone* right now, and sometimes I get really angry and say shit I don't mean."

Elijah winced and shook his head. "No. I want you to know. I've just never told anyone this before, and I never thought I would. I'm worried it'll make you"—Elijah glanced at Adam—"both of you, not want to be around me anymore."

"In case you haven't noticed, you're kinda saving my life, dude. I don't think that's something you have to worry about."

Elijah nodded but didn't smile. Looking down at his hands, he said, "When I was in high school, I met this guy, Brian. We went to different schools. I was in prep school and he went to public school, but we'd see each other at the park playing ball. He was… like no one I'd ever met. First off, for as short as he was, he could beat my ass on the court nearly every time we played. When you first met him, you thought he was this timid, easygoing kid who would let the whole world walk all over him, but after a while, you saw he was secretly feisty, confident, and full of life. He'd show up to play sometimes with blue or black nails, and if anyone gave him shit about it, he'd just smile and challenge them to a game. I fell for him before I even knew what hit me."

Adam swallowed, wondering where the story was going and if it was really a good idea for Elijah to be sharing it with Kollin.

"I guess people were too scared of me to say anything to my face, or even behind my back, because I never had any problems—not that Brian and I ever did anything in public, but I know there were rumors. We became inseparable whenever we weren't at school. He was always at my house. My parents loved him. He only let me come over to his house once, when his parents weren't there. I figured he was embarrassed because it wasn't in a great neighborhood, and well… you know how I grew up. I didn't care, but he always insisted, and at seventeen, it didn't seem like a big deal. There was more to do at my house anyway, and my parents never bothered us.

"He showed up at my house one day. Had a bag over his shoulder and a black eye. His dad had made some derogatory comment about his faggot son, and Brian finally stood up to him. I never even knew he'd had problems with his parents until that day. Brian was out, and everyone knew. It was nearly impossible for him to hide who he was. I just assumed his parents were okay with it. I was so pissed at myself for never thinking to ask.

"I talked my parents into letting him live with us. They didn't know we were together, and my dad was hesitant when he found out why Brian had left his house. So I figured it was best to keep our relationship quiet, for a while." Elijah laughed to himself. "I was sure Dad would come around eventually when I told him how serious it was between us. I figured it'd be better if we were an established couple, could prove our commitment to one another and to our future. Once Dad could see I still planned on taking over Langley Lumber, and I now had the best reason to succeed, he'd be fine. I mean, I know my dad loves me, but he's always been about the bottom line.

"It might've worked if he hadn't caught us together in my room about a week after Brian moved in. We were... uh,"—Elijah paused, looking embarrassed—"rounding third when he walked in, so there was no way to explain it as anything other than what it was. Dad was irate, understandably so. He felt like we'd tricked him and yelled at Brian to leave. I was so mad at my father. We got into a huge screaming match. In between sparring with my dad, I kept begging Brian to stay, but he packed up his bag and left anyway. He didn't want to cause a rift in my family, didn't think he deserved to be fought for."

Adam struggled to not reach out to Elijah, to not touch his hand or leg, to not offer a silent show of support. Elijah was deep into his past, and Adam didn't want to break the spell. Instead, he silently slid off the couch and sat on the floor so he could comfort Kollin, who had tears rolling down his cheeks.

"I let him leave, let him walk out. Dad and I argued the rest of the night, but eventually I gave up. I snuck out later to look for Brian, but I couldn't find him anywhere. I asked around for a few days, and a couple of people told me they'd seen him around, but I never found him. I was devastated. I stopped eating. Stopped going to school. If I wasn't out looking for Brian, I was locked in my room, ignoring my parents. I couldn't understand how Brian had given up on us so easily. I was so mad at him, and I was beyond furious at my dad.

"Finally after about a week and a half, my parents intervened. My dad didn't exactly apologize, but he promised he'd use his resources and help look for Brian if I agreed to stop skipping school and act like a functioning human being again. He said he'd let him stay with us until they could find him suitable help somewhere. It wasn't the best solution, but it was better than him being on the street somewhere."

Elijah took a deep breath and closed his eyes as he pressed forward.

"Two weeks later the cops in Wake County called Dad. They'd found Brian under an overpass by the river. He'd, uh... he'd OD'd on heroin. He'd either started turning tricks to get the drugs, or he'd been raped, and someone wanted to make it look like he'd OD'd. I guess it's hard to tell when you're homeless, and while the police weren't blatantly ignoring his case, they sure as hell didn't make it a priority. I wanted to swear he'd never do that to himself, never sell himself for drugs, but I never thought he'd leave me like that either. I didn't know what to do. I was just a kid. I was terrified, heartbroken—not only by my dad, but also by Brian. Disappointed in myself and ashamed for letting him leave, pissed at the whole world—

the police, his parents, my parents, myself… Brian. I shut down and went through the motions for the rest of the year. I did whatever my parents told me to do, because it was easier than thinking for myself. I knew I was bi, but I had no interest in starting a relationship with anyone after that. So, while I dated both men and women once I went off to college, no one lasted longer than a few dates. It was easier to let my dad think my feelings for Brian were just a phase. I didn't have anyone left to fight for, so when I finished school, I stayed in the closet because it was easier."

Elijah finally looked up and met Adam's eyes. "I thought if I donated all of that money to HOPE, I could let go of some of the guilt, some of the pain. Logically, I knew… know… it wasn't my fault, but what's up here"— Elijah pointed to his head and then laid his palm flat against his chest— "doesn't always make sense in here." Elijah paused, and when he spoke again, his voice was much stronger and full of resolve. "But yeah, that's my big, dark secret. At seventeen, nearly a man in the eyes of the world, I was a chickenshit coward who lost the love of his life, and not a damn thing changed until I met you two. And fuck it all if both of you didn't give me a reason to breathe again. I'm not going to let you down, Kollin. I'm not going to let you run, and *I'm* not going to run. You're not Brian. I can't bring him back, and I can't change the past, but I can learn from my mistakes."

Kollin, in a full-on snot sob, wiped his face with one hand and gripped his hurt side with the other as he nodded. Adam hefted himself onto the couch and wrapped one arm around Kollin's shoulders. His mind was reeling with everything Elijah had just confessed, and he scrambled to compartmentalize the information so he could deal with it later. As off-kilter as Elijah's story had made Adam feel, he could only imagine how difficult it was for Kollin to hear something so close to his own situation turn out so poorly.

Elijah remained on the other couch, looking extremely uncomfortable in his own home. Adam had no idea how to comfort him, so he focused all of his quickly draining energy on the broken fifteen-year-old in his arms, instead of the broken thirty-four-year-old across the room.

CHAPTER 18

IT TOOK Adam nearly thirty minutes to calm Kollin down. Elijah watched helplessly, not missing the fact that neither Kollin nor Adam would meet his eyes. When Kollin finally stopped crying, he asked if he could take his medicine and go to sleep. Elijah remained in the hallway as Adam sat on the edge of Kollin's new bed, speaking to him too softly for Elijah to overhear. He'd let Elijah help him up the stairs but had asked Adam to stay behind for a minute to talk.

Elijah's heart pounded in his chest, and he had to constantly fight the urge to scream that he'd made it all up. He wasn't a monster who was too busy arguing with his dad to ensure Brian's safety. He hadn't allowed the love of his life to run away to his death. He wasn't a coward who'd given up on life and followed in his father's footsteps because it was easier than standing up to him.

But that wouldn't be true, because he was both of those things, and he couldn't lie to the two people in that room.

Adam rose from the bed and leaned over to plant a kiss on top of Kollin's head. Then he joined Elijah in the hall. He led Adam down the stairs silently and was surprised when Adam grabbed his wrist in the foyer and wrapped his arms around him, enveloping him in a tight hug. "I'm so sorry you had to go through that. No one deserves that, especially not a teenager."

Shocked, Elijah slowly slid his arms around Adam's waist and tucked his head into Adam's shoulder. He let out a long, slow breath and fought to hold himself together.

"What happened to Brian was not your fault, and as much as I hate your father right now, it wasn't even all his fault. Stop beating yourself up over it." Elijah sank into Adam's comfort, willing himself to believe Adam's words. He'd told himself the same thing for years, but no one else had ever said it to him, not even his mom.

"Brian was a kid in a shitty situation, made to feel worthless by the two people in the world who were supposed to love him unconditionally. I've seen it too many times. It's a miracle he came to you at all. Those first few years HOPE was open… I don't even want to think about how bad off most of the kids were. They needed someone to believe they were important, that they were just as good as the straight kid down the street or even across the hall. I understand why you feel like you have to do what you're doing, but you need to let go of the guilt over what happened to Brian. Let the what-ifs go. Let the anger go. You've given up enough of yourself to all of that already, and he wouldn't want you to live like this."

Elijah tightened his arms around Adam and held on until he lost track of how long they stayed that way. His back ached and his legs were tired when Adam finally let him go. His brain was screaming at him to believe Adam, to take his words to heart, but his heart was too boxed up—surrounded by vicious vines of doubt, anger, and guilt. Nevertheless, hearing the words come from Adam, from someone he admired and respected more than anyone, buoyed him to stand tall.

"I guess I should go," Adam said when it became obvious Elijah wasn't going to speak.

"Uh, right. I'm sorry. I'm just…."

"It's been a long couple of days, and I know tonight wasn't easy for you. Get some rest. Kollin will be fine. He still loves you, by the way. He wanted me to make sure you knew. Even though he never knew Brian, he's feeling some survivor's guilt and doesn't know what to do with those feelings. It's clear how much you cared about Brian, and it's hard for Kollin not to be glad everything happened as it did because otherwise, he wouldn't have you right now. He's glad you told him, though. Just give him some time." Adam shoved his hands in his pockets and looked at the door.

"Time. I guess we could all use a little of that right now."

Adam huffed. "Guess so. I'll see you tomorrow. Not sure when I'll be able to make it by. I don't want word getting around HOPE about this until we know what we're going to do, so I'm trying not to be too conspicuous. I'll drop by sometime and give you a little break though, and with any luck, Kirsten will have heard about whether or not you can legit be Kollin's foster parent."

"Thanks. I appreciate you looking into that. I should've thought to call my own lawyer. My mind was just…." Elijah balled his hands up and flicked his fingers out as he made an explosive sound with his mouth.

"Ha. Can't say I blame you." Adam laid his hand on the doorknob but turned back again. "Elijah? You had yourself to fight for, you know," he said quietly.

"What?"

Adam took a step toward Elijah, close enough that Elijah thought Adam might kiss him. "Earlier. You said you gave up because you didn't have anyone left to fight for, but that's not true. You had yourself to fight for. You were worth it then, and you're worth it now. Don't ever forget that."

Elijah let out another slow breath and nodded once. Adam gave him a small smile and walked out the door.

TUESDAY PASSED in a tired blur for Adam. Kirsten called with good news as soon as he'd arrived at HOPE. Elijah would be allowed to serve as Kollin's temporary foster parent as long as he passed an immediate background check. Anything beyond that would require a more in-depth investigation, but they could turn Kollin's father in to the appropriate authorities and not worry about Kollin being sent away. As soon as Adam heard the news, he called Amelia, and asked her to cover for him at the center. Then he contacted social services on behalf of HOPE.

Adam went to Elijah's to explain everything to Kollin—who looked equally relieved, terrified, and miserable—and then drove to the police station to make an official complaint. It wasn't the first time he'd gone to the police on behalf of one of his kids, and he was sure it wouldn't be the last. Reporting child abuse was never easy, but the ball sitting in the pit of his stomach as he made his statement felt particularly heavy this time.

When Adam returned to Elijah's four hours later, he had Dr. Will, two police officers, and HOPE's lawyer with him. He'd worked with those particular officers before, and the main reason he'd gone to the station in person was to ensure he could speak with someone he trusted and who would give Kollin fair treatment. Elijah's lawyer showed up several minutes later, and then the long, intrusive, excruciating questioning began.

Kollin sat on the couch, flanked by Adam and Elijah, his face an emotionless mask, while the officers asked him question after question, most of them the same things in different form. Even though Adam knew they had to make sure Kollin wasn't lying, he still struggled to rein in his ire every time they attacked from a new angle. Kollin kept his answers short and to the point, the quiver in his voice and the clench of his fists clearly showing how difficult it was for him to relive the details. Both lawyers remained mostly silent during the interview, but Dr. Will asked for a break whenever Kollin became too anxious. Adam did his best to keep Kollin calm but knew the most he could be was a shoulder to lean on.

They took pictures of Kollin's injuries, which still appeared dark and violent. Then the officers scuttled out with promises to keep Elijah and Adam informed. Everyone left except Dr. Will, so Elijah and Adam moved to the kitchen to give him and Kollin some privacy.

Adam sat at the table and watched Elijah pace around the island as he contacted the school to let them know what was going on. He was relieved to hear Elijah set up a meeting with the guidance counselor to discuss ways to keep Kollin safe when he returned to school. Once Elijah hung up the phone, he plunked himself down in the seat opposite Adam, and they waited—in an unbearably suffocating silence—for Will to finish up with Kollin.

It was the first time they'd had more than a few spare moments together since Sunday, and Adam had no idea what to say. There was still so much uncertainty, so much sorrow and anger, that he felt entirely unprepared to have any sort of meaningful conversation with Elijah.

When Adam learned about Brian and Elijah's issues with his father, Elijah's reticence about entering into a real relationship finally made sense, but Adam couldn't help feeling hurt. He wished Elijah had trusted him sooner—had thought Adam was worth taking a chance for.

Elijah eventually broke the silence. "You okay?"

Adam barked out a laugh.

"Yeah, I guess that was a stupid question."

"Better than the awkward silence we were sitting in." Adam had meant to make a joke, to lighten the mood. Instead, his words came out sarcastic and heavy and real. "Sorry," he whispered.

"I don't really know what to say."

"Honestly, I don't either."

Elijah squirmed in his seat. "I know I've let you down about a million times, but I hope you'll give me another chance."

Adam's eyes shot up to meet Elijah's. *Another chance? At what?* "I'm not sure I know what you mean," he said, hedging his words, careful not to walk into anything he wasn't ready for.

"Another chance to prove myself to you… at anything, I guess. I meant what I said yesterday. I never would've thought my life could be this… big. I lost the desire to connect with anyone when Brian died, and I'd slowly let it turn me into a work-obsessed shell of who I used to be—just like my dad, in other words. When I heard about the fundraiser for the inn, I knew I had to go. I kept thinking if Brian had only had somewhere like that to go, he would still be alive. I would've forked over my entire bank account the night we met to help get rid of even a fraction of the guilt I've carried around." Elijah's eyes were haunted, and he wrung his hands as he spoke.

"My intention was to find out about your business plan to make sure I wasn't wasting money and then donate whatever it took so you could buy the inn free and clear. After I met you, though, after we talked that first time…. God, I wanted you so bad. You were hot and charming and passionate and so comfortable being yourself. So I donated enough to get your attention and figured I'd finagle another couple of meetings out of you while we worked out the rest of the details."

"Elijah…." Adam paused and took a deep breath. "I don't—"

"No, let me say this. I've screwed up everything else, so let me get this out and lay all my shit on the table. I didn't intend to follow you back to the center that night, and I can't even really tell you why I did. I couldn't figure it out then either. I mean, I wanted you—a lot—but I'm usually able to exert at least a little self-control. Once you turned me down, I wanted you even more—want-what-you-can't-have kind of thing, I guess, but I tried to respect your wishes.

"I thought I could just donate the money and run. Then I saw Kollin again, and there was no way I wasn't coming back. They're so different, but still, you have no idea how much Kollin reminds me of Brian. I felt like I was getting a second chance."

Elijah paused and stared down at his hands. "After a while, I realized how much I wanted to be at the center—not because I felt guilty or felt I owed it to Brian, but because I wanted to spend time with you guys. Except nothing can ever be easy, and my father is still my father, so I was still living two lives. When I saw you at the bar that night, I was desperately trying to hold on to my old life. I was happy whenever I was at the center, but when I'd go home or to the office and the rest of the world seeped in, I was lonely and confused—maybe even a little scared. My world had turned completely upside down, and I didn't understand it anymore. Nothing made sense.

"When we were together the other night, for maybe half a second, I believed I could actually deserve you. I was finally doing something with my life to be proud of and not *only* because I felt guilty over Brian. As soon as that feeling settled inside me, all the other shit I've been living with for the past sixteen years started taking over. I *knew* I didn't deserve you. I *knew* I didn't deserve happiness, and I *knew* I didn't deserve love. I even knew it was a chickenshit move to bail the next day, but at the same time, I really believed I was doing what was best for you. I won't do anything but weigh you down."

Adam held up his hand. "Elijah… I get what you're saying. I do. But none of that changes anything, from where I'm sitting." Adam paused and chewed over his words. "I wish I could change what happened with Brian, and I wish I could change the way your dad made you feel. I wish I could give you the past sixteen years of your life back, because you deserve that. I know, to most of the world, you're Mr. Moneybags CEO Langley. And yeah, maybe that's all you were to me, at first. But then you became so much more.

"You were just Elijah, and you loved basketball and rugby. You got a kick out of teasing me and thought you were clever every time you snuck extra cashews out of my half of the Chinese. You spoiled our kids rotten, and you made Kollin smile, and you made *me* smile. You think I changed *your* world?" Adam's voice cracked, and he couldn't quite believe what he was getting ready to say. As brightly as *Stop! Don't go there!* flashed through his mind, he kept talking.

"I could easily say the same to you, Elijah. Only I would've fought for us. I would've done whatever you needed, carried on in private for however long you needed, to let you be who you needed to be to the world, because I felt like I had a piece of the real you. And because it's *you*, that would've been enough for me."

Elijah's face crumpled, and his entire body sagged. Adam had to look away when he continued talking. "I can't do that anymore, and it's not because of your past and what happened with Brian. It's because I can't trust that you'd ever actually give me all of you. If I saw you in public with your dad, and you acted like you didn't know who I was… I just couldn't. I love you for what you've done for the inn and for what you're doing for Kollin. I'd love for us to be friends again, but it's going to take some time. We're both hurting right now, and with everything Kollin is going through—not to mention the inn and the rest of the kids at HOPE—I think it's best we stick to a strictly professional relationship, for now. When the dust settles, we can see where to go from there."

Before Elijah could say anything or Adam could run out of the room so he couldn't take every word back, Will walked into the kitchen.

"He's asleep," he began, either not noticing the tension in the air or not caring. "I won't lie. I'm worried about him. He has a lot of repressed emotions we knew nothing about. If he'd been honest with us from the get-go, this might be easier for him. But on top of everything that's happened with his dad, he feels partly responsible because he's been lying to everyone for so long. I don't believe he's a risk to himself, but the next week or so is going to be rough on him while we work through everything. He's going to need both of you. He seems to feel a special connection to you, Elijah, but he trusts Adam more."

"So, what? You want me to move in here or something?" Adam gaped.

Mildly confused, Will shook his head. "No. That wasn't what I was suggesting at all. Just be here if Elijah will allow it. Drop by every day if you can. And if you can't, let Kollin know why, and let him know that you'll be by as soon as you can. That boy is nothing like the one I've spoken to at the center. He's extremely vulnerable right now, but he's hiding behind his sarcasm."

"What about his parents? What do we tell him about them?" Elijah asked.

"The truth, and big news like that should come from both of you. He needs different things from each of you. I can be here too, if you like, but he may give a more honest reaction without me in the room. Just be tactful—which I know you would be anyway—and give him time to process afterward. He's trying to figure it all out on his own, even though he doesn't need to. Still, it's the way his mind works, and I think he'll come to one or both of you when he's ready."

"Thanks, Will." Elijah stood to shake his hand, and Adam followed them into the foyer.

"Call me if you have any questions. I told Kollin I'd be back Thursday, but if you guys need me, I'm happy to come by tomorrow too."

"I'm going to head out, as well," Adam said. He knew it was a dick move to leave like that, but he wasn't feeling very gracious. He was terrified that if he looked into Elijah's sorrowful eyes one more time, he wouldn't be able to resist wrapping him in his arms and begging him for any little piece of himself that he was willing to give.

Elijah only nodded and muttered a quiet "See you tomorrow" as he closed the door. Adam climbed into his car, waved to Will, and rested his head on the steering wheel. He needed to head back to the center and check on Amelia, but all he really wanted to do was to go home, skip dinner, and sleep through the entire night. With a small sigh, he turned the key in the ignition, pulled onto the main road, and pointed his car in the direction of HOPE.

CHAPTER 19

KOLLIN LAY on the couch, trying to come up with something to do so he wouldn't be bored out of his mind. He was sick of watching TV but couldn't quite muster the will to get up and do anything else. Eli had given him a Kindle, complete with several YA gay romance books already loaded, but he wasn't in the mood to read about two guys falling in love either. He thought about buzzing Eli, who'd gone to his room to catch up on some work e-mails, but figured he should be able to last an hour by himself. Deciding he'd suck it up and fix himself a snack, he threw aside the blanket he was huddled under and slowly stood.

"Hey. What're you doing up?" Eli asked, rushing in. "I told you to call if you needed anything."

Kollin had just wished for Eli's company, but for whatever reason, his concern pissed him off. He knew it wasn't fair, but he couldn't stop himself from snapping back. "I'm not a fucking invalid. I can make myself a sandwich."

He felt like shit when Eli only nodded and backed away. After all, Eli didn't have to deal with any of this bullshit, and now Kollin was acting like an ungrateful jackass, when Eli was only trying to help. Instead of apologizing, though, he shuffled into the kitchen and opened the fridge to pull out everything he needed to make a turkey sandwich. Eli followed and grabbed a bag of chips that was just out of Kollin's reach. He handed it over without uttering even a whisper of "I told you so." Still, Kollin couldn't bring himself to apologize.

Eli sat on the barstool next to Kollin and snatched a chip off his plate. "Could've made me one, you know."

Kollin jerked his head up, eyes wide, and just as quickly as his anger had surfaced, it drained out of him. Grinning, he said, "Shut up, man."

"I'm just saying… I like turkey too."

"Well, I'll be sure to hobble over there and make you one after I finish mine."

"Extra pickles, please."

Kollin shook his head. "Where's your keeper? He can make your damn sandwich. Figured he'd be here by now anyway."

"My keeper?"

"Mmmhmm. Zhe guy alwayz shtarin' at your ash," Kollin said around a mouthful of food. Elijah grimaced as a piece of cheese shot out of Kollin's mouth and landed in front of him.

"Adam?"

Kollin nodded.

"He'll be here soon, but you might want to cool it on the ass jokes. I'm not his favorite person right now."

Eli rubbed at some nonexistent scuff on the counter. He looked tired—exhausted even. Kollin couldn't really blame him after all the trouble he'd been the past few days. Beyond that, though, he looked sad—worse than he had the other night while he was talking about Brian. Kollin frowned.

"You're not... he's not mad at you because of what happened with Brian, is he? That wasn't your fault."

Eli seemed surprised when he looked at Kollin—and then impossibly sadder than he was just a moment before. "No. It's nothing to do with that. I've just made some really stupid decisions recently. Nothing for you to worry about."

Kollin's stomach sank. *Shit.* He'd seen Eli and Adam at the inn together Saturday, and they'd been fine—laughing and joking around. Kollin caught Adam checking out Eli's ass no less than five times. He'd be lying if he said he wasn't curious, but he knew better than to pry into other people's shit. If they'd been fine Saturday, though, something had obviously happened since then, and Eli had spent nearly all of his time with Kollin the past few days. Which meant....

"You're not fighting because of me, are you? I don't want to mess up whatever you guys got going on."

"No." Eli looked horrified enough that Kollin believed him. "Not even a little. We're both on the same page when it comes to you. Don't worry about that, okay?"

Kollin shifted uncomfortably. "You wanna talk about it or something?"

"Nah, but thanks. Let's get you settled before we worry about my love life. Sound good?"

"Sure. Thanks, Eli... for taking care of me like this. It's pretty stellar of you."

"Stellar, huh?"

Kollin shrugged. "Fine. It's pretty fucking epic, and I really appreciate it, even if I seem like an ungrateful asshole sometimes."

Eli gently slid an arm around Kollin's shoulders and gave him a quick hug. "Don't even mention it."

THE DOORBELL rang, interrupting their moment, and Adam walked into the kitchen a few moments later.

"Hey, guys," he greeted them. He looked like an overgrown kid in a black tee that displayed a unicorn covered in glitter, surrounded by the words "Born This Way." Elijah knew from experience that the back had the words "And Proud of It!" written in bold, rainbow-colored bubble print. Elijah loved the shirt for many reasons, the least of which was how tightly it hugged Adam's chest. "What's going on?"

"Elijah wants extra pickles on his turkey sandwich," Kollin quipped. "Better get to it, Jeeves."

Laughing, Adam glanced at Elijah for a moment and then looked away. "I think a task like that is a little above my pay grade. Sorry, man."

"You two are hilarious," Elijah said dryly. His heart sank when Adam refused to look at him. Going through this shitstorm with Kollin was difficult enough, but doing it without Adam's friendship was immeasurably harder. He knew he had Adam's support and gratitude, and there was no question in his mind that Adam would show up at a moment's notice if Elijah needed him. But there was a difference in Adam showing up for Kollin and Adam showing up for Elijah.

Elijah desperately needed someone to show up for him right then.

"It's part of our charm," Kollin said, sliding off the barstool and placing his plate in the sink.

"I have some news…." Adam's words and the ominous tone in which they were spoken made Kollin's face fall. "It's about your parents."

"Well, let's get it over with." Kollin grabbed the Tylenol off the counter and gingerly walked back into the TV room. Adam followed on his heels.

Once they were all sitting on the couch, Elijah and Adam on either side of Kollin, Adam spoke again. "They arrested your dad yesterday evening, as he was leaving his job. He spent the night in jail but posted bond earlier today. They'll arrange a trial as quickly as possible. And if he's found guilty, which is likely, he'll get at least a year of jail time. The max for a first-time offense is seventy-four months."

Kollin sounded hollow when he spoke. "Wow. I didn't think anything would happen that fast."

"You gave them pretty solid evidence. They didn't want to wait and give him a chance to run. And the rest of it will take a while… could be a year or more before he goes to trial."

"What about my mom?"

Elijah laid a hand on the back of Kollin's neck and squeezed gently. He was ready to fall apart. Elijah could practically see his heart breaking in two.

Adam's voice was calm and soft, but his face looked mutinous. "They haven't charged her with anything—yet. She told the investigator she feared for her own life, and her lawyer is trying to paint her as a victim. The police are going to come by again and speak to you, see if you've ever witnessed your dad hurting your mom. Her defense is incredibly weak, especially if you can't confirm her story. It's likely she'll be charged with neglect for not stopping him."

A single tear fell from Kollin's cheek and landed on his lap. Elijah scooted closer and wrapped an arm around his shoulder. They sat in silence, each of them keeping their gaze on the floor.

"It's not fair," Kollin finally whimpered, sinking into Elijah's embrace. "Why do I feel guilty for telling the truth when she didn't love me enough to stop him?"

Horrified and speechless, Elijah tightened his arm around Kollin.

"I don't know, buddy," Adam said. "I wish I could help you make this decision, or at least make it easier. You want me to call Dr. Will?"

Kollin shook his head and wiped away more tears. "No. Tomorrow's fine. I think I want to go to my room for a while, though."

"Of course. Need any help getting up there?" Adam asked.

Kollin shot Adam a grateful look but shook his head. Elijah sank back against the couch and covered his face, feeling completely inadequate. He hadn't said one damn word during the entire conversation.

"You okay?" Adam asked after Kollin left the room.

No. He wasn't anywhere near okay, but Adam had made it perfectly clear where they stood, so he wasn't about to start whining.

"Yeah, just… wish I could handle this as well as you. I had no idea what to say."

Adam shrugged and stood. "Years of practice. Sorry I sprang the news on you. The cops called me on the drive over here, or I would've talked to you first."

Elijah waved him off. He hadn't thought twice about it, and truth be told, he was glad Adam had handled the situation.

"I guess I'm going to head out. Word's gotten around at the center, and I don't want to leave it all up to Amelia and Kirsten to field the questions. Plus, no one has even touched the inn this week, so I need to go by there and take inventory. We need to get back on track."

"Shit, man. I hadn't even thought about the inn. I'm sorry."

"Don't be. You're where you need to be. Even if Kollin wasn't one of ours, I wouldn't expect you there." Leaving Elijah sitting on the couch, Adam walked toward the formal living room and paused in the archway. "You're doing great with him, you know? It's a small miracle he was smiling at all when I got here. It's not always about knowing exactly what to say. Just make sure he knows his feelings are valid, no matter what they are."

Elijah couldn't say he agreed with Adam, but he took a small measure of comfort in his praise. Quelling the urge to beg him to stay, he said, "Thanks. Call me if you have any questions on the inn. Kollin is moving around better and making noises about getting out of the house. Maybe I can bring him by tomorrow, just to give him something to do. He can't do any work, but at least he'll have a four different walls to stare at."

"Will do," Adam said. With an awkward wave, Adam walked out, leaving Elijah staring after him.

Feeling lost and abandoned, Elijah grabbed a throw pillow and hugged it to his chest as he fell to his side on the couch. Burying his face in the cushions, Elijah gave in to the overwhelming turmoil he'd felt since Saturday night and wept.

"NO. I'M not sticking my nose in where it doesn't belong, Derek." Kirsten glanced at her GPS and flipped on her left turn signal. "I'm just going to check on Kollin and see if Elijah needs a break. If he happens to want to talk while I'm there, though, I won't tell him no."

Kirsten held back a grin when Derek huffed into the phone. "You do realize we're married, right? I know how you operate."

"You love how I operate." Derek grunted in Kirsten's ear as the entrance to Elijah's gated community came into view. "Oh, I think I'm here. I'll call you when I'm on my way home. Love you."

Kirsten hung up before Derek had a chance to say anything else. They both knew she was going to do what she wanted, so what was the point in listening to him fuss? Besides, *someone* had to fix this clusterfuck of a situation between Elijah and Adam, since neither of them seemed capable of doing it.

She breathed a sigh of relief when the code Adam had given her opened the gates as promised. Elijah didn't know she was coming, and she preferred to keep it that way.

Kirsten pulled into his driveway, grabbed the gallon of warm soup she'd brought, and hurried through the cold to ring his doorbell. She had to hold back a giggle when Elijah opened the door and his tired face showed nothing but surprise.

"Hey, Elijah," she chirped, walking past him. "I thought you boys could use some company. Or maybe some soup?"

"Uhh…. Kollin is asleep. It's kind of late, Kirsten."

Kirsten widened her eyes and made a show of checking her watch. "Oh. You're right. How'd it get to be nearly ten o'clock?"

Elijah stared at her, still looking slightly bewildered.

"Well, since I'm here, we might as well have a drink. I haven't seen you in ages. Plus, you can tell me how Kollin's doing. Adam's too moody to relay all the details."

Elijah scratched his head but motioned for her to follow. "Sure. In here." Kirsten looked around as Elijah led her through a very formal, very stuffy, and very un-Elijahlike space, into what looked like a rec room. There she could see touches of Elijah everywhere. The sofas were large, a deep chocolate-brown leather, soft to the touch and made for comfort. There was a Yale Blue La-Z-Boy recliner with a white *Y* on the back, tucked between the couches. The walls were dotted with memorabilia of Elijah's favorite sports teams, most of them signed and likely worth a pretty penny.

"You entertain a lot?" Kirsten asked, gesturing toward the fully stocked bar taking up most of the back wall.

"Not really. Just like to be prepared for the unexpected visitor." He gave her a wry smile.

"Touché." Kirsten grinned and nudged his arm. "Seriously, though, I just wanted to check on you, see how you're doing."

Elijah shrugged as he pulled out two glasses. "I'm okay. Hanging in there. What's your pleasure?"

"Whatever you're having is fine with me."

Elijah's eyebrows rose. "Sure about that?"

Grinning, Kirsten nodded. "Do your worst, buddy."

"Nah. I like you too much to do that. I'll hook you up, though. If you're anything like Adam at all, you'll love this." He bent down and pulled out a squat bottle that Kirsten immediately recognized as Patron. But instead of the amber color she was used to, the liquid inside was dark brown, almost black. "You like coffee?"

Kirsten nodded.

"You like tequila?"

"Oh yeah."

Elijah grinned, plunked two ice cubes in her glass, and poured in two fingers of the coffee tequila. He slid the glass across the bar and his face fell as he studied Kirsten warily. She merely smiled and raised the glass to her lips.

Kirsten knew he was squirming, and yeah, she was there to try to get things patched up between him and Adam. But he'd still hurt one of the people she loved most in the world. It wouldn't be the worst thing ever if she made him nervous before fixing everything. The drink was strong, but Kirsten enjoyed the burn as it slid down her throat. Elijah remained silent and took his own, heftier sip of tequila.

"So, how're you doing?" Kirsten finally asked. Elijah started to wave off her concern, but Kirsten stopped him right away. "Don't give me that bullshit. Adam's miserable, and not just because of Kollin and Julie. Tell me how you're really doing."

"*Julie*? What happened to her?" Elijah asked, setting his glass back down on the bar.

Closing her eyes, Kirsten sighed. "She's fine. She had some discoloration around her eye, but she swears no one hit her. Things have never been good for her at home, but she won't admit to anything. You have your hands full with Kollin, though. We'll take care of Julie and let you know if we need anything."

Elijah didn't look the least bit comforted, but he nodded. Kirsten took another sip of her drink and waited patiently. She raised an eyebrow when Elijah continued to stare at her.

"What do you want me to say? He's your brother, and we both know you're going to take his side. I was an ass. I apologized, but even I can't be surprised he's not willing to give me another chance."

"But you want another chance? A real one?"

Elijah's eyes met hers, and the despair shining out of them nearly bowled Kirsten over. "I'd do anything but give up Kollin if he'd give me another chance—even just for our friendship. I know he has no reason to trust me, especially after I told him about my past. I can't promise I won't mess up again because I'm so fucked up inside. But I won't run ever again."

Kirsten squinted her eyes and glared at Elijah. "Well, you're wrong. You weren't just an ass. You were a colossally huge prick who hurt someone who would've done anything for you. *Any*thing." Kirsten paused. "Regardless, I think your sorry ass is good for my brother, so I'm willing to help. But Elijah, I swear, if you flake again—"

"I won't. I swear I won't."

"I'm not going to pretend like Adam hasn't told me a little of what's going on, but I don't know the whole story, nor do I need to." Kirsten held up her hand when Elijah looked like he was going to interrupt again. "That's your business. If you need a friend to listen, I'm here for you. But don't make that decision now, when you're already emotionally compromised. What I *can* tell you is that Adam will not be anyone's dirty little secret—at least not for long. We all have our baggage. I don't doubt yours is worse than most, but don't forget Adam has his own not-so-happy past that he doesn't want to go back to. He's fought damn hard to get where he is today and to put his demons behind him."

Elijah's shoulders slumped. "I hadn't even thought of it like that. He's never told me about his past."

Kirsten cocked her head to the side. "Have you asked?"

Elijah linked his fingers together and dropped his head between his arms on the bar. "No."

To his credit, Elijah sounded completely miserable. Kirsten reached out and scruffed the top of his head. "That's okay, you know? Adam is incredibly generous and incredibly patient. He's open about his birth parents because he has to be. It's the nature of his job. Just… don't forget he's human too. Don't put him up on a pedestal, because he'll never live up to it. He's stubborn. He's cranky in the morning. His feet stink, and he cheats when he plays poker. All of those things are okay, because no one's perfect, and Adam knows his faults better than anyone. When you spout off about how he's too good for you, especially when you're pretty damn amazing yourself, it doesn't really add up in his head. Besides, you're kind of his hero for helping to save these kids."

Elijah remained still for a long while. Finally he turned his head to the side and peeked up at Kirsten. Seeing Elijah, normally so strong and self-assured, looking so crestfallen and sad made Kirsten's heart melt a little. She slid down the stool so she was directly in front of him and wrapped her arms around his broad shoulders. "Seriously, Elijah. He really likes you, but he's scared and maybe a little too proud to let his guard down again. Give him a reason to be proud of *you* instead."

CHAPTER 20

ELIJAH PACED around the living room and set out a bottle of his best whiskey along with a couple of tumblers. He fluffed the pillows on the couch Kollin wasn't occupying, grabbed the ice bucket to set on the counter, and sat in his La-Z-Boy. Then he stood, put the ice bucket in the freezer, and set a wine glass next to the tumblers.

"Will you stop fluttering?" Kollin groused, sitting stiffly next to the arm of the couch, nursing a ginger ale. He'd tripped on an area rug earlier in the day but caught himself on an end table before falling onto the floor. He hadn't hit his ribs, but he'd had to twist awkwardly to catch himself and had been favoring his side ever since. Elijah thought he needed to take something stronger than Tylenol, but whenever Elijah asked, Kollin insisted he was fine and didn't need anything. "Relax," Kollin said. "It's not like your dad can ground you."

Elijah snorted.

"Sorry. I didn't mean to be like that. I know it's not easy. I just… it's weird to see you so nervous. You're usually like Superman or something."

Elijah looked up. He recalled using that very same description, except he had been referring to Adam. Did Kollin really think Elijah was someone to be idolized?

Kollin's next words were spoken so quietly, Elijah barely heard him.

"If it's easier, you don't have to tell him why I'm here."

Elijah shook his head. "It's not you. You're not the problem here. You got me?"

Kollin nodded but remained silent.

Staring at Kollin, Elijah cocked his head to the side. "I'm serious. Yeah, I'm nervous as hell to tell my dad what's going on, but it's not just because of you. I'm damn proud of the work I've done at the center and the inn, and I'm proud of you for finding help and being true to yourself. It's not something to be ashamed of. Coming out to my dad after lying to him for so long, though—it's not really going to be my shining moment. And if I'm being completely honest, I'm terrified of how he's going to react."

"You sure you want me to be here?"

"I want him to meet you. He already knows you're here, so that won't be a surprise. I wouldn't do that to you, and I'll wait 'til after you've gone to bed to tell him about Adam."

"What do you think he's going to say?"

Elijah shook his head. "I have no idea, but if he thinks it's bad for business, he's not going to be happy."

Before Kollin could ask another question, the doorbell rang. Elijah tensed, but seeing how nervous Kollin suddenly seemed, he forced himself to calm down. "If you start to feel uncomfortable, just let me know, and I'll get you to your room. Okay? No matter what they say, you're here to stay as long as you want. This is your home, not theirs."

Kollin nodded again, and Elijah hurried to answer the door. He steeled his nerves with a deep breath and quickly pulled the door open.

"Hey, Mom, Dad." Elijah gave his mom a quick hug and motioned them inside. "Kollin's a little nervous and in some pain. I told him to let me know if he needed to get away. Don't take it the wrong way if he bails. He's had a rough week."

"Of course we wouldn't, son." Elijah's mother smiled at him. "I'm so proud of you for taking him in like this. I know it can't be easy. Especially… well, you know."

Elijah's eyebrows rose. That was the closest his mom had ever come to mentioning Brian. He knew she was the main reason his dad finally called in some favors and started a search for Brian, but she'd never once spoken directly to him about it. He loved his mom, but she was the textbook definition of a Stepford wife. She never spoke against her husband and supported him unconditionally, even when she knew he was wrong. There's no way in hell she would ever admit that Elijah Senior might've made a mistake—not even to comfort her son.

"It wasn't really a difficult decision. He's a great kid. I have the means to keep him safe, and he trusts me."

She patted his arm with a small smile on her face. "Nevertheless, it's quite noble, and I'm proud."

Elijah returned her smile and finally looked at his dad, who only dipped his chin. Apparently he didn't share his wife's sentiments.

"Right. Well, he's in here." Kollin looked completely miserable when they entered the room, so Elijah gave him a quick thumbs-up and a smile. "Mom, Dad, this is Kollin. I met him at The Center for HOPE, a place in town that reaches out to LGBT youth. I've been volunteering there for a while and I'm helping them renovate the old Tarboro Inn so other youth who are turned away or in danger will have a safe place to stay." Elijah glanced down at Kollin and smiled again. He'd already told his parents all this, but he wanted to make sure Kollin heard him say the words as well. "Unfortunately for Kollin, he lost a bet playing basketball and is stuck with me until further notice."

Kollin actually chuckled and made to stand, but Elijah held out his hand to stop him, and Elijah's mom rushed forward. "Don't get up, sweetie. I'm Gloria Langley, and this is my husband, Elijah." She gestured toward her husband but didn't let him speak. "I'm so pleased to meet you. E. J. is positively enthralled with you."

Kollin's eyebrows rose, and he looked at Elijah. "E. J.?"

"She's the only one allowed to call me that, so don't even think about it."

Smirking, Kollin barely even tried to look chastised. "I wouldn't dream of it. Does Kirsten know about this?"

"C-SPAN, man." Elijah pointed his finger at Kollin as he gave the warning, but there was no real threat in his voice.

In a move Elijah suspected surprised everyone in the room, his dad walked around his mom and held out a hand for Kollin. "It's nice to meet you."

Looking more than a little hesitant, Kollin took his hand. "Thank you, sir."

Shocking Elijah even further, his dad sat next to Kollin on the couch and crossed his leg over his knee. "I'm sorry to hear about what happened, but I'm glad Elijah decided to take you in." He paused for a beat and glanced briefly at Elijah. "I'm quite proud of him."

While his dad spoke, Elijah's mom busied herself at the bar, pouring whiskey into the two tumblers and handing them to her husband and son. Then she poured herself a glass of wine and grabbed a cold can of Coke from the fridge. She handed Kollin the Coke and perched on the edge of the La-Z-Boy. "I assumed the Cokes were for you since E. J. has never liked them," she said when Kollin just stared at her.

"Uh… yeah. This is great. Thanks."

Unsure of what to do, or who the two people sitting in his living room were, Elijah sat on the remaining couch and tried to keep his mouth from hanging open. He didn't think his parents would be rude to Kollin by any means—they had too much class for that—but he hadn't expected them to be pleasant either and definitely not after the cold greeting he'd gotten from his father at the door.

"Will you be returning to school Monday?" Elijah's mom asked.

Kollin winced but nodded. "Yes, ma'am. Eli collected some of my work from the school yesterday. I did a little of it today, but I think it's going to take me a while to catch up."

"You should consider enrolling him in Killington, Elijah. He'll get a better education there."

Elijah stared at his father. "I… I hadn't really thought about it. I just assumed he'd want to stay where he is, where his friends are."

His dad shrugged. "Just something to consider. Might have an easier time there too. They have a very strict antibullying policy."

Elijah looked at Kollin, who looked just as bewildered as he did. Of course he did. Elijah had been freaking out all day about his parents visiting, and here they were, appearing to be the most supportive people in the world. He'd expected as much from his mom—maybe not to that extent—but not from his dad. He knew his dad would respect his decision, but Elijah had been sure his dad would have told him to find Kollin a safe place to go somewhere else, not encourage him to enroll Kollin in their alma mater. Kollin scrunched his eyebrows, making a "whatever" face, and Elijah had to hold in his laugh. Whatever was up with his parents, he wasn't going to borrow trouble.

The next two hours passed quickly. Both Langleys took a genuine interest in Kollin and his story. The more they got to know him, the harder they fell for him as his naturally charismatic personality shined through. When they found out Kollin's parents had thrown all of his clothes into the pouring rain Sunday night, and he'd been wearing the same two outfits Adam had brought over from Walmart on Monday, Elijah's mom offered to take him shopping for new school clothes. She gave Elijah a disapproving look and promised to drop by the next day and get Kollin out of the house. Elijah blushed and sat back in his seat, properly reprimanded. When Kollin started yawning, Elijah gently hinted it was time for him to head up to his room.

"It was nice meeting you both. Thanks for not flipping out," Kollin said with a grin as he trudged out of the room with a little wave.

As soon as he was out of earshot, Gloria turned to Elijah. "Oh, E. J., he's something else. I can see why you wanted to help him, and I know it can't be easy."

Clearing his throat, Elijah's father drew their attention. "I know I said it earlier, in front of the boy, but it bears repeating. I'm proud of you. While this is very honorable, I was ready to come over here and give you all the reasons why you should find an alternative solution. That kid, though… when I saw him, I…. I know I was never in the running for father of the year, but how anyone could ever physically hurt his own child… I just don't get it. You've performed a commendable deed taking him in. I'll help out at the office for as long as you need while you two figure this out."

Elijah basked in his father's praise. He never expected to hear those words come from his dad, especially in a situation not involving work. He closed his eyes and took a moment to commit the moment to memory, certain he was about to ruin it all.

"Actually there's something else I need to talk to you about."

ADAM LAY on his couch, watching TV—*Seinfeld* reruns—for the first time in months. Amelia had dropped by the center and shoved him out the door with orders to go home and rest. He was so weary he didn't even pretend to act like he didn't need it. He collapsed in front of the TV as soon as he arrived home and hadn't moved since. His stomach had started growling half an hour ago, and he was to the point where he would need to get up and do something about it soon, when his front door swung open.

"Hey," Kirsten called as she walked in. "Mom said she gave you the night off. Thought I'd drop by to see how you're doing." She set a Subway bag on his coffee table, dumped the rest of her stuff on the floor, and claimed the only chair in the room.

"Hey, Kris. Come on in," Adam said, sarcasm dripping from his voice.

"Thanks." She grinned. "How's it going?"

Biting back a snarky reply, Adam sighed. "Not so well," he said, pushing himself up and grabbing his sub.

"Yeah, about that… maybe we should try to focus on something we *can* change, instead of all the things we can't."

"I can't change any of this shit," he grumbled.

Kirsten waited for Adam to take a bite. "You could talk to Elijah."

"No." Adam shook his head to emphasize his point since his mouth was full of food. He swallowed and continued. "I can't keep putting myself on the line… for him just to get my hopes up and have them crushed again."

"Well, I didn't mean you should jump into bed with him without talking first and then expect him to be ready for two kids and a dog," Kirsten deadpanned.

Adam narrowed his eyes at her as he raised his sandwich to his mouth. Just as he was about to take a bite, he slowly raised his middle finger and sneered. Kirsten rolled her eyes but otherwise ignored his gesture.

"What am I supposed to do, Kris? It really sucked hard when he dumped me Sunday night without even giving us a chance. I would've done whatever he needed."

"Sounds to me like he needed some time and maybe a little understanding."

"Are you fucking kidding me? You're supposed to be on my side."

"I am on your side, idiot. That's why I'm trying to make you see this from his point of view. Yeah, what he did was shitty, but you just said you would've done anything for him, so why did that change because he made one mistake?"

"*One* mistake?" Adam set down his sandwich and held up his first finger. "He practically attacked me the night we met in HOPE's parking lot—"

"Which would've been a fabulous story if it had worked out."

Adam ignored her and held up another two fingers. "He completely ignored me when he was out with his parents, and then, when he did acknowledge that he knew me, he glossed over the fact that I run an LGBT-friendly center, because heaven forbid Daddykins finds out where Elijah donates his time and money."

Kirsten winced. "But he apologized for that, and you forgave him, so you can't hold it against him anymore."

He lifted another two fingers. "He slept with me and kissed me and held me and made me think there was a chance…." Adam clamped his mouth shut. *Dammit.* He didn't want to get into this.

"I know he messed up. A lot. A lot lot," Kirsten began, her voice soft. "And his past doesn't excuse him for making shitty decisions now, but can't you at least give him a chance? I see what you two have together. You guys make each other better just by being around one another, and you're obviously both happier when you're together. If he were one of the kids at the center, you'd give him as many chances as he needed."

Adam's heart clenched as if tiny, sharp points of barbed wire were digging into his flesh. Everything Kirsten said was true, but she didn't understand. That's why it was so much more difficult to forgive Elijah. He'd dealt with rejection his whole life—from his family, his friends, from too many supposed caregivers. Even with as much love and energy as he poured into HOPE and the kids, too many dismissed his help. He didn't want to worry whether the man he went home to at night would suddenly change his mind one day, and Elijah had yet to give him a reason to believe otherwise.

Adam dropped his head and looked down at the floor as he spoke. "I'm not kicking him out of my life, but I can't go there again with him. I was so busy falling for the guy, I never thought about what our life would be like. How long before his dad would start asking why he's not showing up at functions without one of his blonde bimbos on his arm? What about on Thanksgiving or Christmas? He'd be welcome at our family dinners, but I wouldn't even rank a mention at his parents' table. I won't do that to myself, and I really hope you'll respect my decision. I deserve better than to be shoved into the closet because the person I've chosen to spend my life with is too ashamed to step out of his."

Kirsten's hand landed gently in his hair. "You're right, and I'll stay out of it from now on. I'm glad you're not selling yourself short. You deserve someone who'll be proud to call you his."

Sighing in relief, Adam grabbed Kirsten's hand and turned his head to kiss her wrist. "Thanks, Kris."

"Mmmhmm," she murmured. "Now finish your dinner and get some sleep. You look like death warmed over."

"Don't flatter me," he groused and grabbed his sandwich. He really *was* starving.

Kirsten dropped a kiss on Adam's head and walked to the door. "Take care of you, Adam, and remember, all I really want is for you to be happy."

CHAPTER 21

KOLLIN STARED in the mirror, his eyes raking over his face. Behind him, Gloria winced as she looked over his shoulder.

"I'm sorry I couldn't do any better," she said, her eyes confirming every word.

Tracing the most obscene bruise, the one framing his jaw, Kollin met her stare in the mirror. "It's okay. I thought since they'd turned this fabulous shade of puke yellow, they'd be easier to hide. Just wasn't expecting it to still be so obvious. At least most of the swelling is gone."

Eli's mom fretted, worrying her bottom lip between her teeth. "Are you sure you're ready to go back today? They'd probably give you another few days off."

Kollin shook his head. "Might as well get it over with. Besides, I have a few friends who will stick with me, and maybe, since people can actually see the bruises, they'll realize it sucks to have your parents beat the shit out of you, and they'll leave me alone."

"Oh, Kollin." Gloria wrapped an arm around his shoulder gave a small squeeze. "Well, at least you look good. I love the clothes we picked out."

Kollin raised an eyebrow and looked over his outfit. She'd spared no expense when they went shopping on Saturday, and he had a blast spending the day with her. With his interest in fashion, Kollin had always dressed well. His parents weren't poor, and his mom had indulged most of his clothing requests, but she never would've let him drop a hundred dollars on a pair of jeans. When he tried to put back the first outfit after seeing the price, Gloria shoved the clothes back in his hand and went on her own search for several outfits she thought he'd like. Then they hit a few more shops where Kollin helped her pick out a few outfits for herself.

"Thanks again for taking me. I was way past ready to get out of this house, and I think Eli needed a break too."

"Don't you worry about Elijah," she said, cleaning up the makeup she'd brought over to camouflage the bruises on Kollin's face. "He's a big boy and can take care of himself. He knows his limits. Besides, I adore shopping. I was so upset when E. J. wouldn't let me help him buy clothes anymore. He was just a year or so older than you when he decided I wasn't necessary and shoved me out of his closet." Kollin snorted, and Gloria looked up, wide-eyed. "I didn't mean it that way."

Kollin waved her off. "I know what you meant."

Gloria smiled and gave him a quick peck on the cheek. "Let's get you downstairs before Eli paces a hole in the floor. He always hated being late."

"I heard that," Eli called from the hallway.

"Of course you did, dear. You've been standing there for the past five minutes." She patted Eli's arm as she walked by. "Now, Kollin, I know you have Elijah's and Adam's numbers, but if you need me for anything, don't hesitate to call. I don't care what it's for. You two have a good day. And Elijah, try not to worry yourself to death, okay?"

They reached the bottom of the stairs, and with a wave over her shoulder, she opened the door and left the two boys staring after her.

Kollin looked at Eli. "Your mom…. She's something else, man."

Eli scratched his head and tugged at his hair, a trait Kollin thought he'd picked up from Adam. "Yeah, she is. I wish she'd been like this when I was a kid… or any of the years after it."

Kollin's face fell as he walked to the closet to get his jacket. Eli's antagonistic comment struck a nerve. He knew it was irrational. Eli was allowed to have a bad past with his parents. Just because they didn't beat him didn't mean his life was sunshine and roses. But instead of biting Eli's head off like he would've done a week before, he murmured, "Maybe she was and you just never noticed."

"Maybe," Eli replied, though his tone didn't sound like he agreed at all.

Kollin shrugged it off. He really didn't want to think about Eli's mom in any light other than how he knew her. And even if she was more reserved when Eli was younger, at least she was trying. "Do you really have to come in with me once we get to school?" he asked, instead.

"Yes." Eli's tone brooked no arguments, but he continued anyway. "Even if I didn't want to send a clear message about who people will have to deal with if they mess with you, I have to sign a few forms."

"Fine. Just please don't go all parental and embarrass me. Please?"

"Wouldn't dream of it, kid."

"You going to be at HOPE later on?"

Eli opened the door for Kollin. "I don't know. I have a lot to catch up on at the office, and with CPS coming over tonight, we need to make sure everything here is perfect."

"You can't avoid him forever, you know," Kollin said, dismissing the pitiful excuses. Eli side-eyed him and grunted. "I'm just saying. I don't care what he *said*. He's gonna wanna know you told your dad."

Eli grunted again. "Aren't you supposed to be taking advice from me, instead of the other way around?"

"No offense, dude, but I am never taking guy advice from you. You kinda suck at it."

Eli gently shoved the back of his head. "Shut up and get in the car."

NEWS ABOUT Kollin's abuse traveled fast. He was so well liked that it was no surprise to Adam when everyone chipped in and bought special snacks for his return. They all worried together, and they all celebrated together. They were the only family some of them had.

When Kollin first walked in, Julie ran from the room without saying a word to anyone. Adam found her huddled in one of the lecture rooms, crying quietly. She finally confessed her dad was, in fact, responsible for her occasional bruises, but that he always apologized afterward.

Later Adam stood in the doorway of the multipurpose room and watched Julie break through the crowd to wrap Kollin in a fierce hug. She whispered something in his ear, and Adam smiled when he saw Kollin tighten his hug on Julie. He wasn't positive about what Julie said to Kollin, but given the conversation he'd just had with her, he could guess.

Adam's already fragile heart wept as Julie explained that her mom did her best to stop him, or at least minimize the damage by stepping in front of her, but every now and then, she failed. Julie honestly believed she was the problem. Her dad hated her for being different, and once she was eighteen, she could leave without a fuss from anyone and get a job to support herself. She thought her mom and sister would be safe without her in the house.

She had no idea how flawed her reasoning was, and Adam nearly broke as she explained that once she was officially an adult, her father would no longer have a say in her life. On the off chance that her dad started in on her sister after she left, Julie thought she'd be old enough to legally take care of her. When Julie saw Kollin, still favoring his left side where his ribs ached and with his face noticeably bruised, the overwhelming fear that her dad might one day hurt her sister was suddenly real. When she agreed to talk to Dr. Maggie the following day, Adam breathed a sigh of relief. As grateful as Adam was that Julie had finally confessed to everything happening at home, he found himself once again stuck with a difficult decision to make.

Well, that wasn't true. With another minor involved and a parent who showed consistent signs of abuse—not only to a child but also to his wife—Adam knew he had to report Julie's dad. But his first instinct was to always keep the kids with a parent, if possible, and it sounded like Julie's mom had tried to protect her daughters. They just needed to find a way to keep all three of them safe.

Adam knew what he wanted to do for her and her family. There were two empty rooms at the inn waiting for someone who needed them. Julie's mom didn't technically meet the criteria and he had no idea why she stayed in the relationship. She tried to protect her daughter, but that didn't mean she'd be willing to leave her husband. Adam needed to find out whether she'd even be willing to accept help.

Adam scrubbed his hand through his hair, turned back to his office, and made a mental list of everything he needed to do for Julie. He opened his office door and jumped when he found Elijah sitting at his desk, typing away on his computer.

"Shit. You scared me."

"Sorry." Elijah glanced at him and returned to the computer. "Kollin was busy, so I thought I'd revamp our plan for the inn, since we had to abandon it last week."

Adam sank into the chair on the other side of the desk. "Thanks. I was going to do it this afternoon, but some stuff came up."

Cutting his eyes toward Adam, Elijah stopped typing. "Good stuff or bad stuff?"

Adam screwed up his face and shook his head.

"Oh God. What happened now?"

"Technically nothing new, but Julie finally confessed her dad's been hitting her. Her mom tries to stop him, but she gets thrown around too. Julie has some crazy idea she can escape when she turns eighteen. She thinks she can take her sister with her and that they'll be fine as long as they're together. She has no idea what would actually happen, but that's why she's refused help before."

"Fuck," Elijah sighed, drawing the sound out as he sat back in Adam's seat.

"Yep," Adam agreed. "It's good she finally told us. But this goes beyond the scope of hitting your kid because she's gay, and it's not a situation I'm familiar with. It sounds like her dad would be abusive no matter what, and he uses her as his scapegoat. I need to somehow figure out what Julie's mom is willing to do and see if HOPE can help them with a place to stay at the inn. We've never housed an adult, and as tacky as it sounds, I'm not sure if we can set that precedent. This isn't supposed to be a shelter for battered women, but if we have the room, I can't stand the thought of turning away someone who needs help."

"I'd have the lawyer double-check, but you might lose some of the government funding if they catch an adult in there. That money is a bonus, though. We don't technically need it right now, since the building and renovations are paid for." Elijah rubbed his temples. "We could always pass her off as the night guard, maybe even pay her a little something. That way it's legit if someone questions us."

Adam stared at Elijah, shocked he'd solved one of his problems in a matter of seconds. He sometimes forgot how smart Elijah was and how well they bounced ideas off of each other. "That's... brilliant," he finally said. "Thank you. Now I just have to figure out how to convince Julie's mom to come along."

"If she's willing to protect Julie, she's probably willing to protect her sister too. I'd work that angle. If this is anything like Kollin's case, the guy is going to spend a night in jail and be home a day later."

"Yep, and once that happens, we lose momentum. Julie's mom has been here a few times. We'll try to get her here tomorrow to talk with Dr. Maggie too. If she doesn't agree, I don't know what Julie will do. But I guess we'll cross that bridge when we come to it."

"Sorry, man. It's been a rough couple of weeks. Anything I can do?"

Adam stared at Elijah and resisted the urge to ask him for a simple hug. Too dangerous. Instead, he shook his head. "Just take care of Kollin. Seems like he had a pretty good day. I didn't get to talk with him much because of Julie."

Elijah smiled. "Yeah. He texted me a few times during the day to tell me he was fine. Plus he called me on the way over here and said mostly everyone either left him alone or gave him pitying looks. A few people were even nice to him, and one of the cheerleaders complimented him on his outfit. I'm sure Mom was tickled pink when he told her."

"She's really taken a liking to him, huh? When I stopped by yesterday, he wouldn't stop talking about how much fun he had shopping with her."

Elijah laughed, his eyes bright and amused. "I never would've believed it if I hadn't seen it with my own eyes."

"Maybe you haven't had your eyes open in a while." He spoke the words without really thinking, but Adam only half wished he could pull them back. Yeah. His comment ruined Elijah's good mood—something he was sure was a rare thing lately—but maybe it was something Elijah needed to hear.

"Kollin said the same thing to me this morning. I may have been walking around numb and blind, but Mom wasn't there for me when Dad kicked Brian out. She saw how it destroyed me, but she never once reached out to tell me it wasn't my fault. I'm not saying she was a bad mom, but I can't help thinking my life would be different right now if I'd had a little support back then." Elijah's voice sounded angry and frustrated, but his face was contorted in sorrow.

"I'm not defending your mom. I'm really not, but try looking at it from her point of view. I love these kids, but you've heard them. They're in love with someone new every other damn week. I suspect, up until the very moment you were caught with your pants down, your parents had absolutely no clue you might be bi. You've carried a grudge against them for an awfully long time for not believing how serious you were about Brian, when they didn't even know those types of feelings were *possible* for you with another guy.

"Parents aren't perfect either. They make mistakes and learn from them, just like the kids here do. Maybe that's what she's doing. But if you're this upset with her, you should talk to her." Adam paused. "She deserves to know all of you, Elijah. They both do." It was as close as he'd ever come to telling Elijah to come out to his parents. Now that any chance of a relationship between the two of them was off the table, the words seemed to spill out.

Before Elijah could tell Adam to mind his own business, the door swung open and Kollin walked in, all smiles. "Hey, Eli. I didn't know you were here already."

"I left work a little early to update the plans for the inn. I have you hanging drywall tomorrow after school. Sound good?"

Without missing a beat, Kollin tapped his fists together toward Elijah. "Funny guy. I wouldn't touch that shit, even if I could."

Elijah chuckled and shook his head. "You know, when I first started coming here, you apologized for cussing in front of me. Whatever happened to that respect?"

Kollin shrugged. "You know us crazy teenagers. Finicky as hell these days. You ready? I have a ton of homework to do."

"Sure. Let me e-mail this to myself. I can work on it tonight."

Turning to Adam, Kollin asked, "You're going to be there for the interview, right? You should come for dinner too."

Adam had been shocked when Elijah and Kollin called him over the weekend and asked if Adam would be Kollin's secondary caregiver. He accepted immediately, consequences be damned. There was no way he was letting Kollin down at this point. "Yeah. I'll be there. I have a ton of shit to do here, though, so I'll have to take a rain check on dinner."

Elijah nodded. "Bring some stuff with you if you want, and I can help once the smartass goes to sleep."

Kollin huffed, crossed his arms, then winced when his arms bumped his ribs. "I can't believe you're giving me a bedtime."

"When I don't have to throw ice water on your head in the morning to wake you up for school, you can stay up as late as you want," Elijah replied, unfazed by Kollin's pouting.

"I can tell you two are a match made in heaven," Adam said.

"More like hell," Kollin grumbled.

Ignoring both of them, Elijah looked at Adam. "CPS will be there around seven. And seriously, bring whatever if it's something I can help with."

Adam nodded noncommittally. "Try not to kill each other before I get there. Okay?"

"I make no promises." Kollin's singsong voice floated back into his office, and Adam delved into his work with a smile on his face.

CHAPTER 22

"YOU NERVOUS?" Kollin asked as they pulled into Elijah's driveway.

Elijah glanced at Kollin. Damn straight, he was nervous. But he wasn't about to tell him that. "'Course not. The guy who ran my background check was nice enough, and from what I hear, it's all a formality here on out. Why? Are you?"

Kollin shrugged one shoulder. "I just hope I don't say something to mess it up."

"You're not the one under investigation tonight. I am. You have nothing to be nervous about."

"I guess." Kollin turned to face him in the car. "They obviously know I'm gay, but do they know you're bi?"

Elijah stared at Kollin, trying to figure out where he was going with his line of questioning. "I doubt it, since I'm not really out to anyone but you and Adam... and now my parents."

"I'm pretty sure everyone at HOPE knows too."

Sighing, Elijah rolled his eyes. "Whatever. I don't see how CPS would know or why it would matter."

Kollin scratched an imaginary spot on his jeans and looked out the window. "I've heard sometimes it matters. If we get some homophobic asshole, they could just make shit up and decide I'm better off with my mom. Don't they always try to keep kids with their parents?"

"I think we need to take this one step at a time. All they're doing today is making sure I have a suitable home. We can worry about the permanent stuff later. Okay? And if we get someone who tries to pull some BS because of our sexual orientations, my lawyer will take them down without even blinking an eye."

Kollin grinned and glanced back at Elijah. "Yeah?"

"Oh yeah. Now come on. We need to scarf down some food before this woman gets here, and I have no idea what we have to eat."

Elijah and Kollin ate a quick and unsatisfying meal of roast beef sandwiches and chips and then sat in the rec room to watch TV while they waited. Not even five minutes into their show, the doorbell rang. Elijah gave

Kollin a smile and a thumbs-up and stood to answer the door. Sounding a little panicked, Kollin asked, "Why isn't Adam here yet?"

"Probably just running a little late. He had some unexpected stuff to take care of today. He'll be here."

Elijah plastered what he hoped was a genuine smile on his face as he answered the door and was surprised to see a matching one on the woman standing behind it. He expected Ms. Vick to be an older woman, with graying hair swept up in a bun and huge glasses that dangled on a beaded rope around her neck. In his mind, she'd looked an awful lot like his old high school librarian, instead of the young, curvy Latina with long dark hair and a *huge* rack—who was tilting her head sideways to bring Elijah's attention back where it should be.

"Mr. Langley?" she asked as his eyes popped back up to her pretty face. "I'm Vivian Vick. I've been officially assigned to Kollin's case."

"Yes. I'm sorry," Elijah said, holding out his hand. "Please, come in."

She shook his hand and scanned his foyer as she walked in. "Thank you. You have a beautiful home."

"Thanks. I was actually thinking of selling when it was just me, but maybe not, now that Kollin's here." Elijah forced himself to stop speaking before he started rambling—he had no idea why he'd brought up moving— and tried to quell his nerves as he watched her shrug off her leopard-print backpack with pink straps. She dug around inside and pulled out a stack of papers and a clipboard along with a pen. "Is that something I'd have to ask to do, prior to moving now?" he asked belatedly.

Grinning up at him, she laughed lightly. "Not as long as you stay in the area and aren't downgrading to a dumpster. Depending on how permanent this arrangement becomes, we may need to know where you move, so we can keep in contact with you."

Elijah glanced down at the floor and shoved his hands in his pockets, embarrassed. "Right. Makes sense."

Ms. Vick took a step closer, drawing his attention back to her face. Her teasing smirk replaced by a genuine and sympathetic smile. "Look, Mr. Langley, I'll be honest. Your background check cleared already, so this is the last piece of the puzzle. You don't have anything to worry about. There aren't many people who would take in a kid who's in trouble and has nowhere else to go. It's a huge responsibility, even without what he's been through and the challenges ahead that he—and now you—will face. You'll be seeing a lot of me until you're officially licensed, but just remember that

I'm on your side. I want what's best for Kollin, and from everything I've discovered, right now that's living with you."

Breathing a sigh of relief, Elijah nodded. "Thank you."

"You're welcome." She smiled again, and Elijah's nerves eased a little more. "Now, can I meet Kollin?"

"Of course. Right through here. He's a little nervous too."

Kollin stood as they entered the room, and Ms. Vick greeted him just as warmly as she had Elijah. She told him not to be nervous and that she only had to make sure Elijah wasn't using him as slave labor at Langley L&C.

Kollin laughed. "I'm pretty sure I'd be a bigger liability than an asset there, as long as I'm in this condition."

"You know who to call if he puts you to work once you're all better." She winked and turned back to Elijah. "Why don't we start with a tour, and then I just have a few questions to ask, and I'll be out of your hair. Will your partner be joining us?"

Elijah's eyes shot up to meet hers, and he felt the blood drain out of his face. Did she think he was married? Was he supposed to be? "My partner?"

"Adam Lancaster? You have him listed as the secondary caregiver. I assumed... I mean, usually...." She trailed off, and Kollin sniggered.

Elijah glared at Kollin and shook his head. "No, Adam is just a friend—a business partner actually. He's known Kollin longer, though, and Kollin specifically requested him. Is that okay?"

Ms. Vick nodded, and Elijah was surprised to see her blushing. "Of course. I'm sorry. I know who Adam is. We've met at a couple of LGBT awareness events. And I know he's.... I just assumed you two—"

She was cut off by the doorbell, immediately followed by the sound of the door opening and Adam calling out, "Sorry I'm late."

"Don't worry, Adam. You're right on time," Kollin shouted back, his tone gleeful.

"Well, this is embarrassing," Ms. Vick said as her cheeks tinged a light pink.

"Don't worry about it, and you behave." Elijah pointed at Kollin as Adam walked into the room.

"Did I miss anything?" Adam asked.

"Nope, we just finished introductions," Elijah said before Kollin could speak up. "Ms. Vick, this is Adam. Adam, Vivian Vick. She's in charge of Kollin's case."

Adam stepped closer and took her hand. "Right. I remember you. We've met a few times. Good to see you. We're lucky you're in charge of Kollin's case."

"Thank you. I'm just glad we don't have to put Kollin through the stress of placing him, after everything he's already been through. You guys ready to get started?"

Elijah took over and gave her the grand tour of the house. That took all of two minutes, and they moved to the kitchen table to answer Ms. Vick's questions. The longer the interview went on, the more Elijah relaxed. He didn't want to sound conceited, but answering questions about his income and the safety of his home only made him sound like an all-star guardian. Listing the people Kollin would be alone with the few times Elijah wouldn't be around was simple. His parents and Kirsten and Derek were the only ones making the list. The only time he'd worried was when Ms. Vick asked who Kollin's pediatrician would be. Elijah floundered for a minute and then assured her he'd find the best pediatrician in the area. When Kollin piped up and said he'd just as soon keep the one he'd been going to his whole life if it was okay with everyone else, she grinned and jotted down the doctor's name.

When Ms. Vick finished asking her questions, everyone huddled in the foyer and watched her zip up her book bag. "It's been a pleasure, gentlemen. You guys have nothing to worry about, as far as I'm concerned."

Adam shook her hand. "Thank you so much. I'm heading out too, so I'll walk you. You coming by HOPE tomorrow, Kollin?"

Kollin shook his head. "My teachers are being pretty cool about all this work I have to catch up on, but I want to get it over with. Eli said I could hang out at his office, after school, since it'll be quiet there."

"That's what I like to hear," he said, holding his hand out for a fist bump. "Call me if you need me."

Ms. Vick smiled and offered Elijah and Kollin a wave. "You guys have a good night."

Elijah closed the door behind them and breathed a sigh of relief, knowing Kollin would be safe with him, for the time being. Raising his eyebrows at Kollin, he didn't even try to hold back his excitement. "Looks like you're stuck with me, kiddo. What d'ya say we celebrate with some ice cream?"

CHAPTER 23

OVER THE next few days, Kollin stuck to his promise and stayed away from HOPE so he could catch up on all of the work he'd missed. Elijah knew Adam and Kollin were keeping in touch, chatting every day. But Adam hadn't made any effort to speak to Elijah since the home inspection. Elijah was at a loss. It's not like he'd been making progress with Adam when he saw him, but now that they weren't speaking at all, he was starting to believe they'd never even be friends again.

After school on Thursday, Kollin returned to the center, and Elijah arrived early to pick him up so he could feel out Adam. He got his answer almost immediately when Adam only gave him a stiff nod of acknowledgment—making it clear that he had no intention of returning to their prior carefree friendship, much less anything else. When Kollin laid a heavy guilt trip on Adam, begging him to come over for dinner because they hadn't seen each other all week, Elijah didn't know if he should hug him or strangle him. Elijah had never fixed a real meal. Ever. All signs pointed to the entire evening being a complete disaster.

He decided to make chicken fajitas because they seemed fairly simple. Just toss some chicken, onions, and peppers together with the packet from the store, cook it all up, and stuff the wraps. There didn't seem to be much room for error, as long as he didn't burn them. Elijah desperately wanted to show Adam he was serious about the changes he'd made in his life.

"You're welcome, by the way." Kollin grinned at Elijah as he sat at the bar in the kitchen and watched him.

Elijah glanced over his shoulder and cut the plastic wrap covering the chicken. "And just what am I thankful for?"

"Inviting Adam over for dinner."

Elijah plunked the chicken onto the cutting board and nudged open the cabinet where he hid his trashcan. When he realized he also needed olive oil and fajita seasoning from the cupboard, he pushed the hot water on and washed his hands and grabbed what he needed, remembering at the last minute to pull out a Ziploc bag so he could coat the chicken. He'd seen someone do it that way on TV once, and it seemed much easier than flopping it around in a dish.

"You think you're doing me a favor by inviting a guy I like over for dinner, when he kind of hates me right now *and* I can't cook?"

"Obviously. Someone needs to make you two work this out. Being in the same room with both of you is torture. If you can't get your shit straight, you can at least stop being awkward and avoiding each other."

Not bothering to clarify that Adam was the only one doing the avoiding, Elijah sliced the chicken. He slid his uneven chicken chunks—apparently cutting them into small, uniforms strips was trickier than he'd thought—into the bag. Then he poured the seasoning on top, zipped the bag, and started shaking.

"Um," Kollin hedged, "maybe we should just order fajitas from that place down the street."

"What? Why?" Elijah poured some oil into a pan and set it on the stove to let it heat up while he cut the vegetables.

"I've watched my mom make these before. I'm pretty sure you cook all the food first and then add the seasoning with some water, after it's all done."

Water? Elijah's heart sank a little as he glanced at the empty packet of seasoning lying on the counter. He hadn't even thought to look at the directions.

"Shit."

"You know, it's probably okay. Can't make too much of a difference. It all ends up in the same place."

Elijah spun around and looked at Kollin. "Do you really think that, or are you just saying it?"

Kollin shrugged. "I dunno. Cook it all up and see what happens. Who cares if it tastes like shit? Maybe it'll be better this way."

Elijah closed his eyes. "Fuck," he whispered. Taking a deep breath, he calmed himself down. Kollin was right. This wasn't a big deal, and he had to start somewhere. Still, it would've been nice if the first meal he cooked for Adam wasn't a disaster before any food actually made it to the stove. He turned back to the peppers and resumed slicing. "If I can find a way to blame this on you, I'm doing it."

"Go for it. Adam already loves me."

Squelching his urge to laugh, Elijah grabbed the seasoning packet and looked at the back. Sure enough, he'd done it incorrectly. "Do you think I should add the water before I cook it, since I've already added the seasoning?"

"I have no idea. I ruin hot dogs and Easy Mac. Wouldn't that boil the chicken?"

"It doesn't even call for a cup of water. I think you need more than that to boil chicken."

"Then go for it." Elijah peeked over his shoulder at Kollin, who raised his eyebrows a few times and popped a handful of cashews in his mouth.

"You're way too happy about this," he muttered and dumped all the food in the pan together. The hot grease sizzled and popped. A few splats landing on his hand and made him jump back.

"Maybe you should wait to add the water," Kollin deadpanned as Elijah turned down the heat and stirred the vegetables and meat.

"Why don't you do something useful and set the table?"

Kollin grumbled but complied. Fifteen minutes later, they were setting the food out when Adam rang the bell and walked in.

"It smells great in here," he said and pulled out a chair next to Kollin.

"Let's hope it tastes as good as it smells," Kollin chirped.

Elijah glared and tossed a fajita wrap at him. "Just eat."

"Did I miss something?" Adam asked, grabbing his own wrap.

"Just Kollin trying to push his bedtime up."

"What?" Kollin exclaimed. "Dude. You already make me to go bed at nine. It's been years since I had to go to bed that early."

"Do you really make him go to bed at nine?" Adam's eyes were wide, but the hint of a smile played on his lips.

"I let him keep his TV on for an hour," Elijah said, feeling ridiculous and a little overprotective. Kollin would be sixteen in a few months. A bedtime that early was kind of unheard of.

But the kid needed his rest.

"No. It's good," Adam offered. "Anyone with a brain can see he needs a tight leash."

"Ha ha. You're so funny," Kollin sniped, wrapping up his food.

Somewhat mollified, Elijah scooped some chicken and peppers into his wrap. The fajitas weren't terrible, but Elijah wouldn't call them tasty either. While he hadn't burned the food, he'd still overcooked everything. The chicken was pretty tough, and the vegetables were mushy enough to make baby food. Adam and Kollin ate them without complaint. Kollin even asked for seconds and proclaimed they were the best fajitas he'd ever had. He could be a pain in the ass with his sassy mouth, but he always meant well and never let Elijah down when it counted. Elijah also liked the idea of Kollin being in his corner where Adam was concerned. He respected the hell out him, and it meant a lot to know Kollin wanted them to work their shit out nearly as much as Elijah did.

When they finished eating, Kollin managed to convince Adam to stay for one game of basketball on the PlayStation.

Not even one minute into the game, Kollin suddenly dropped his controller. "Ah, shit. I have a French test tomorrow, and I haven't studied yet."

Elijah, who had been watching from his La-Z-Boy, snapped his head toward Kollin. He'd taken his French test that afternoon and had already told Elijah he was certain he'd aced it.

Adam was already setting his controller down. "We can play some other time—"

"No," Kollin shouted. "Stay. I just need about thirty minutes to review the verb conjugations, but I don't want to put it off in case I can't get it. Stay here while I study, and if I'm not down by seven, you can head out."

Elijah rolled his eyes as he watched Kollin practically run out of the room.

"He hasn't moved that fast since the incident," Adam mused. Elijah, feeling incredibly awkward, had no idea how to respond, so he grunted. Adam looked at him and tilted his head. "You put him up to that?"

Elijah shook his head. "No. I knew he had a hidden agenda when he invited you over, but I thought he'd given up when nothing happened over dinner. Obviously not."

"Well, if he's not actually studying for a test up there, I'm going to head out. Tell him bye for me?"

"Sure," Elijah agreed, his heart sinking. He hadn't really thought Kollin's plan would work, but it hurt that Adam didn't even want to sit in a room with him for half an hour. A lot.

"I guess I'll see you guys at the inn this weekend," Adam said, standing. "It'll be good to start working on it again. I can't believe we took two weeks off."

"I told my dad about you," Elijah blurted out, staring at the ground.

Adam stopped in his tracks and turned around. "About me?"

Elijah looked up and stared directly into Adam's eyes. He wasn't going to be ashamed anymore. He was done hiding how he felt. "I mean, I told my parents about *me*. I told them I'm bi, and I told them about the money and all the work I've been doing at the inn. I told them how hurt I was after Brian died and that I've been carrying around a lot of guilt and resentment ever since. I told them about the other guys I've been with, and I told them about you."

Adam slowly sat on the couch, his face showing his genuine surprise. "What about me?"

Emboldened by the fact that Adam hadn't just kept walking, Elijah rose and sat next to him on the couch. "Please don't freak out. I heard you the other night, when you said we could never be anything more than business partners. I did this more for me than I did to prove anything to you, but it doesn't erase the fact that you're a big reason I had the balls to even consider this."

Adam nodded, and Elijah reached out and took his hand. Even this small touch felt good to him. They'd had absolutely no physical contact over the past two weeks, and Elijah had hated every minute. Adam was a demonstrative guy and had never been shy about shoving Elijah or swatting him on the chest or arm. He never thought twice if their sides were pressed together while they worked or if Adam brushed something off Elijah's shirt. This, though—this was different. And the fact that Adam was willing to leave his hand in Elijah's filled his heart with hope.

"I told them you're the first person I've truly cared about since Brian and that I was willing to do whatever it took to keep you in my life, not as my business partner but simply as my partner. I told them how amazing you are, how funny you are, how big your heart is, how good you are—not only with those kids, but also with me. I told them how I'd messed everything up, and that I would never be as brave as you or Kollin, but I was damn well going to start trying."

Elijah took a deep breath and continued, "And finally, I told them if they had a problem with me, or Kollin, or you, they wouldn't be welcome in my life anymore. I'm not going to subject Kollin to that type of bigotry and expect him to think it's okay just because it comes from my parents. I even told my dad I'd resign from the company, if I had to."

Adam stared at Elijah, his mouth open, and Elijah thought he'd probably finally said something Adam didn't have an answer for.

"And what did they say?" he finally choked out.

Elijah sighed. "Uh… Mom cried. A lot. She blames herself for me never being happy. Dad mostly stayed silent. I'm not really sure what he's feeling. It was awkward as hell, but he did admit I've seemed truly happy over the past couple of months. He thought I was secretly seeing someone—just didn't expect it to be you and Kollin and the inn. They were both enamored with Kollin. Dad's even called me a few times to check up on him."

Adam looked down at their joined hands and turned his over so their palms touched. His thumb grazed Elijah's pinky for a moment. Then he slowly pulled his hand back into his own lap.

"I don't think I know what to say," Adam said quietly. "Do you mean you want me as your boyfriend, even out in public?"

Elijah's heart raced, and the fajitas in his stomach churned. "Yes," he said much more boldly than he felt. "I know that's a lot to ask. And as much as I wish I could just magically make you believe it's okay to trust me this time, I know I can't. But would you think about an 'us'? Or at least think about being friends again and see where it goes?"

Slowly Adam nodded, his eyes wide and his mouth slightly open. "I should go now, though."

He was already across the room, grabbing his jacket off the other couch before Elijah could catch up. "Wait a second."

"I'm sorry, Elijah," Adam said as he turned, his face panicked. "I can't handle this right now. It's just too much. Tell Kollin I'm sorry?" With a quick turn on his heel, Adam was out the door, leaving Elijah alone in his foyer.

Feet pounded down the stairs, but the hopeful look on Kollin's face faded as soon as he saw Elijah. "No deal?"

Elijah closed his eyes, leaned against the door, and shook his head. He couldn't believe he'd lost his last chance with the first person who made him feel alive in over fifteen years. Maybe he'd been wrong about life. It wasn't just a sequence of random events completely devoid of karma. There was no way in hell the last few weeks weren't a giant "fuck you" from the universe.

Chapter 24

THE FOLLOWING morning Adam did something he'd never done before. He called in late and told Chloe that he'd be there by noon. He promised he'd bring lunch from her favorite deli to make up for his absence. She was used to being alone for a morning here and there, so it wasn't a huge deal, but he still felt a little guilty because he didn't have a valid excuse.

Well, a valid excuse beyond wanting to find a cave in the middle of nowhere until everything in the world righted itself.

Adam spent most of the morning just as he'd spent most of the night—tossing and turning in bed. His mind raced so fast that he couldn't hold on to a thought long enough to analyze it. He was tired—and not the good kind that came from a hard day's work or helping one of his kids through a difficult time. Adam felt drained, bone-deep exhausted, and helpless to make anything better.

Being around Elijah was akin to torture. Adam's chest physically ached whenever he was in the same room with him. As Kollin's injuries continued to heal—his face nearly back to normal with only the faintest hint of a bruise along his jaw and a dark pink scar next to his eye—using him as a distraction or a buffer was no longer an option.

Adam hated what Elijah had lived through. He hated the burdens it had placed on him at such a young age, and he hated that Elijah allowed his past to keep them from having something real together. But *dammit*, he'd finally made peace with his decision. Keeping his distance from Elijah was agonizing, but he'd already accepted they'd never be together.

Heartbreaking, brutal honesty from Elijah was something Adam had never expected—not at this stage of the game.

Adam looked at the clock for the five hundredth time that morning and figured he might as well get up and go to work. He'd be a little earlier than he originally planned, but Chloe's sandwich would keep until her lunch break. He showered and dressed quickly, once again bypassed his contacts for his glasses, and absently noted it was time for a haircut. He pulled on a hat and grabbed his jacket on the way out. The weather lately was thinking about warming up but today wasn't one of those days.

Adam pulled up to Etman's Delicatessen ten minutes later. He shoved his hands in his pockets as he hurried across the parking lot, his head bowed to keep the biting wind from reaching too much skin. He was so focused on the ground in front of him that he didn't see the other person reaching for the door until they bumped into one another.

Raising his head to apologize, he was surprised to hear a familiar voice. "Adam?"

"Bruce. How are you?"

"I'm good. After you," Bruce said and held the door open. Hurrying out of the cold, they joined the back of the line together. The deli was the most popular place to grab breakfast, brunch, or lunch in Cary, so Adam wasn't surprised they were busy. Their food was fresh, homemade, and not too pricey. If they ever expanded to serving dinner, they'd be packed from sunup to sundown.

"How've you been? How's the inn?" Bruce asked as he scanned the menu board behind the counter.

"I'm good. A couple of my kids have had some rough times lately, but it's looking like we'll be able to help both of them, and the inn is open. We still have a lot of work to do, but most of it is behind us. We're hoping to open five new rooms a week until they're all livable."

Bruce glanced at Adam and looked impressed. "Wow. That's great. I know you were thinking it would take a lot longer."

The line moved forward and they shuffled along with it. "I did, but Elijah really stepped forward and took over the planning and organizing the help. If it'd just been me, we'd still have a ways to go."

"Ah, right. Elijah." Bruce shoved his hands in his pockets and looked down at the ground. "How're things with him?"

Adam peered at Bruce from the corner of his eye. He hadn't forgotten Bruce's accusation the last time they'd spoken, nor that he'd vehemently denied being attracted to Elijah. With everything as fucked up as it was right then, Adam had no idea how to answer, so he went with the truth. Sort of. "Elijah is fine. Like I said, he's really excelled with his work at the inn, and he's been a big help with one of the teens who was recently abused by his parents." Adam felt a small twinge of satisfaction when he continued, even though he was grossly misrepresenting his relationship with Elijah. "If you're asking if we're together, though, we're not."

Bruce's head snapped up, and he looked at Adam. "You're not?"

"No." Adam wanted to leave it at that, still hoping to save face, but Bruce stared him down. Either he didn't believe him or he was waiting for more of an explanation. Adam blew a long breath out as the line moved forward. "Okay. You might've been a little right, but we both realized pretty quickly it wasn't going to work out. I'm sorry if I hurt you. It was never my intention, and you deserved better."

To Adam's surprise, Bruce smiled. "Thanks, and no worries. I was a little harsh with you that night. I just… I really liked you, and it seemed so obvious what was going on. I just wanted you to admit it."

Adam shook his head sheepishly. "I think I was the last one to figure it out."

Before Bruce could respond, the woman behind the counter called Adam forward, and he ordered two chicken salad wraps. He stepped aside to pay while Bruce ordered, and his food was ready by the time Bruce finished paying. They walked out together, and this time Adam held the door for Bruce.

"Listen, I don't know where you're at right now with everything." Bruce waved his hand around in the air. "And I'm in no way asking you out again right now, but if you're ever serious about seeing what could happen between us, don't hesitate to give me a call. I'm not going to sit around waiting or anything, but it's not off the table if you're ever interested again."

Adam considered Bruce's offer and remembered how easy everything had been between them, how much he enjoyed laughing and talking with him. He thought about their first kiss—how it had made his dick twitch—and he figured he'd have to be stupid not to take Bruce up on his offer.

But then unbidden images came to mind. Elijah laughing. Elijah nudging him when one of the kids was acting like a fool. Elijah tugging on his hair when he was frustrated because his numbers weren't working like he wanted. He remembered Elijah carrying a broken and bruised Kollin through the front doors of HOPE. And the image that would forever be seared into Adam's brain—Elijah's haunted yet determined eyes when he said he'd take Kollin home with him. The last one lingered….

Adam's heart ached, but this time with pride. More memories flooded his mind. Elijah kissing him in the HOPE parking lot. Elijah pulling Adam's shirt off and sinking his teeth into Adam's neck. Elijah's body pressed against his as he slowly entered Adam. Elijah's face as his orgasm ripped through his body. And finally Elijah grabbing Adam's hand as he told him he'd give up everything to be part of Adam's life. Butterflies danced in Adam's stomach, threatening to escape and tell the whole world exactly how he felt about Elijah Langley.

"Yeah. That's what I thought," Bruce said, pulling Adam out of his reverie.

Sighing, Adam shrugged his shoulders and offered a halfhearted smile. "I'm sorry. The timing is just all wrong."

"Nah. I get it." Shocking the hell out of Adam, Bruce leaned forward and brushed his lips lightly against Adam's cheek. "Just... don't forget you deserve someone who's willing to kiss you no matter where you're standing."

Adam nodded and remained silent. It seemed cruel to tell Bruce he already had that in Elijah. He just needed to pull his head out of his ass and accept everything Elijah had offered him. Bruce walked off with a small wave, and Adam turned to his car with what felt like the first real smile he'd had in weeks plastered on his face. He and Elijah had a *lot* to talk about, but he felt like they were finally both on the same page.

He'd only taken three steps toward his car when he saw Elijah himself standing right next to it, staring at him. Adam's smile widened, and he lifted his hand to wave. Then he noticed the crushed look on Elijah's face. Turning, he followed Elijah's gaze over his shoulder, and watched Bruce open his car door and get in. Frustration and anger ripped through him when he turned back to explain—only to see Elijah already in his car, starting the engine. Adam started to jog toward him, but Elijah was already pulling away.

ELIJAH TEXTED Kollin from his car, telling him he was in the parking lot and ready to go home. No way was he going inside after seeing Adam with Bruce. He'd already ignored two calls and hadn't responded to Adam's text begging Elijah to let him explain.

He'd decided early on to pick up lunch for Adam at the deli, knowing it was one of his favorite places and that he rarely found the time to actually go. He didn't want to push him, but he thought randomly bringing a guy lunch was a check in the good-boyfriend column. Even though they weren't dating, he wanted to prove he could be worthy of that title if Adam ever gave him the chance. Never in a million years did he expect to see Adam already there, sucking face with his ex.

Okay. Maybe they weren't sucking face, but still.... It was more than Elijah had gotten to do with Adam in too long. He went back to his office and brooded the rest of the day, mad at himself for taking too long to grow the fuck up and mad at Adam for moving on so quickly. While he was at it, he was mad at that fuckface, Bruce, for being the kind of person Elijah should have been in the first place.

"You could've come in. No one bites," Kollin said, startling Elijah as he opened the car door.

Ignoring Kollin's jibe, Elijah mumbled a quiet hey. His voice sounded sullen even to himself. He needed to pep the hell up before Kollin caught on—he wasn't in the mood to rehash the day's events.

"You know," Kollin continued as if Elijah hadn't spoken. "I'm old enough to get my learner's permit now. Do you know how boss I'd look driving this around?"

Elijah barked out a laugh. "In your dreams, buddy. We're finding you something with a lot less horsepower and something a lot safer than this, but we can start looking this weekend if you want."

Silence engulfed the car as Elijah pulled onto the highway. He'd expected a witty comeback, or at the very least, some excitement. Peeking at Kollin, he saw him staring back with his mouth wide open. "What?"

"You're serious?"

"Hell, yeah. I'm serious. You're not getting behind the wheel of this thing while you're *learning* to drive. I love you and all, but I'm not an idiot."

"You're going to buy me a car?"

"How else are you going to learn?"

"I just…." Kollin's voice shrank. "I figured I'd have to wait until I could support myself. I didn't actually expect you to get me a car."

Elijah tightened his grip on the wheel. He didn't like the implication. "You and me, man. We're in this together. Right? I promised I wouldn't run, and I'm going to do my best to give you the kind of life you deserve. You have some heavy shit to go through in the next few years. I'm not saying a car will make it all go away, but if having the freedom to get away when you need to or being able to drive your friends around helps in some small way…. " Elijah took a deep breath. "I have the means to provide that for you, so I'm going to. But mark my words, you get in trouble, and the car will be the first thing to go."

Kollin sank down in the seat and stared out the window. "Thank you," he finally said, obviously trying to hold back tears. Elijah didn't say anything else. They'd had a few moments over the past week where Kollin seemed unable to believe that Elijah was in it for real. Elijah had quickly learned it was best to say his peace and drop it. To allow Kollin to work out his emotions on his own. Sometimes Kollin would come back with more questions, and sometimes he wouldn't. Dr. Will assured Elijah he was handling the situations appropriately. Kollin would need constant reassurance for a while, and Elijah was determined to be as patient as Kollin needed him to be.

Elijah finally broke the silence when they were pulling through the gates to his community. "So, what do you want me to ruin for dinner tonight? I have stuff to make spaghetti, or we can grill hamburgers."

"Oh. I forgot to tell you," Kollin said, perking up a little. "Adam is bringing dinner over, in like fifteen minutes."

"What?" Elijah yelled. "Why?"

"Ugh...." he groaned. "I was supposed to tell you I invited him over. I brought up driving this car because I knew there was no way in hell you'd let me. Figured inviting Adam over wouldn't sound so bad after that, but then you had to go ruin it by being all awesome."

"Dude."

Kollin threw his hands up in the air. "Adam said I owed him for tricking him into coming over last night so you could talk to him. I told him you honestly had nothing to do with that, but he didn't seem to care, and he promised me he'd fix everything, if he could just talk to you."

"Fix everything?"

"Yep."

Elijah pulled into his driveway, completely bewildered. "Fifteen minutes, huh?"

"Give or take." Kollin grabbed his book bag from the floorboard and climbed out of the car. "Hope you're in the mood for Chinese. I thought it was cute how you two shared last time, so I asked him to bring it again."

"Fucking kid is going to kill me," Elijah mumbled under his breath as Kollin laughed his way to the door.

Elijah jogged upstairs and changed into a pair of jeans and a long-sleeved tee. He didn't want to be overdressed. Besides, he knew how much Adam liked him—or more specifically, his ass—in jeans. No matter what Adam had to say, he wanted to at least look good while he listened.

Ten minutes later Elijah was fixing himself a drink when the doorbell rang. Adam walked in as Kollin appeared at the top of the stairs and gently bounded down the steps. Elijah watched them speak quietly. Then Kollin grabbed one of the bags of Chinese food and raised his voice. "Thanks, Adam. I have so much homework to do, I think I'm gonna eat this in my room tonight. Is that okay with you, Eli?"

Elijah scowled at Kollin but reluctantly waved his hand. "Go ahead."

Kollin shot Elijah a quick thumbs-up and jogged back up the stairs. Adam walked into the kitchen and held up the remaining bag of food. "I brought a peace offering."

Elijah squinted at him. A peace offering? Did he really think some damn Chinese food would make everything okay? He'd given Adam everything he had to offer, and it still wasn't enough. Rather than say something he might end up regretting, Elijah turned to get two plates out of the cabinet.

"I have a lot to say to you, but I don't think you'll really listen unless I get this part over with first. I've never lied to you, and I'm not going to start now. What you saw today wasn't what you thought it was."

"No? It looked like your ex was kissing you good-bye, after you two had lunch together—less than twenty-four hours after I laid my heart on the line for you and you ran over it with a Mack truck." He bit out the last few words, anger and resentment lacing each one.

Adam glanced down and then met Elijah's eyes. "I'm sorry I hurt you last night. I wasn't expecting you to say any of that—ever—and I handled it poorly. But I would never have gone out with someone else without talking to you. I just happened to run into Bruce at the deli. We exchanged a few words. He even asked about you. When I told him we weren't together, he implied he was still interested, and I realized"—Adam huffed—"quite definitively the only person I want to be with is you."

Elijah blinked, certain he'd misheard Adam. But then Adam walked around the island, stopped a few inches in front of Elijah, and mirrored his pose against the counter. He slowly reached for Elijah's hand and tugged him a step closer. Elijah studied their hands as Adam twisted them together and eventually linked their fingers. Adam raised their joined hands to his mouth and pressed a light kiss on Elijah's knuckles.

"I'm sorry I hurt you, Elijah. I'm sorry I left like that, and I'm sorry it took me so long to come around." Adam spun Elijah's hand around and kissed his wrist. "You are one of the bravest, most selfless people I know. I am so proud of you for overcoming your past, for being honest with your parents, and for being honest with yourself." Pulling Elijah even closer, he pressed their foreheads together. "If you still want me, I'd really, really like it if we could give this thing between us an honest-to-God chance."

Elijah held his breath, scared that if he even blinked, he'd wake up and find it was all a dream. But then he looked into Adam's eyes, and he knew… he knew the truth was looking right back at him.

With a gasp that sounded too much like a sob, Elijah shook his hands free of Adam's and cupped his face. He closed the last two inches of space between them and poured all of his happiness, pain, anger, joy, sorrow, frustration, and love into a kiss. Adam circled Elijah's waist with his arms. He pulled them flush as he eagerly returned the kiss, their lips and teeth and tongues crashing together over and over again. Elijah finally pulled back, unable to hide his massive smile, but Adam chased down his lips for one last kiss. He chuckled and gently rubbed Adam's cheeks with his thumbs. "Is this real? Because it sure as hell doesn't feel like it."

Adam tucked his head down and rested it on Elijah's chest to hide his face. "I missed you so much."

"You could've had me a week ago, if you weren't such a stubborn ass," Elijah teased.

Adam looked at Elijah, his face full of mock outrage, but before he could say anything, Elijah kissed him again. Squirming in Elijah's embrace, Adam pulled away, only to throw his arms around Elijah's neck and sink his fingers into his hair. Adam made a low, growly noise in the back of his throat and thrust his hips against Elijah's.

"Holy shit," Elijah mumbled, tearing his mouth away from Adam's to catch his breath. He gripped Adam's ass and thrust their groins together.

"We have to stop. Kollin…" Adam said even as he sank his teeth into Elijah's neck and rubbed his jean-covered cock against Elijah's.

Elijah groaned and stilled his hips, though he gave Adam's ass one final squeeze. He wasn't willing to let go of Adam yet, but Adam was right. They couldn't do anything else with Kollin in the house. "Damn kid wants us together so badly, he'd probably cheer us on if he walked in on us."

Laughing, Adam pulled away but didn't stop touching Elijah, seemingly just as reluctant to lose contact. "That's wrong on so many levels. Let's eat before we talk to him. Let him stew a little."

They grabbed two forks and split their meals, standing at the counter and not even bothering with plates. Taking turns feeding each other with the chopsticks, they laughed every time bits of food landed on the counter, on their clothes, or even halfway across the kitchen. They lingered over the meal and found ways to kiss each other after every few bites. If Elijah had seen the two of them out in public, he surely would've rolled his eyes and found the whole scene entirely too sickeningly sweet, but he couldn't bring himself to give a shit.

When they finished eating, Elijah stuck the leftovers in the fridge, grabbed Adam's hand, and pulled him closer. Then he kissed Adam just because he could. "You know we still have a lot to talk about," Adam mumbled, his words almost lost between their kisses.

Elijah grunted. "Tomorrow. Today is for kissing."

"Somebody's gonna have whisker burn tomorrow." Kollin's singsong voice floated into the kitchen, scaring the hell out of Elijah and making him jump away from Adam. He felt guilty for making out with someone in their kitchen while Kollin ate alone up in his room. "Don't stop for me," Kollin said innocently. "I thought today was for kissing."

Adam laughed long and loud, while Elijah floundered. "Shut up," he said, grinning like a fool.

"You cool with this?" Adam asked Kollin as he grabbed Elijah's hand and tugged him closer again. Elijah went willingly. He wasn't going to make out with Adam in front of Kollin, but now that he could touch Adam whenever he damn well pleased, he fully intended to take advantage.

"Cool with it? Of course I am. I was tired of seeing you two mooning over each other," Kollin said. "Seriously, I'm really happy for you guys."

"Thanks, buddy," Elijah said, motioning him forward and pulling him into a hug. "And just so you know, this doesn't change anything for you and me. You still come first. Okay?"

Kollin nodded and turned his face to hide it in Elijah's chest for a moment. When he finally pulled away, his eyes were a little glassy, but his smile was huge. "So, who's ready to get their ass beat in *Madden*?"

CHAPTER 25

ELIJAH PULLED into Ruth's Chris Steak House parking lot ten minutes before their reservation, jumped out of his car, and ran around to open Adam's door. Adam raised an eyebrow but smiled and murmured a quiet thank you. He goofed around with Kollin on the short walk inside, so Elijah rushed ahead to open the door for them, let the hostess know they had arrived, and then wrapped his arm around Adam's waist. Adam looked him up and down but didn't say anything or move away. When they were shown to their table a few minutes later, Elijah scooted his chair closer to Adam's and draped his arm across the back of Adam's seat.

"Dude," Kollin said. "Why're you acting weird?"

Elijah glared at Kollin. "I'm not acting weird."

Shit. Even Elijah could hear the lie in his voice. In addition to officially telling his parents about Adam at dinner, that was his first real date with a man, and he had no idea how to act. He wasn't entirely comfortable showing affection in public, but he didn't want Adam to think he was ashamed. With a little time, he'd get there, but his life had taken a fucking one-hundred-eighty-degree turn in the past month, and accepting change—even change he craved—wasn't one of his strong suits. He wasn't willing to lose Adam just because he was a little nervous, though.

"Uh…." Adam hedged. "Yeah. You are. What's all this about?"

"Oh. Are you marking your territory?" Kollin asked. "Scared someone's gonna steal him from you?"

Elijah jerked his arm back from Adam's chair. "I am not marking my territory. Don't be ridiculous."

Adam laid a hand on Elijah's knee under the table, and to Elijah's relief, offered a small smile instead of teasing him further. "So what's going on, then? Not that I don't appreciate it or anything, but opening my car door and putting your arm around me and"—Adam looked Elijah up and down—"sitting so close. It's different."

"I wanted to show you that I'm not ashamed to be with you in public," Elijah said.

"Oh geez." Kollin rolled his eyes. "I don't know whether to barf or congratulate you. This is why I'm never asking you for dating advice."

"Shut it, you."

Adam grabbed Elijah's hand. "I appreciate that more than you know, but I can tell you're not all that comfortable doing this. And honestly, I'm not either. I'm not huge into PDA. I won't ever deny who you are to me or pretend like we aren't together, but we don't have to be touching every second we're in public either."

"Oh, thank God," Elijah said, sliding his chair back over.

"It was sweet, really. But maybe for now, we just act like we always have in public? Besides, we should probably break the news to your parents before they walk in and see us hanging all over one another."

Elijah felt like his throat dropped into his stomach. He'd managed to forget about his parents while he'd been humiliating himself in front of Adam and Kollin.

Two weeks had passed since Adam and Elijah had officially become a couple. Surprisingly, Adam had been the one to suggest waiting to tell their friends and family about their relationship. He'd never dated anyone so heavily involved at HOPE and wasn't sure how the kids there would react to the news.

While Elijah would have gladly announced their relationship to everyone at the center right away, he understood why Adam wanted to wait. Secretly he'd been pleased by Adam's decision, as it would also give him extra time to introduce Adam to his parents. Just because they knew he wanted to date Adam didn't mean they'd welcome his boyfriend with open arms, and he cherished the judgment-free time he and Adam spent together.

As it turned out, keeping a secret that huge had felt more like lying than either of them had anticipated, and they made plans to come clean after little more than a week together. Adam called Amelia and Matthew right away, and both offered their support without seeming surprised in the least. For some reason that Elijah was now regretting, he'd thought taking his parents out to a nice dinner to officially introduce Adam as his boyfriend would be a good idea.

"They just walked in," Kollin said, whispering. He cocked his head. "You okay? Y'all can do this some other time, you know? Adam won't care, and I can keep a secret."

Elijah's heart warmed. He smiled at Kollin and thought, not for the first time, how lucky he was to have the kid in his life. No matter how the night turned out, the two people sitting at the table with him were all he really needed. "I'm fine. Theoretically they already know. This shouldn't be a big deal."

"Doesn't mean it's not," Kollin said under his breath as he stood to greet Elijah's parents. He hugged Gloria tightly, waved to the senior Elijah, and sat down again. Elijah offered both of them a weak smile while Adam greeted them with a handshake.

"I hope you're ready to eat the best steak of your life, Kollin," Elijah's dad said.

"Yes sir, though I may be more excited about the dessert. Eli said the chocolate sin cake is amazing."

"It was his favorite growing up." Gloria smiled at Elijah and took a sip of her water. The knot in Elijah's stomach turned over.

The waiter arrived, took everyone's orders quickly, and shuffled off all too soon for Elijah's taste.

"So, we wanted you to join us tonight to share some news with you."

"Oh?" his mom said, her eyes flicking back and forth between Elijah and Adam.

"Yes." Elijah took a deep breath. "I wanted you to know that Adam and I are dating."

Adam pressed his leg lightly against Elijah's underneath the table, but Elijah couldn't bring himself to take his eyes off his butter knife to acknowledge the gesture.

Finally his father spoke. "I thought you'd been dating this whole time. Isn't this the man your big speech was about?"

Elijah looked up and gaped at his father. Gloria huffed. "Honestly, dear. Did you not listen at all to what E. J. said that night?"

"Of course I did. He said he was in love with this boy and was going to throw the family business away if I had a problem with it. In what world does that *not* mean they're dating?"

Elijah buried his head in his hands on the table while Kollin chuckled. "I just want to go on record and say I love everything about this night," he said, grabbing his water glass.

Adam's knee bumped Elijah's again, a little more insistently this time, until Elijah turned his head to peer at Adam. "You told them you love me, huh?"

"Oh God," Elijah said, groaning.

Kollin leaned toward Gloria and stage whispered. "In case you're having trouble keeping up, they haven't used the *L* word with each other yet."

"Well, it should've been obvious when Elijah threatened to give up the company over it. Damned fool is so stubborn, he couldn't possibly come up with any solution aside from all or nothing."

"Dad," Elijah exclaimed. "What in the hell has gotten into you?"

"Don't talk to your father that way, E. J. You may not have noticed, but retirement has changed your father. Maybe if you'd visited us more than once a week or talked about something other than that company you run, you could've seen that for yourself."

"What?" Elijah looked at Adam and silently begged him for answers, even though he didn't know what questions to ask. Looking back at his parents, he said, "What are you talking about? Dad always dominated the entire dinner conversation with work."

"Maybe at first," Elijah Senior said. "But when you took over, you needed the advice. Then it just seemed like you didn't want to talk about anything else. Besides, what would we have even talked about? Before you met these two, you never did anything but work."

"And what did you ever do besides work?"

Elijah Senior's face softened. "You're right."

The waiter returned with their salads, so everyone sat back and waited. The tension at the table was palpable, and they all remained unnaturally silent—except for Kollin—who cheerfully asked for more ranch dressing.

Once the waiter was gone, Elijah's father spoke again. "To say I was surprised when you told us about your feelings for Adam would be an understatement, but once the idea settled, I talked it over with your mother. Even I can see these two are good for your soul. I hoped you'd realized sooner than I did that there's more to life than Langley Lumber. I spent too many years consumed with being the best. And while I'm proud of the success of my business, your mother has helped me see there's more to life."

Gloria barked out a laugh. "I told him he'd given forty years to that company, and now it was my turn."

Elijah's dad tilted his head with a wry smile on his face, acknowledging the truth of his wife's words. Elijah's head spun as his dad continued. "We noticed when you gradually started slipping in details about the center. Granted, we didn't know, at first, exactly who the center was for. And I don't even think you realized you were speaking of it so frequently, but we noticed. I should've told you before not to make the same mistakes I did, but I thought you'd see my regrets plain as day and figure that out for yourself. Or who knows? Maybe I was just too chickenshit."

"Dad!"

Elijah's father rolled his eyes and looked at his wife. "He's allowed to date a man, but I'm not allowed to say chickenshit?" Returning his attention to Elijah, he continued. "Kollin set me up on the Facebook, you know. You should be happy to have a father so in touch with today's youth."

"You tell him, Elijah," Kollin said, grabbing a roll from the basket in the center of the table.

Elijah's dad turned to Adam. "What I'm saying is… you clearly make my son happy, and though I realized it a little too late, that's truly all I want for him. My apologies if I ruined the big reveal for you, but it seemed quite obvious to me, and most likely everyone else, how much he cares for you."

Adam smiled. "Thank you, sir, and no apologies necessary." He looked at Elijah, and his smile morphed from "I put everyone at ease" into something softer—something meant only for Elijah. Adam leaned over, closed the gap between them, and bumped Elijah's shoulder. Then he turned back to his plate.

Elijah grinned and looked back at his father, who offered him a silent "Whoops" with a twist of his mouth. Elijah snorted out a cross between a guffaw and a whimper. He had no idea how his dad had the ability to deliver the most heartfelt speech he'd ever heard and then manage to sound condescending with the very next breath.

The rest of dinner passed smoothly. Elijah remained quiet, letting his father's words sink in and enjoying the carefree air surrounding their meal. At the end of the night, Elijah acknowledged it had been one of the best nights he'd ever had with his parents, and they hadn't spoken of work even once. Kollin kept the conversation going in the beginning. But after a while, Adam held his own and engaged both of Elijah's parents with stories about the youth who passed through HOPE's doors. By the end of the night, Gloria had offered to volunteer at the center, and Elijah Senior had slid a check across the table, made out to HOPE.

Elijah shivered as they stepped into the cool night air. The weather was beginning to warm up, but once the sun set, nights were still quite chilly. Before they reached his parents' car, Elijah's mom pulled him aside.

"E. J.," she said, looking up into his eyes. "I'm so sorry about Brian. I know it was a long time ago, and you're over him now, but your father and I had no idea how much you cared for him. I don't want to make any excuses, but it just came as such a shock at the time. Suffice it to say, we didn't handle the situation well at all, and then after he was found… well, it felt like we lost you, and I had no idea how to get you back." She looked down at the pavement for a moment. When she looked back up, her still-pretty face was marred with sorrow. "I don't have many regrets in life—only one in fact—and it's how your father and I handled that situation. I should've told you long ago how sorry I was… how sorry I am… but until recently, I wasn't sure if it would've made one damn bit of difference. Still, I should've told you."

Elijah nodded, choking back tears from what felt like a lifetime of shame and guilt easing off his chest. He wrapped both arms around her shoulders, buried his face in her neck, and held on until the feeling passed. When he eventually pulled away, he brushed a soft kiss across her cheek. "I love you, Mom."

"Love you too, E. J."

WHEN HE heard the soft tap on his office door, Adam looked up to see Elijah filling the frame and looking stupidly handsome in one of his millions of suits. Grinning, Elijah walked in and propped his ass cheek on the side of Adam's desk.

"What're you doing here?" Adam asked. He clasped his hands behind his head as he leaned back in his chair.

"Thought maybe we could go to lunch, if you have time. I finished up early at the office."

"You wear a suit to work on Saturdays?"

"You don't like it?"

"Oh, I like it all right, but most people dress down when they come in on weekends."

Elijah shrugged. "Maybe I wanted to look good for you. What's so wrong with that?"

Adam barked out a laugh. "Whatever. You're such a snob."

"Shut up, asshole. I'm so used to dressing like this, I don't even think about it."

"Oh, babe… that's kinda pitiful."

Elijah rolled his eyes, entirely unruffled by Adam's teasing. "Then I'll start borrowing your clothes so I can slum around in jeans with holes in them from now on. You want to go to lunch or not?"

Adam grinned as Elijah straightened his tie until he was satisfied with his appearance. "Can you gimme five minutes?" he asked.

"Of course. I'll go bug Chloe." Elijah leaned forward to whisper. "Does she know?"

Adam rolled his eyes. "I haven't had time to send out my office-wide memo yet."

"Kollin said she's been pressuring him for inside information."

"What the hell? Does everyone know?"

"Everyone *here* apparently."

"Why'd we keep it a secret, then?"

Elijah shrugged. "I don't know, but can we talk about it over lunch? I'm starving."

"Yeah. Go fill Chloe in, and I'll finish up here."

Bits and pieces of Elijah's conversation with Chloe filtered into Adam's office as he entered the last few monthly expenses into his spreadsheet. He'd just clicked Save when Chloe's voice climbed an octave.

"Honestly, Elijah. How do you know this girl isn't just after you for your money? I thought you had better sense than this."

"I'm telling you, she's the real deal. I never believed in love at first sight until last night."

"Well, does she know about Kollin? What if she doesn't want to be an instant mom?"

"I'm sure she'll love Kollin. How could anyone not?"

"There's a difference between loving Kollin and wanting to play house with him."

The desperation in Chloe's voice skyrocketed, so Adam locked his computer and grabbed his keys.

"You're a good man, Elijah Langley. I don't want to see anyone taking advantage of you. Besides, what about... you know...?"

Adam walked out of his office, drawing the attention of both of them.

Elijah winked and then turned back to Chloe and asked, "Know what?"

Laughing, Adam hip-checked Elijah. "Stop being mean. I need her here."

"Mean? Me?" Elijah grabbed Adam's hand, laced their fingers together, and placed their joined hands on top of Chloe's desk. "Never."

"Ohh," she exclaimed, her eyes widening as she flicked her wrist toward Elijah. "You are such an *ass*. Excuse my French, but you're trying to kill me. Don't you know I'm fragile?"

"Please. You're tough as nails, woman. I'm more fragile than you."

"Maybe so. Either way, I'm thrilled for you guys. You both deserve happiness, and anyone can see you make each other better versions of yourselves." Chloe hustled around her desk to hug each of them.

"Thanks, Chloe." Adam basked in her praise as he squeezed her tightly. "We're heading out for lunch. Want us to bring you anything?"

"Nah. I'm out of here in fifteen. Thanks, though. Have fun. And behave."

"Yes, ma'am."

Within fifteen minutes, they were seated at a small window table at Etman's. Adam noted Elijah walked a little closer than normal and still opened the door of the restaurant for him, but nothing screamed, "We're on a date." Best of all, he looked completely content and relaxed.

"Anything new going on at the center?" Elijah asked when their waitress left.

"It's been a quiet week, thankfully. Julie's mom is officially acting as night supervisor at Home for Hope. Did I tell you she balked at the idea when I first presented it to her?" Elijah shook his head. "There was so much going on then, I must've forgotten to mention it when we got back together. Anyway, when we talked to her that first day, she seemed interested but asked us to wait until she could get everything straight at home."

"Obviously that didn't happen."

Adam shook his head. He'd dealt with Julie and her parents when he and Elijah weren't speaking to one another. On the one hand, it had been an opportune distraction to take his mind off Elijah, but on the other, he would've much preferred consulting Elijah. "I couldn't wait. Couldn't risk him hurting Julie again. She waffled on it a while until Julie broke down and begged her to get out. They spent about a week down in Georgia with Julie's grandmother before coming back here."

Elijah sat back as the waitress set their drinks on the table and then sauntered away with a promise that their food would be ready soon. "So, what happened with Julie's dad? I know he spent two nights in jail. Has he been around since they came back?"

"No. They filed a restraining order, and thankfully he's adhered to it. He's not allowed near HOPE, the inn, or either of the girls' schools. I didn't ask for any details, as it's not really my place, but Julie gave me the impression her mom admitted the abuse has been going on for years and that she'd tried to take the girls away once, when they were young, but ended up going back to him."

"Why the hell would she go back?"

Adam shrugged. "I don't know for sure. Like I said, Julie was vague about it, and I didn't want to push. Could be any number of reasons, though. Maybe she was too ashamed to reach out to her family, and without that support, she felt helpless. Or maybe her family wasn't willing to help, at the time. Or maybe she didn't want to be a burden on—"

"Okay." Elijah held up a hand. "I get it."

"Sorry," Adam said. He pushed his drink aside for their server to set down their food. After several silent moments, Elijah pulled his plate closer and picked up a chicken finger.

"You okay?" Adam asked.

"Yeah. Just trying to wrap my head around everything."

Adam hesitated. "Maybe you should talk to Will or Maggie sometime." Elijah grunted noncommittally, so Adam continued. "I've actually seen both of them, from time to time. There's no shame in it, and you've had a lot going on in the past few months. Dropping into our world like this isn't easy, even without your own ghosts."

"I'll think about it."

Adam could hardly make out Elijah's words, but he didn't want to push too hard, so he dropped the subject and took a bite of his sandwich to give the moment time to settle.

"So...." Adam attempted to waggle his eyebrows in a poor effort to make Elijah laugh. "What do you want to do tonight?"

"How about a movie at my place? Maybe we could even go out to see one. I haven't been to a movie theater in forever."

"I'm game, as long as we get popcorn. And hot tamales."

"First rule of our relationship... we can't watch a movie without chocolate-covered peanuts."

Adam reached across the table to cover Elijah's hand with his own and dropped his forehead to the table. "Oh my God, it's like we were made for each other."

"You're an idiot," Elijah said, laughing.

"Guilty. It's why the kids love me."

Elijah's smile widened. "Movie and junk food it is. I'll tell Kollin. He's coming with me to the inn this afternoon."

"Yeah? That'll be good for him. He needs to get out of the house."

"I know. Ri's been calling a lot. He doesn't tell me what they talk about, but I've heard Kollin tell him that he's not allowed to go anywhere. I've not given him any restrictions, so I guess he's using me as an excuse. But I'm giving him some time before I push him on it. I think he's scared to go anywhere but school, the center, and home."

Adam nodded. Both of them had noticed the missing spark in Kollin's eyes recently. Dinner with Elijah's parents had been the first time in over a week that Kollin had been animated and excited, so Elijah had already made plans to have more family get-togethers. Dr. Will and Adam assured Elijah that Kollin's mood fluctuations were normal and that he'd continue to have them for a while. Knowing he'd eventually turn another corner never made it easier to watch him struggle, though.

"He'll get there. You're doing so well with him. I'm incredibly proud of both of you," Adam said.

"Yeah, yeah. No need to go emo on me. Eat your damn sandwich, and let's get out of here."

CHAPTER 26

THEY SPENT the afternoon at the inn, followed by a late movie. Kollin was wiped and went straight to bed, so Adam and Elijah hung out in the living room, not really paying attention to the TV while they talked for hours. Eventually Adam decided it was time to go home, but after a lengthy make-out session in the foyer, Adam found himself pressed against the front door with Elijah's stiff cock rubbing against his own.

Elijah hooked his fingers in the waistband of Adam's jeans and tugged him up to his room. They took their time undressing one another—the polar opposite of their first time together. Instead of a desperate urgency to touch, grab, and consume, they lingered over every kiss and caress as their clothes came off. At the end of the bed, Elijah stood behind Adam and ran his palms up and down Adam's chest and stomach while his mouth traced the top edge of the foreign lettering across Adam's back.

"You ever gonna tell me what this means?" Elijah grazed his lips up Adam's neck.

Arching his back, Adam leaned into Elijah's kiss and shoved his bare ass against Elijah's still-covered cock. "Mmm… sure am."

Adam turned in Elijah's embrace and wrapped his arms around Elijah's neck, but instead of answering him, Adam peppered kisses along his jawline. They teased each other with quick, light kisses and licks, but Elijah's hands never stopped. He learned every dip, muscle, scar, and imperfection on Adam's body and was perfectly content with the languid pace they'd set.

Adam slipped his hands beneath the soft fabric of Elijah's boxer briefs and squeezed Elijah's hard, plump ass. With a chuckle, Elijah flexed his glutes and made Adam groan. Dropping to his knees, he pulled Elijah's underwear down. When Elijah's cock sprang out, fat and ready, it smacked Adam right in the face.

"Easy, now." Adam grinned and rubbed his nose against the velvety skin of Elijah's shaft.

"You're killing me," Elijah said, trying not to come from the sight of Adam on his knees, gazing up at him.

"I'm trying to," he said and nuzzled the other side.

"I thought you'd learned…. I'm an impatient man." Elijah thrust his hips forward, jutting his dick against Adam's mouth and pulling back just as quickly so Adam would know he wasn't serious. He'd take all the teasing Adam wanted to dole out and love every minute of it.

Adam ran his hands up Elijah's thick thighs. "Oh, I learned. I just don't care."

He swept a hand under Elijah's balls and gently cradled them while he ran his tongue up the crease of Elijah's thigh and bit his hip. Goose bumps erupted on Elijah's skin, pebbling his ass as Adam gnawed his tender skin, occasionally dipping his tongue between Elijah's cheeks just far enough to pique his interest.

"Please." Elijah whimpered. Adam assaulted his flesh with strong hands and stubbled cheeks. "Please stop teasing."

Adam growled. The sound emanated deep in his chest. "If you insist," he said and then sucked Elijah's cock deep into his mouth.

Elijah cupped the back of Adam's head and pushed forward, easing off at the last moment so as not to choke his boyfriend. But Adam gripped the back of Elijah's thighs and tugged him forward. He forced Elijah down his throat, and swallowed several times around Elijah's aching dick. With the wickedest look in his eyes, Adam sat back on his haunches, opened his mouth, and waited.

Eager to take over, Elijah settled his hands along Adam's jaw and slid his cock between Adam's lips. Watching his dick disappear into Adam's mouth over and over again brought Elijah to the edge way too soon. He quickened his pace, grunting every time Adam's teeth grazed his shaft. The tip of his cock brushed against the back of Adam's throat, and his thrusts became uneven as he watched Adam jerk himself off in rhythm with Elijah's movements. When Elijah felt Adam's insistent fingers playing behind his balls, he couldn't hold back any longer.

He came in thick spurts down Adam's throat. Elijah teetered as his knees buckled during his orgasm, making him topple onto the bed behind him. As his cock popped out of Adam's mouth, jizz shot in a perfect arc over Elijah's head and landed above him on the soft comforter. Completely spent, Elijah rolled to his side so he could watch Adam pump out his load, his face contorted in the sexiest expression Elijah had ever seen.

"Holy fuck. Your mouth is amazing," Elijah said.

"Mmph." Still panting, Adam kissed the inside of Elijah's thigh. "I got jizz on your carpet."

Elijah laughed, incoherent and giddy. "S'okay. Carpet's white. It'll match. Besides, mine got on the bedspread."

Adam rested against Elijah's knee and slowly regained control of his breathing. He held his hand out and beckoned for Adam to join him, but Adam held a finger up and pointed to the bathroom, instead. While Adam cleaned up, Elijah grabbed a tissue to clean the dab of come off the comforter and crawled beneath the covers. After a few moments, Adam emerged from the bathroom and joined him in bed.

"Mmm...." Elijah sighed and tugged Adam so close his head rested on Elijah's chest. "You gonna stay?"

Adam draped an arm across Elijah's stomach. "I don't know. You think I should? What about Kollin?"

"You could always leave before he wakes up, or even sleep in the other room. He asked me this week when you were going to start spending the night."

"Of course he did. What'd you say?"

"Told him your feet stink, and I didn't want them in my sheets."

Adam laughed and lifted his head so he could see Elijah's face. "You did not."

"I really did. And it made him laugh, so it was worth it." Elijah shrugged unapologetically. "He said he's fine with it, though."

"Yeah?" Adam propped his elbow on Elijah's chest. "I don't know. I don't think it's a great idea just yet."

"Me either actually. I don't ever want him to worry that he's not my number-one priority. Besides, even though he's almost sixteen, he doesn't need to see anyone coming out of my room in the morning, even if it is you."

"Why Mr. Langley," Adam drawled, "how very old-fashioned of you."

"Shut up." Elijah yawned and tightened his arm around Adam, flattening Adam against his body. "I'm not ready to let you go yet, though. So I vote you sneak out in the morning, just this once. He's never up before nine anyway."

"Just this once, huh?"

"Yeah, I might have to amend that, depending how long it takes us to move in together. I think I could get used to this."

Elijah yawned again as the weight of the day and the bliss of sex with someone he loved settled over him. Adam nestled himself closer, and contentment sank deep into Elijah's bones as he drifted off to sleep.

WARMTH FLOODED Adam's chest when Elijah brought up their inevitable cohabitation with the same confidence he possessed in every other aspect of his life. But the feeling was bittersweet because the edges of that warmth were tinged with anxiety. He and Elijah had spent a lot of time talking about their relationship and their future over the past two weeks. While they knew anything could happen, they both agreed they were in their relationship for the long haul. Willing to do whatever it took to fight for each other, they wanted to eventually move in together and maybe even start a family beyond Kollin. They also agreed there was no rush. They were determined to take things slowly.

Adam knew he had to tell Elijah about his past before they took that next step, though—and he wasn't looking forward to it. He wasn't ashamed of what happened to him, but sometimes people treated him differently when they heard the specifics of his life before the Wrights. And after everything they'd been through, Adam wouldn't be able to handle that from Elijah—not right away.

Besides, Elijah was already lightly snoring, and the dawn would bring a new day.

Keep reading for an exclusive excerpt from

Resurrecting Hope

Home for Hope: Book Two

By Shell Taylor

Adam Lancaster can't imagine how his life could possibly get any better. He's on the cusp of moving in with his boyfriend, Elijah Langley. Their charge, Kollin Haverty, finally has a loving, stable home environment, and Home for Hope is up and running, keeping over fifteen LGBT youth off the streets at night. One phone call from his birth mother, Jessica Lancaster, is all it takes to unravel Adam's carefully constructed new life.

Informing Adam his grandfather has died, Jessica expresses remorse for abandoning Adam to the state and begs him for a chance to be part of his life again. Jessica's true colors eventually shine through her façade, and Adam is devastated all over again when he discovers she is only using him to get her hands on the valuable inheritance his grandfather left him. Jessica's betrayal forces Adam so far inside his own hell, not even Elijah or Kollin can keep him from abandoning all of his responsibilities and running away. Adam will have to dig deep to find the strength to confront his birth parents, heal once and for all, and earn back his place with his new family.

CHAPTER 1

As THE jurors filed into the courtroom, Adam Lancaster slipped one arm around Kollin's shoulders and gently nudged Elijah Langley, to remind his partner that he wasn't alone. Elijah leaned into the touch but didn't let go of Kollin's hand to reciprocate.

"Ladies and gentlemen of the jury," the judge began, nodding to the panel. "I am informed that you have reached your verdicts."

"Yes, Your Honor."

"Please hand the verdicts to the clerk, and Mr. Marshall, will you hand the verdicts to me?" The judge silently read the small piece of paper and handed it back. "I direct the clerk to read the verdicts."

"We, the jury, find the defendant, John L. Haverty, guilty of child abuse, class E felony offense."

Adam closed his eyes and slowly exhaled. One down. One to go. Beneath his arm, Kollin sank further into himself.

The clerk continued. "We, the jury, find the defendant, Susan S. Haverty, guilty of child abuse, class E felony offense."

Tears sprang to Adam's eyes as Kollin fell forward and buried his head in his arms. Adam gripped Kollin's shoulder and tugged him into a one-armed hug. Elijah didn't let go of Kollin's hand, but he tilted his head back to stare at the ceiling. With a heavy sigh, Elijah closed his eyes while the judge continued.

"I'd like to thank the jury for their service and diligence. Sentencing will be announced at a later date and is dependent upon the defendants' cooperation. Court is adjourned."

Kollin's parents shuffled out the side door without a spare glance in his direction, and the handful of people in the audience filed out the back murmuring quietly to one another. Kollin didn't stand, so Adam and Elijah remained in their seats, flanking him on each side, protecting him from the worried eyes of their extended family huddled in the corner. Adam's and Elijah's parents, Adam's sister, Kirsten, and her husband, Derek had insisted on attending the court reading for moral support. But when Kollin started to shake beneath Adam's arm, he wondered if allowing them to come had been a mistake.

After several more minutes of silence, Elijah knelt in front of Kollin and Adam. Wrapping an arm around each of them, he huddled them all together.

"I'm so sorry, Kollin. I'm so fucking sorry. I'd spend every last dime I have if it meant ensuring you never had to go through this. I don't want you to ever doubt you're wanted and loved exactly the way you are in my home. It's already our home to me."

Kollin choked out a sob and threw one arm around Elijah to bury his face in Elijah's neck. "I love you." He whispered so quietly Adam barely heard him.

"I love you back, buddy," Elijah said. "Let's go home."

CHAPTER 2

"BULLSHIT, KRIS!"

Kirsten threw down her cards and glared at Adam. "How in the hell are you doing that?"

"I'll never tell," Adam sang, pitching his voice high to mimic Brittany Murphy in *Don't Say a Word*.

"Ahhh, la la la la la." Kirsten plugged her ears. "Stop it. You know that creeps me out."

"I'll never tell." He mimicked the chant again more softly.

Elijah sat back in his chair. "I will never understand how you two lived together."

Pushing himself off the couch where he'd been watching everyone play cards, Kollin said, "I think the real question is how Matthew and Amelia put up with them."

Kirsten scrunched up her face and made a sound closely resembling that of a dying seal. "You guys are so funny. Seriously, though. Adam's the worst Bullshit player ever. Like ever, ever in the history of time. How are you kicking my ass right now?"

"I'll—"

"Don't you dare."

Derek collected the cards and peered at Adam through the shaggy blond hair that always seemed to cover his eyes. "She's right. In the six years I've been around you guys, I've never once seen you win this game."

"That doesn't mean he can't," Kollin said, leaning against the La-Z-Boy.

"Thank you, Kollin."

Kirsten flumped back against her chair. "I guess the sun really does shine on every dog's ass once in a while."

Elijah eyed Kollin and took the deck of cards from Derek. "Why're you defending him? You're usually the first one to make fun of Adam."

Kollin shrugged. "Y'all are being kinda mean."

Eyes widening, Elijah pointed at Kollin. "You helped him. Didn't you?"

"Whaaaaat?" Kollin held his hands up and shook his head. "I would never."

Derek's eyes flickered from the couch, where Kollin had been lying, to Kirsten's seat. "You could see her cards."

"Whaaat?" Kollin said again.

"Oh, please. Don't even try. We all know you're a horrible liar."

Kollin's face broke into a grin, and he clamped his hand down on Adam's shoulder. "Sorry, man. I tried. Oh, and FYI, I could see your cards in the mirror too, Derek."

"You dirty cheater," Kirsten said.

"You set this up beforehand," Elijah said and pointed at Adam.

"That's just sad, Adam," Derek said. "Involving a minor in your deceit. You're supposed to be a role model."

Unable to control his laughter any longer, Adam threw up his hands. "It feels so good to finally win, I don't even care. My losing streak started long before you came around."

"That's pretty lame," Kollin said.

"Yeah. Well, you didn't have to fold so quickly. All you had to do was deny with a modicum of believability."

"Whatever, dude. Can you please tell them why you asked them over so I can go to my room?"

Kirsten grinned at Kollin. "Phone date with Jase?" she asked.

Kollin narrowed his eyes at her slightly, but Adam didn't miss the way his cheeks tinged a darker shade of pink. Jase had shown up at HOPE for the first time about three weeks before, and Kollin had glommed onto him quickly. They bonded over their mutual love of basketball, but Adam saw the flirtatious glances the boys sent each other when they thought no one was looking. He was one of the few black kids at the center, and Adam hoped that Jase's presence was the result of their efforts to reach the entire community, to let them know everyone was welcome.

"No one has phone dates anymore, Kirsten," Kollin said with all the derisiveness a sixteen-year-old boy talking to a stone-aged, out-of-the-times adult could muster. "We text or Snapchat."

Raising one eyebrow, Kirsten spoke primly. "Is that so? I'll be sure to remember for future inquiries."

"Anyway," Adam said, "we wanted to let you guys know I'm officially moving in with Elijah and Kollin—"

Kirsten shot up from the couch and threw her arms around Adam's neck. "Oh my God. You're getting married."

Adam's eyes widened, and Elijah choked on his drink and quickly pounded himself on the chest three times.

"Um, no, Kris. But thanks for that," he said, gently pushing her away.

"Shit. Sorry." Kirsten sat down and covered her face in embarrassment. "But you've basically been living here for two months. I didn't think it required a big announcement."

Having regained his breath, Elijah stepped next to Kollin and Adam. "There is a little more to it—we hope." Elijah cast a sideways glance at Kollin and continued. "Adam probably should've started by telling you guys that I've contacted my lawyers about formally adopting Kollin. After talking it over between the three of us, Kollin and I decided this was something we felt we needed to do, even though he's almost an adult. We're trying not to get too excited, because a lot could still go wrong—particularly Kollin's biological parents refusing to sign over rights."

Adam could count on one hand the number of times Kirsten had been rendered speechless, but there she sat on the couch, hand covering her mouth, several slow tears sliding down her cheeks. She placed her hands in her lap and offered them a watery smile. "Well, that's even better news."

Kirsten stood, hugged Kollin first and then Elijah, whispering to each of them. Derek followed behind her to offer his congratulations.

"I guess it's time we go home before I weep all over your house," Kirsten said.

Derek hugged Adam and offered a simple, "Congrats, man," and then followed his wife to the foyer.

"See you guys later," Kollin said as he jogged up the steps with a wave over his shoulder.

"Thanks for coming tonight. We'll have to do it again sometime soon." Elijah one-arm hugged Derek and bent down to hug Kirsten again. "I have some stuff to do in the office before I turn in, so I'm going to head up. You guys be safe."

Kirsten turned to Derek. "Can I have a minute?"

"Of course. I'll be in the car."

Adam waited until the door shut behind Derek. "You okay?"

Kirsten nodded. "Are you?"

Adam shoved his hands in his pockets. "'Course I am. This is the best thing for Kollin."

"Well, duh. But what about you? Why aren't you doing this together?"

"Come on, Kris. Elijah and I have been together half a year. Adopting a teenager with me is not even close to being on his radar."

"I doubt adopting a teenager fell on his radar at all a year ago, but life happens, and things change. There's nothing you could say to make me believe Elijah and Kollin wouldn't be 100 percent on board if you wanted to adopt him as well."

Adam sighed. "Even so, it's better for everyone involved if I stay out of it. And Elijah and Kollin agree. We'll set up the legal papers so I become his guardian if something happens to Elijah. But I don't feel the need to do this the same way Elijah does. I'll always love that kid as if he were my own, but this is Elijah's thing with Kollin. This is a healing thing for them that I'm not a part of, and I'm more than okay about it. Besides, I know Kollin's different, but I'd feel weird legally adopting someone I met through the center and guilty I couldn't do it for the next one who comes through and needs a home."

Kirsten stepped forward and wrapped her arms around Adam's waist. "You're right."

Adam rested his chin on her head. "Really? That's it?"

"Yeah. That's it. I get it." She looked up to meet Adam's eyes. "I guess I always assumed if this happened, it would be all of you together. You're so damn selfless…. Are you sure this is what you really want?"

"I promise. I'm excited and happy for both of them. I can't think of two better people who deserve this more."

Kirsten pursed her lips as she pulled away. "Hmmph. I can."

"Yeah, yeah. Trust me on this one. Okay? Now get out of here. It's not nice to keep your man waiting."

"Like you know anything about keeping my man happy."

Adam laughed and then pulled Kirsten back in for a hug. "I love you."

"I love you too, brother."

ADAM'S PHONE rang, jerking him out of the haze of inputting expenditures. He checked the time and saw the "So You Want to Go to College?" course he'd signed up to teach that month had started five minutes before. He'd never remember anything without HOPE's receptionist's constant reminders.

Adam grabbed his desk phone as he locked his computer. "I'm coming now, Chloe. Thanks for the reminder."

"Wait, Adam. You have a call on line one. She wouldn't leave her name and didn't want to leave a message when I told her you were getting ready to step into a meeting. She said she'd call back, but I told her I'd check with you first."

Adam groaned. He didn't want to be late—later—for his class, but he never knew what kind of trouble the person on the other end of the line could be in.

"I'll take it, but can you let the group in the training room know I'll be a few minutes?"

"Of course. She'll be there when I hang up."

A moment later, the line clicked over, and the loud background noise of the center disappeared.

"This is Adam. How can I help you?"

Silence followed his greeting, and Adam's heart sank. Calls starting out this way rarely ended well.

"Hello? Are you okay?"

Silence.

"Listen. I'll do whatever I can to help you, but you have to talk to me first. Okay? I promise whatever you tell me right now is strictly confidential."

"Adam?"

The voice sounded scared, or maybe skeptical, and made the hair on the back of his neck stand up.

"Yes. This is Adam. Is there something I can do to help you?"

"Adam.... Lancaster?"

Adam's heart sped up and butterflies fluttered around his stomach as his mind searched for the owner of the somewhat familiar voice on the other end of the phone.

"Yes," he all but breathed out. "Who is this?"

"I… I can't believe I actually found you."

The butterflies danced and twisted, threatening to empty everything in his stomach as his mind led him to a door he'd not only closed but locked long ago.

"I never thought I'd hear your voice again," the woman continued.

Slowly shaking his head, Adam fell into his chair and pleaded for his brain to back away from that door.

"Adam? Are you still there?"

Adam squeezed his eyes shut and tightened his grip on the phone as he held it to his chest. The voice on the other end called his name one more time and Adam could no longer take the sound. He slammed his phone down in the receiver and tried to take a deep breath. But it turned out choppy and short, so he drew another right behind it.

Same result.

He struggled to suck in oxygen, but once again, was unable to breathe deeply. So he tried again.

And again.

And again.

True panic crept in. Adam had no control over his body. He was going to pass out.

Calm down.

Breathe slower.

But his lungs wouldn't cooperate. He struggled to remember what he needed to do to pull himself out of a downward spiral, but he hadn't had a panic attack in so many years, everything he knew felt fuzzy and out of reach.

Panic filled every nook and cranny in his body.

Adam could barely inhale before his body forced him to gasp for another breath. Lightheaded and desperate for more oxygen, Adam dropped his head between his knees. Several moments later he was able to take his first deep breath. Closing his eyes, Adam pressed his palm against his chest and began counting, slowing his breathing a little at a time.

A light tap sounded on his door, and the loud squeak of the hinges quickly followed. "Oh my God." Chloe rushed around the desk to kneel at Adam's side. "What happened? Are you okay?"

Adam took another long, slow, deep breath and nodded gently.

"What can I do? Do you need water?"

He shook his head and then rested his forehead on his knee and turned to look at Chloe. "Can you apologize to the kids in the application course and tell them I can't make it today?"

"Of course. Anything else?"

"Umm. I hate to ask, but could you call Elijah for me? I don't think I'll be able to drive for a bit, and I need to go home."

"I'm on it. Don't you move."

"Thanks. And Chloe? Please don't tell the kids why I can't be there." No need for them to worry. Chloe would do enough of that for everyone.

After Chloe left, Adam managed to raise his head enough to lay it on the desk in front of him while still focusing on his breathing. True to her word, Chloe returned in less than two minutes with a bottle of water.

"Elijah's on his way. He's likely to break the sound barrier getting here. I didn't know what to say that wouldn't worry him, so I told him you'd explain." She fussed with the pitiful, limp throw pillow Adam kept on his couch and then kneeled next to him again. "Want to try moving to the couch?"

Adam accepted her shoulder to lean on, fumbled his way over to the couch, and then took the water she'd opened.

"Thanks. I'll be fine if you need to get back out there."

Chloe sat on the edge of the couch by Adam's feet and patted his leg. "Nope. Julie's covering the desk for me. I'm not leaving you until Elijah's here."

Adam nodded, feeling guilty for keeping Chloe in the dark, but exhaustion from his panic attack kept him from explaining. Adam hadn't heard his mother's voice in almost twenty years, and he knew without a doubt he could've gone twenty more without hearing it again.

SHELL TAYLOR is a full-time mother of three exuberant and loving kiddos and one fur baby, a tiny but fierce Yorkie-poo named Rocco. As a Christian who practices love and grace and humility rather than hatred and judgment, she tries her best to instill these same virtues in her rowdy kids. She just recently learned how to crochet to start bombarding new mothers with matching hats and booties. She is a huge Marvel fan and, because of the superhero-plastered tees paired with jeans and Chucks, has been told when helping out in her son's classroom that she looks more like the students than a parent. Her favorite way to procrastinate is to binge-watch entire seasons on Netflix. Best of all, she's been married ten years to a man who's turned out to be everything she never knew she needed.

Also from Dreamspinner Press

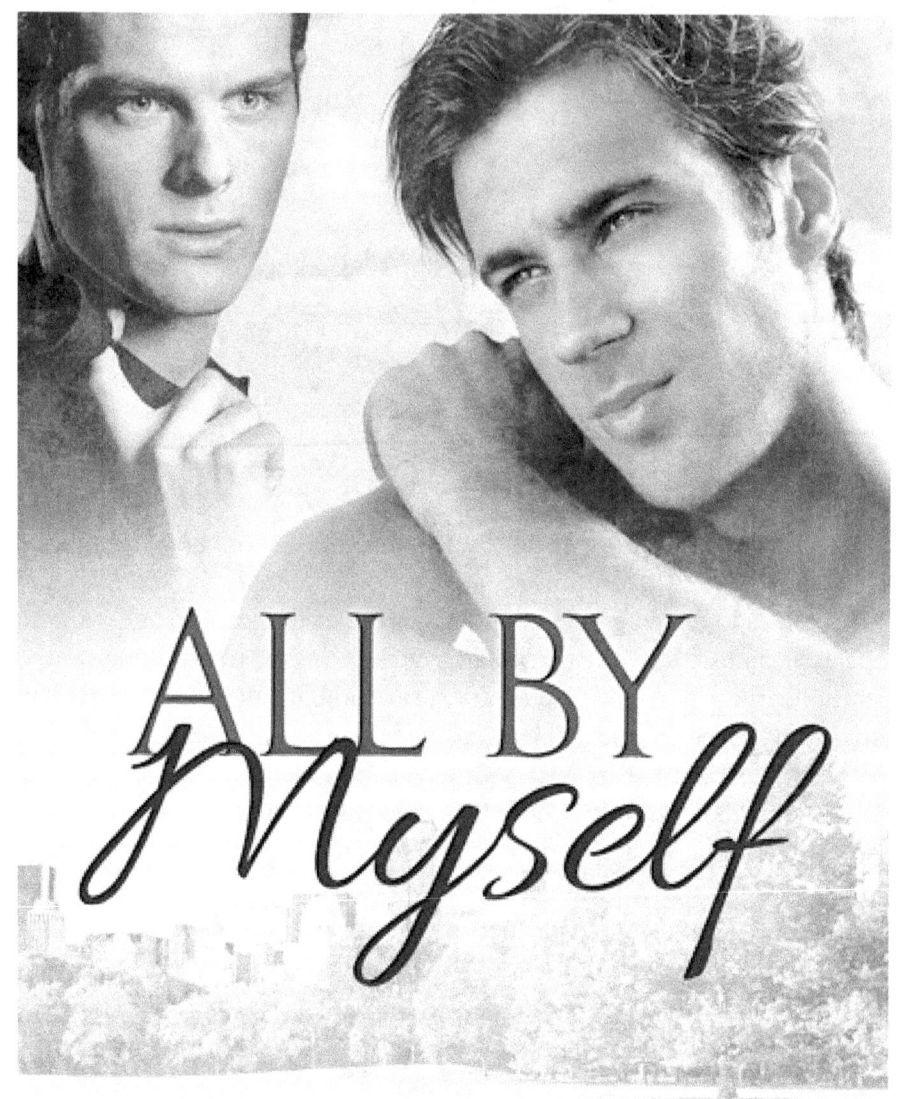

ALL BY
Myself

KEN BACHTOLD

www.dreamspinnerpress.com

Also from Dreamspinner Press

Also from Dreamspinner Press

NESTED HEARTS: BOOK TWO

Bowerbirds

ADA MARIA SOTO

www.dreamspinnerpress.com

Also from Dreamspinner Press

GET YOUR
SHINE ON

NICK WILGUS

www.dreamspinnerpress.com

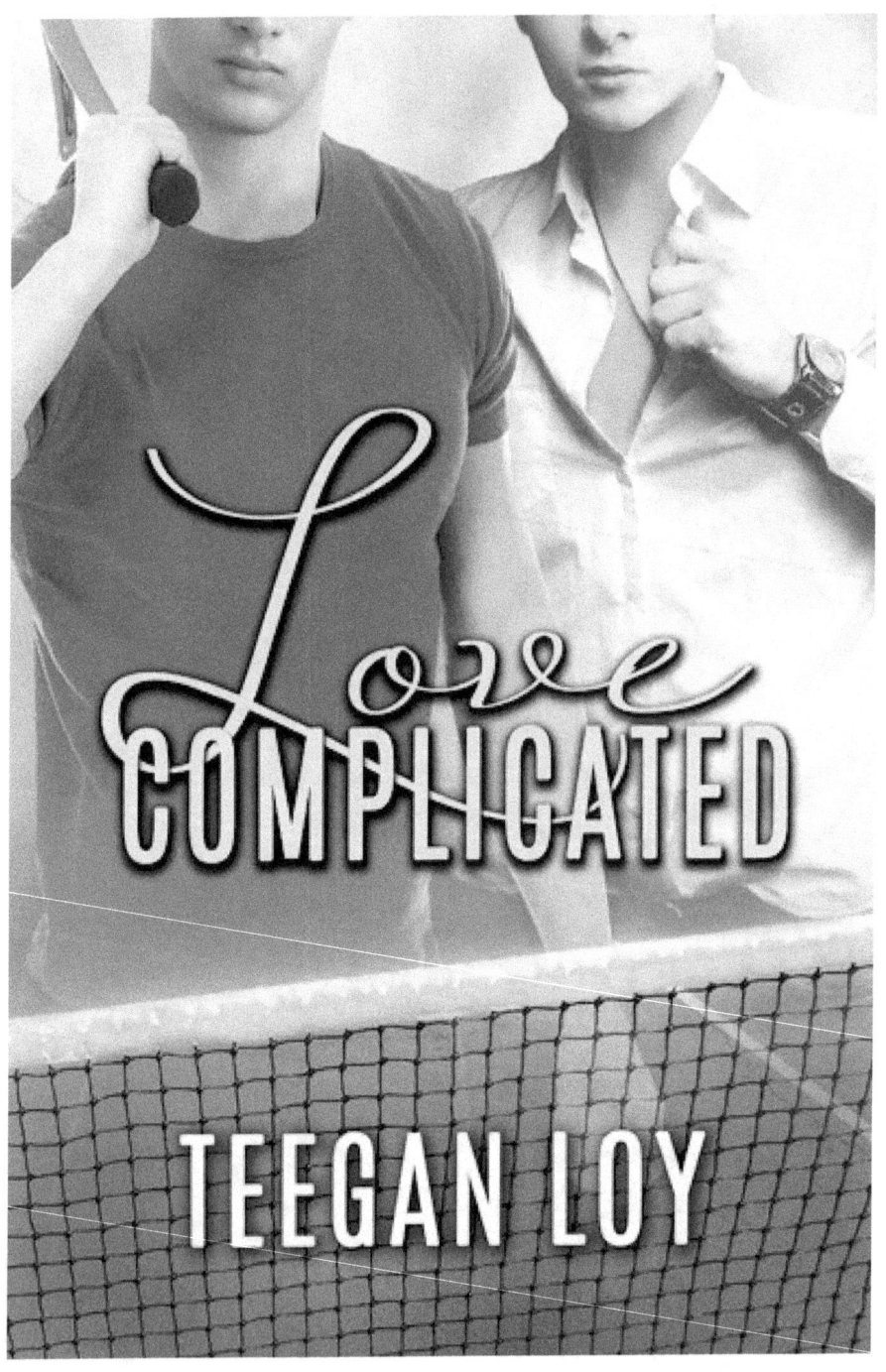

Love COMPLICATED

TEEGAN LOY

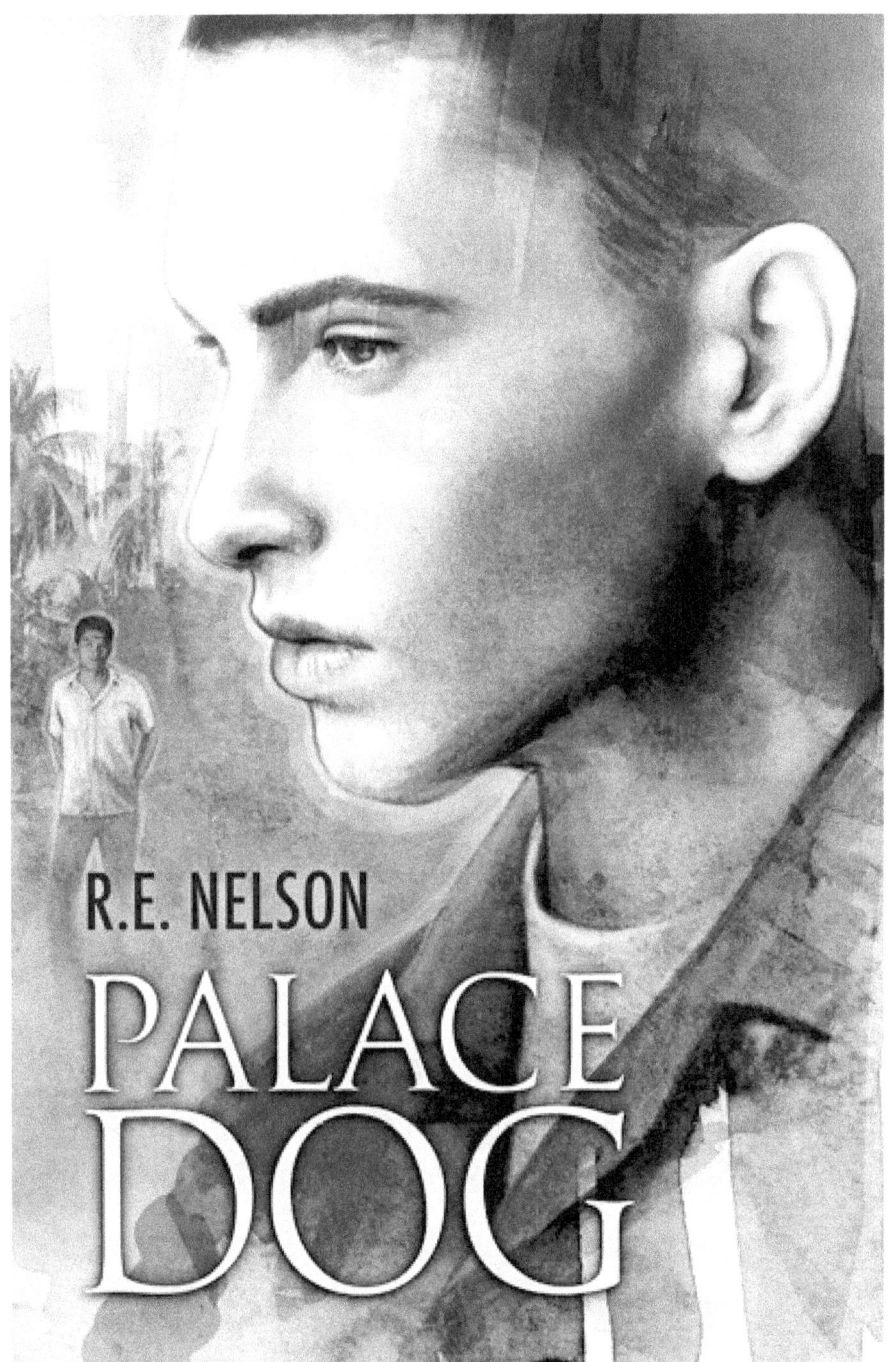

Also from Dreamspinner Press

RATTLESNAKE

KIM
FIELDING

Welcome to
Rattlesnake
pop. 2317

www.dreamspinnerpress.com

Also from Dreamspinner Press

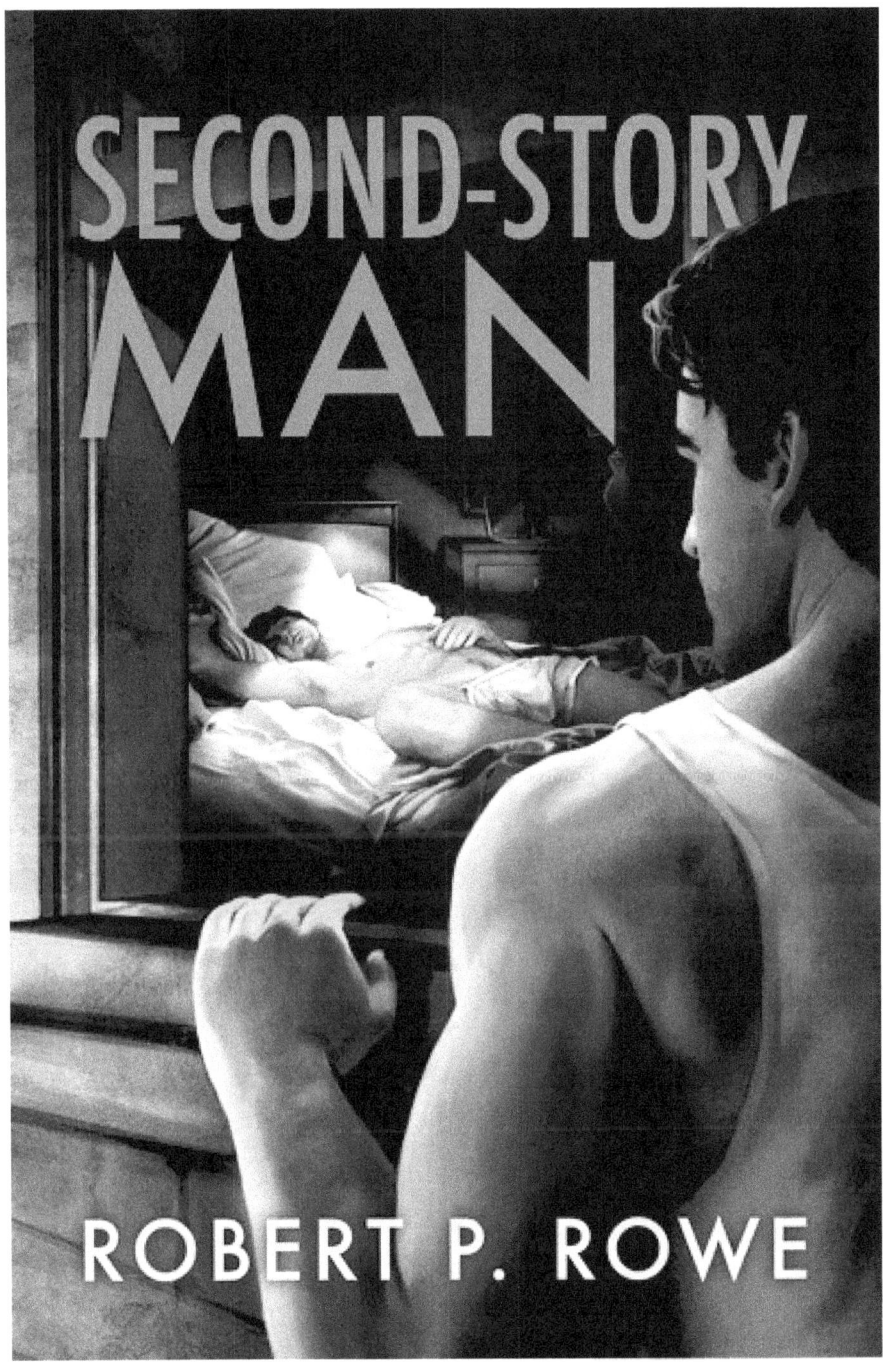

SECOND-STORY
MAN

ROBERT P. ROWE

www.dreamspinnerpress.com

Also from Dreamspinner Press

Thrown
A CURVE

KATE McMURRAY

THE RAINBOW LEAGUE

Also from Dreamspinner Press

The Truest Type

D.W. MARCHWELL

www.dreamspinnerpress.com

FOR **MORE** OF THE **BEST** **GAY** ROMANCE